Carol MacLean lives in the Glasgow area. She began by writing pocket novels, having 18 published before deciding to write historical saga. When she's not writing, Carol can be found visiting museums or walking around the city looking for traces of old Glasgow to inspire her next novel.

Also by Carol MacLean

The Kiltie Street Girls

Kathy's Courage

CAROL MacLEAN

hera

First published in the United Kingdom in 2024 by

Hera Books
Unit 9 (Canelo), 5th Floor
Cargo Works, 1-2 Hatfields
London SE1 9PG
United Kingdom

A CIP catalogue record for this book is available from the British Library.

Print ISBN 978 1 80436 485 7
Ebook ISBN 978 1 80436 484 0

This book is a work of fiction. Names, characters, businesses, organizations, places and events are either the product of the author's imagination or are used fictitiously. Any resemblance to actual persons, living or dead, events or locales is entirely coincidental.

Look for more great books at www.herabooks.com

Printed and bound in Great Britain by Clays Ltd, Elcograf S.p.A.

For Mum and Dad

Chapter One

'Go and get the messages, will you love? There'll be a queue at the butcher's but Mr Heaney will have kept a wee something special back for me under the counter.' Mary pushed a string bag and her purse into Kathy's hands.

'Why do I have to do it? It's my first day off in over a week and I'm that tired, so I am. Can't Jeannie do it when she gets in?' Kathy griped.

'Honestly, it's no wonder my hair's turning grey,' Mary sighed. 'It's not very fair on your sister if she has to go shopping after a day's work when you can just as easily go now, is it? Besides, she's suffering with morning sickness and needs looking after. You're not so big that I can't give you a clip round the lugs, so off you get.'

'You'd have to catch me first before you could clip me.' Kathy grinned, her mood changing quickly.

'Kaa,' Dennis bellowed, staggering towards her on his sturdy little legs. He hugged her and buried his head into her skirt.

She picked him up and swung him around, loving the sound of his throaty chuckles.

'You'll make him sick,' her mother warned.

'Och, he's fine, so he is. Take more than that to make you boak, won't it Den-den?'

I

He looked up at her adoringly, from his horizontal position, cradled at her hip. She shoogled him and he giggled again. It was on the tip of her tongue to suggest to Mammy that she look after Dennis while Mammy did the shopping but when she set the toddler down on his own two feet he began to wail, sticky hands waving at her to pick him back up.

'I'll away and get the messages then,' she said hastily, grabbing up the abandoned string bag and purse from where she'd thrown them so she could pick Dennis up.

Kathy turned to the front door, but not before she saw Mary's sorrowful look. She tried to ignore the flash of guilt. It wasn't Kathy's fault she couldn't stand the tears and tantrums that a wee boy could produce. Besides, Mammy had taken on that responsibility when she agreed to be Dennis's mother. Hadn't they all agreed it was for the best? Kathy got her freedom back after falling pregnant to a man who had said he loved her and wanted to marry her; only it turned out he already had a wife and children. Mammy got another beautiful baby to love and care for just when she was feeling sad about her youngest, Bob, growing up.

The blast of hot August air hit her skin as she scampered down the stone steps from their tenement home and out onto Kiltie Street. It was lovely not being on the factory floor today with all its noise and heat and the supervisor, Miss McGrory, always on her tail complaining about Kathy's tardiness or sloppy work. She hated working there but there hadn't been much choice. Mammy and Harry had been adamant that she needed to stay close to home after what had happened, and Jeannie had found a place for her quickly when one of the girls at the Fearnmore munitions factory had got married and moved away.

Nobody had asked what Kathy wanted. They all thought they knew best. Harry wasn't even her dad, just her step-dad, and even he was over-protective of her. That wasn't fair of her, she knew. Kathy sighed. It wasn't Harry's fault. She was very fond of him and he made Mammy happy. Mary had been so sad since their dad died, it cheered them all up to see her laugh and smile and sing round the house since she'd married Harry less than two years ago.

What *did* she want? Kathy swung the bag, weighted by Mary's purse, as she sauntered along Kiltie Street and turned up at the corner onto the main road where she'd find the butcher's shop alongside the greengrocer's and baker's and, after a bit of a walk, Franny's Emporium, where she used to work before her call up for war work. The fact was she didn't know exactly what she wanted. She knew what she didn't want – Miss McGrory's endless reprovals, the boring days at the munitions factory and being stuck at home while there was all the excitement of the war. She only had to walk in to the centre of Glasgow to see all the men and women in their uniforms striding about purposefully, not to mention the American GIs with their gleaming white teeth and glowing skin and drawling, exotic accents. Then there were the Canadians, like Jeannie's husband, Bill, and the Polish officers and all sorts of different tongues being spoken right there on Glasgow's shabby wartime streets.

It was heady stuff, but she wasn't a part of it. She had to be home, helping Mammy and taking a share in looking after Dennis, who was supposed now to be her wee brother. And she loved him. She really did. But she didn't have the patience for bathing him or washing nappies or seeing him through teething when he was up

3

all night gurning. That was Mammy's job. She had taken that on so that Kathy didn't have to.

There was a pout to her lips that she didn't realise was there as she joined the long queue outside Mr Heaney's butcher shop. The queue consisted of tired housewives with bags of shopping who had already queued for bread and vegetables or been to the Buttercup Dairy for milk and butter rations. Kathy recognised some of their neighbours from Kiltie Street who nodded to her and some of the women from the other nearby streets, Kilmun and Duart and Duncruin.

She let their voices wash over her, still absorbed in her own tale of woe.

'Not a bloody onion to be had. I'd gie ma right leg for an onion, ah tell ye,' a large, raw-boned woman was saying to the woman in front of her in the queue.

'Aye, and I'd gie ma left leg an' aw.' Her companion nodded. 'But there's no point greetin' about what cannae be had. Ah've got a bunch of sad-looking carrots, Sadie. I'll swap ye a few for that cabbage ye've got there, hen.'

'You're on, Agnes,' Sadie boomed. 'Here, put them in ma bag. What ye after at Heaney's the now?'

'Whatever the auld man has got,' her friend said. 'Ah heard he's got a few pork chops the day.'

Kathy swung the bag half-heartedly, already bored with queuing. She flicked back her glossy red hair which hung loose to below her shoulders. She had helped herself to Jeannie's Tangee lipstick so that her lips were bow-shaped and orange-red. It was patriotic to wear make-up, whatever Mammy thought on the subject. Kathy liked to look nice even though it was a challenge when she had no money, clothing was rationed and the only choice was utility or second-hand. She didn't mind rummaging

4

through the market though as she often found a bargain. The summer dress she was wearing now was one such bargain. Jeannie had sewn pockets over the faded patches, embroidered the hem and sleeves for her and there she had it, a lovely new outfit.

'I know you like to look good,' Mammy had said recently, 'but you don't want to attract the wrong sort of attention.'

'What do you mean?' Kathy had bristled.

Mammy hadn't met her gaze as she folded freshly dried washing from the line in the back close but Kathy had seen the worried groove that so often appeared between her mother's eyebrows and relented.

'I'm not trying to flirt, Mammy. I just want… to be pretty,' she said softly.

'I know, love, but it's a fine line between being neat and smartly turned out and wearing too much make-up, which gives certain men the wrong signal.'

Kathy felt tears prick the backs of her eyes and she blinked them away. She had been a silly wee fool at the tender age of sixteen and had been taken in by a soldier much older than her. Thinking they were going to get married, since he had given her a ring, she had let him have his way and the result had been Dennis. Then she'd found out he was already married and when she tried to find him to tell him she was pregnant she discovered he'd been transferred to another base. She remembered her fear and loneliness at being sent away from home to have the baby. Even though she had learned to love Miss Main, who had taken her in for Mary's sake. And she loved Dennis with a fierce love that she could never have imagined before she had him. But she hadn't been ready to be a mother, even if it was possible. She wanted her childhood and her freedom to be young and have fun.

Mary and Harry agreed to raise Dennis as their own son while Kathy got to be his big sister. She didn't regret that decision at all. The only thing she regretted was that now her family was so protective of her she felt smothered at times.

'...no better than she should be.' The muttered words penetrated her musings and she stiffened and glanced up.

The women she knew from Kiltie Street, Mammy's friends, either smiled sympathetically or pretended to be busy with their shopping bags. Ahead, the women called Sadie and Agnes had their heads together talking and Kathy was sure it was them. She didn't recognise either of the women but reckoned they came from the tenements in streets nearby. Gossip travelled fast between the streets and although everyone was told that Dennis was Mary Woodley's, anyone totting up the weeks and doing the arithmetic could work out that there were less than nine months between the wedding and the arrival of a baby and very little sign of Mary being pregnant.

Kathy was frozen for a moment. She clutched at the string bag, her heartbeat picking up speed. Should she flee? Then she lowered her shoulders and took a couple of breaths in. Why should she? She had every right to be in this queue. She was Dennis's sister and no one could prove differently even if they had their doubts. Besides, Mammy would be very disappointed if she came home without the meat for dinner and Mammy being disappointed was much worse than Mammy being angry. None of them liked to upset their mammy, they loved her so much.

She tried to blot out the muttering ahead and the dirty looks that the large woman, Sadie, was now throwing back

6

in Kathy's direction. There were only the two women in the queue ahead of her now. She was uncomfortable but she could hold out. She held her head high as if nothing was the matter. She saw Mr Heaney's shiny forehead under his butcher's hat as he doled out the tiny rations from behind the counter. He had a cheerful word for all his customers despite the summer heat and the smell of blood and sawdust in the shop. The sunshine glinted off the metal meat slicer as his quick hands pushed the meat through, avoiding the sharp blade.

He winked at Kathy when it was her turn. She was about to step up to give Mammy's order when a basket glanced painfully off her hip. As she gave a small cry, Sadie pushed past without so much as an apology, her friend Agnes following her, eyes narrowed at Kathy. Behind her, she heard someone laugh and, still feeling the sting from the blow she'd received, she turned to see Judith Lennox grinning maliciously from the end of the queue.

Kathy hardly heard Mr Heaney's pleasant greeting, and the exchange of ration cards and money for a little package from under the counter passed in a blur. Judith's mirth and scorn was ringing in her ears as she thanked the butcher and almost ran out of the shop. Judith's foot turned out as she passed but Kathy didn't trip. She managed to avoid it and now she was out of the shop and speeding along the street, desperate to get away and not looking where she was going.

'Ahhh!' The cry was wrung from her as she slammed into a solid shape and Mammy's precious parcel went flying.

Strong hands steadied her arms and placed her back on her feet before she could fall. She looked up into a pair of green eyes under black brows and saw the air force blue

7

uniform. She stepped back quickly out of his reach but he had already dropped his hands from her and gave her a grin that creased the sides of his mouth in a way that made her heart give a little lurch.

They both moved towards the scattered pork chops on the pavement at the same time and their shoulders collided.

'We really must stop bumping into each other like this,' he said lightly.

Kathy flushed.

He thrust his hand at her. 'Alisdair Meikle at your service.'

'I'm Kathy... Kathy Dougal.'

She shook his hand, his skin warm and dry against her own, and a little hot flame licked along her nerve endings, making her want to gasp. She watched him hunker down to collect the chops and noticed the way his uniform jacket stretched over his broad shoulders. His hair was dark, almost black, but the sun caught coppery strands within it. She caught herself staring as he turned back to her, standing up and presenting the pitiful parcel, now wrapped again.

'Mammy's going to kill me,' Kathy said. 'That meat's been all over the road.'

'The pavement, technically, but never mind, I dusted them off. Run them under the cold tap for a few minutes and they'll be good as new.'

His voice was Scottish but had clearly had the benefit of a private education because she was hard put to say where exactly he came from. She was suddenly conscious of her second-hand dress and her dishevelled hair, plus she was fairly certain her lipstick was smeared from their collision as she'd wiped the back of her hand across her face. Yes, there was a deep orange-red stripe on her skin. Wonderful. What must he think of her?

'Look, I've given you a terrible fright,' he said, sounding thoughtful, his sea-green eyes fixed on hers. 'Why don't I make it up to you and buy you a coffee? There's a little place not far away does a reasonable scone. What do you say?'

She knew she ought to say no. Mammy would definitely want her to thank him politely and leave with the pork chops and never see him again. Yet, she lingered, the parcel dampening in her grip with the meat juices seeping out.

'I… I can't,' she said. She held up the parcel. 'I have to get this home.'

He shrugged carelessly but she saw the disappointment flash across his face before it vanished in a polite smile. He touched a finger to his brow in salute and turned away.

'Wait!' she called. There was a tempo in her chest as her heart beat rapidly.

He quirked a brow but didn't speak.

'I could meet you a wee bit later. If you give me an hour to get myself sorted. I know a nice café in town if you don't mind a bus ride? Maggie's Café, you can't miss it on Gordon Street.'

'Splendid. I'll see you then, Kathy Dougal.' His voice was warm and his grin infectious.

She was kicking herself as she walked home to Kiltie Street. What on earth was she doing? She shouldn't be arranging to meet a strange young man in a café in the city centre. Wasn't this just what Mammy was always warning her about? Yet a flicker of excitement ran through her. Oh, but it was grand, so it was. He was handsome and tall and in the RAF and she liked him. She liked him!

9

She ran lightly up the steps and into their home with its hallway, kitchen, two bedrooms and tiny parlour. Harry was out at his allotment and Jeannie was at work. She hoped that Mammy had popped out for some air with Dennis but no such luck.

'What in the name of the wee man have you done with our tea?' Mary cried.

'Sorry, I dropped it on the way home.' Kathy unwrapped the meat and ran it under the tap.

Mary sighed but took it from her and dried it and then put it on the cold slab to keep. 'Never mind, at least we've got chops for tea. That's something. Harry will be pleased. A bit of mash and gravy and no one will notice the chops have been through the mill.'

Kathy hugged her. 'I love you, Mammy. I really do.'

'Aye well, I love you too but honestly, what a footer you are, dropping these.'

Kathy landed a kiss on her mother's soft cheek and smelled Mammy's talcum powder that she used so sparingly these days. It was impossible to get more. Sure, didn't she smell lovely just with Lifebuoy soap.

'I'm away out for a couple of hours but I'll be back for my tea.'

'Mind you shut the door quietly, Dennis is napping.'

Kathy nipped into the bedroom she shared with Jeannie. They had more room with Isa and Bob, their younger sister and brother, evacuated to the countryside and their older brother, Jimmy, away fighting in the war. She'd rather they were all here but it was nice to have space for herself.

She changed her dress by borrowing one of Jeannie's. It was blue with white polka dots and it set off her red hair very well. She matched it with Jeannie's white summer sandals. They had seen better days and the buckles were slightly tarnished but her sister looked after her belongings carefully, unlike Kathy, so that despite their age, the sandals were still respectable.

–

Alisdair Meikle hummed a tune under his breath as he sauntered back to his nana's home in the tenements overlooking the river. The brown water never smelled too good and the stink brought back childhood memories of visiting, until his parents decided that Nana Mackie should always come to them and paid for the train tickets. He remembered being sad that he no longer got to visit the cramped, dark flat with all its little china ornaments and knitted blankets and the tin of sweet biscuits which Nana would offer. He had spent hours as a child hanging out of the top-floor window looking for ducks on the river below.

His thoughts turned to the young woman who had crashed into him. She hadn't been looking where she was going and he'd been unable to get out of the way before she fell into his arms with force. His first impressions were of shining red hair, horrified grey eyes and high cheekbones with a generous sprinkling of freckles. She was gorgeous. He had reluctantly removed his fingers from around her upper arms, sorry to lose her closeness.

He thought she was going to flee once he'd retrieved the sorry-looking package of meat from the ground. Luckily, for once, his mouth had got ahead of his brain and he'd asked her out to a café. It was most unlike him. He had a reputation in his squadron for being careful, measured and thoughtful. And choosy when it came to women. His chums were making the most of the war and girls' eagerness for adventure in all forms. He was teased because he rarely asked a girl out, preferring to spend his brief leisure hours reading.

The truth was, he hadn't met someone who intrigued him. Until now. He couldn't get her out of his head as he made a pot of tea for his grandmother and laid the small table for her.

'Use my good linen,' Beatrice Mackie said, pointing at the press as she watched him from the kitchen doorway, her hands grasping at her stick.

'All right, Nana. I can manage. Why don't you go and sit down and I'll bring it in to you?' Alisdair suggested, good-naturedly.

'The good linen, Alisdair. Did I say that?'

'Yes, you said. Have a seat and I'll not be a minute,' he said.

She moved slowly from the kitchen doorway, her movements stiff. He watched to make sure she used her stick. Nana could be stubborn enough and didn't like getting older. Unfortunately, she was frail and he worried about her falling. He had been round the flat, fixing loose carpet and rugs for her.

'Are you on holiday?' she asked him, when he went through with the tea things.

'I've got a forty-eight-hour pass. I told you that,' he said patiently.

'Och, yes… you did,' she frowned.

He was currently stationed at RAF Bishopbriggs, near a pretty little village north-east of Glasgow. The camp was surrounded by fields and farms and there were other villages, Auchinairn and Kirkintilloch, nearby. He had cadged a lift from another RAF officer into town and the same friend had agreed to pick him up and take him back.

'I wanted to call in on you while I'm in the area. I told Mum and Dad I'd see that you were managing.'

'Of course I'm managing,' Beatrice's voice rose a little. 'What gave you an impression otherwise? I'm getting on a wee bit but I'm not in my grave yet, young man.'

Alisdair laughed easily and was pleased to see the corners of his nana's mouth twitch up in shared amusement. She might be frail but she still had her sense of the ridiculous.

'So, are you up here for long?'

'I have no idea, and even if I did, I couldn't say much. Loose lips and all that, Nana.'

'Aye,' she nodded. 'This terrible war, it's changed everything and everyone. Anyroad, I'm glad you're here. Why have you put the good linen out on the table? The everyday cloth would have done.'

'I met a girl today, Nana. Actually, I literally bumped into her. Or rather she came running straight into me.' He wanted to talk about her.

'Is she a nice girl?' Beatrice asked, picking up her biscuit with a shaky hand and inspecting it before taking a nibble.

'She seemed very nice. I think you'd approve of her. She has the most amazing red hair.'

Beatrice nodded. 'A highland lassie, then?'

'She sounded local. In fact, I'm meeting her for a coffee soon. I'd better get ready. Will you be all right on your own?'

'Sure, since I live on my own, Alisdair, I'm certain I'll be just fine for an hour or two while you go chasing women. Off you go and have fun. You're only young once.' Beatrice winked.

He would report back to his parents that Nana was doing well for her age. They couldn't leave their shop in the Borders to come and visit. It was so difficult getting transport with the war on and the trains were often too full or were cancelled or delayed. They couldn't risk it, they told him, when their customers depended on them for their rationed food. They sent her food parcels when they could and her neighbours looked in on her too.

'I'll cook the meal when I get back. Give you a rest.'

Beatrice had insisted she cook when he'd arrived yesterday evening. He hadn't liked to argue even though he noticed she was unsteady on her feet and had trouble opening tins. She had brushed his concerns aside. But she didn't protest now, simply nodding and closing her eyes. She was asleep before he had time to say goodbye. Tenderly, he put one of her knitted blankets over her knees and kissed the top of her head.

He went outside, conscious of people's approving gazes as he walked along the street. He knew he looked smart in his uniform and he found himself hoping that Kathy would approve too. He couldn't wait to see the warm admiration in her lovely grey eyes. God, he had it bad. He'd only met the young woman for a few minutes, most of which were spent scrabbling for meat on the pavement. Why then was his heart beating so fast at the thought of her?

He was thinking on all of that and he was lucky not to have a similar collision with another person waiting at the end of the street. It crossed his mind briefly that the rather stout girl standing there *wanted* him to bump into her. She had her arms crossed and a curl on her lip that was quite off-putting.

Murmuring an apology, he moved past her and walked swiftly on, conscious that he needed to catch the right bus to find the café that Kathy had described. He didn't notice the girl behind, following.

Chapter Two

Kathy's favourite café was in the city centre, not far from where the bus dropped her off. She liked it because it was far away from Kiltie Street, in a place where no one knew her and she could be herself. She liked to window-shop down Buchanan Street as she wandered along, dreaming about owning the clothes and shoes on the mannequins. Not that there was much in the shop windows these days. Just big promises that products would return after the war. The windows were criss-crossed with tape against bomb blast and the clothes on display were all utility, with its drab colours and lack of frills or anything frivolous.

She tripped on a sandbag and moved further out onto the pavement. She wasn't in the mood for shop windows today anyway. She was eager to get into Maggie's Café and wait for Alisdair. Maggie smiled as Kathy went in, the door chiming to let her know another customer had arrived. Kathy smiled back and was pleased to see her usual table was free. She liked to sit at the window in the corner so she could watch the people coming and going outside.

'Hello, hen, what you having today?' Maggie asked, cheerfully.

'I'm waiting for a friend.'

'I'll come back when she arrives, then, shall I?'

Maggie nodded and was away to take an order at the next table before Kathy could tell her that actually her friend was a man and that possibly this was a date. Not that she'd say that part out loud, of course.

The door rang again and Alisdair came in, his green eyes lighting up when he saw her. Kathy's mouth widened in a spontaneous smile.

'You found it then,' she said.

'Very good directions,' Alisdair grinned, sitting opposite her.

The table seemed suddenly small. She flicked her hair behind her ears, uncertainly. She didn't know him at all. What should they talk about? But it turned out she didn't have to worry. Alisdair put her at ease, asking about her work and her family, and they were deep in a chat when Maggie returned for their order.

'How about a pot of tea for two and some scones?' Alisdair suggested.

She liked that he asked her and nodded in agreement. Maggie wrote it down and bustled away after a curious glance at the two of them. Kathy was always in the café alone so this was unusual.

'What about you?' Kathy asked. 'Are you from Glasgow? I've spent all the while talking about myself.'

'I was born in Glasgow but we moved to the Borders when I was two. My parents have two shops in Kelso, but I was sent to boarding school when I was seven so in a way I don't feel I belong anywhere particularly.'

'I can't imagine being away from home at seven,' Kathy said, horrified.

Alisdair shrugged. 'You get used to it.'

She wondered if that was true. His mouth had tightened. She changed the subject quickly.

'What were you doing near Mr Heaney's? Are you based at the barracks?'

'Ah, I saw the barracks were busy yesterday when I arrived. No, I'm based outside Glasgow, but I'm on a pass to visit my nana, who lives in Culmore Road.'

'Oh, that's near the river, isn't it?'

'That's right. You can tell that from the awful smell coming off the water.'

What a lovely smile he had. And a twinkle in his eye as he joked with her. Kathy's heart sang. He liked her. He must do. The trouble was that Mammy and Harry wouldn't like it if she brought him home. She could just see their worried faces. Didn't they realise she was very careful now? She had no intention of letting a man near her physically. She loved Dennis so very much, but she had paid a heavy price for her mistake. She decided she wouldn't tell Alisdair where she lived. Just in case he ever decided to call on her unexpectedly.

She was torn between wanting to see more of Alisdair Meikle and shying away from what he might want from her. Would he be satisfied with a few kisses? Or would he lose interest in her quickly? She caught herself on the thoughts. Goodness, the man had only asked her to meet for a cup of tea and here she was practically marrying him off in her mind. Mrs Alisdair Meikle. It had a nice ring to it. Stop it, Kathy Dougal. Stop it right now.

'My Nana Mackie is getting on a bit,' Alisdair was saying in his warm, rich voice. 'I told my parents I would call in and check on her. I'm very fond of her.'

'That must be nice, having a nana. I don't have any grandparents.' Kathy paused before asking what she really wanted to know and trying to sound casual. 'Are you based up here for long?'

Alisdair laughed and Kathy noticed other women glancing at him and the way they smiled at the handsome young man. She felt proud that she was with him and not them.

'As long as a piece of string,' he said. 'We simply go where our orders take us.'

Maggie arrived with a pot of steaming tea and a plate of butterless scones and they tucked in, spreading a little pot of jam onto the scones and sharing a knife to do so. Their fingers touched and that ripple of awareness spread up Kathy's hand and arm again. The way Alisdair stared at her made her think he felt it too. How could he not? It was so very powerful a feeling.

'You're not keen on the factory work then?' he said, filling the small silence that had blossomed between them after the touch of their fingers.

Kathy shook her head. 'No, I hate it, but there's no choice.'

'You're doing your bit for the war effort. That's important,' Alisdair said.

'It's noisy and the supervisor picks on me. The girls are all right and my sister, Jeannie, is on the same floor as me but it's so dull and boring,' Kathy sighed.

'Have you thought about joining the forces?'

'I couldn't though, could I? I'm already doing important war work as they see it. I wouldn't be allowed to chop and change.' Besides, Mammy would have a fit if Kathy suggested it.

Alisdair finished his tea and set the cup down on its saucer. 'If you were set on it, I don't imagine they would stop you.'

'Oh...' She hadn't thought on it at all before now. It felt like that was for other women, not her. It was for the glamorous girls she saw walking confidently around Glasgow in their smart uniforms with their plummy accents and that air that being well off brought with it. Surely it wasn't for a girl from Kiltie Street?

'They take all sorts of people from different backgrounds,' Alisdair said, as if he'd read her mind. 'I've made good friends with some chaps I'd never have met ordinarily. Decent sorts.'

'Do you two want anything else?' Maggie swept in to pick up the teapot and the plates with their scattered crumbs.

Alisdair glanced at his watch. 'Sorry, I'm going to have to head off soon. Let me pay for this and perhaps we can get the bus back together?'

Maggie waggled her eyebrows and smiled at Kathy from behind Alisdair. Kathy tried not to smile back.

'Aye, that'd be nice,' she said.

They didn't speak much on the bus back due to the noise of its engine and the chatter of the other passengers, but it was thrill enough for Kathy to sit next to him and feel the occasional brush of her leg against his as the bus swayed round the road corners. She was glad she had made the effort to dress up and put on some lipstick. She sensed his admiring looks on the journey.

'I'm here tomorrow before I have to go back to camp,' Alisdair said as they got off the bus in Maryhill. 'Do you fancy another trip to the café?'

'I've got tomorrow afternoon off. I'm due that even if Miss McGrory disapproves, which she does. Yes, I'd love to.'

They arranged to meet at the café the next day at two o'clock and parted ways, with Kathy heading down to turn into Kiltie Street, careful to make sure he didn't see where she turned off, while Alisdair headed in the opposite direction to his nana's flat near the river.

Kathy was humming the tune of 'We'll Meet Again' as she strolled along, enjoying the sensation of the sun burning hot on the top of her head and warming her legs. She was so absorbed in happy thoughts that she didn't notice Judith Lennox standing on the steps up to number five in the street until it was too late.

'Well, if it isn't Miss Perfect. Except you're not, are you. You're no better than anyone else. Did you enjoy your "trip" this morning?' Judith mocked.

She stood, arms folded, her stout body leaning forward aggressively. Her face was blotchy pink and white as if the sun disagreed with her. Kathy was wary. She wasn't one to stand back usually if someone gave her lip but Judith had a reputation for being handy with her fists. She had been a bully at school and once knocked an older boy's tooth out. Kathy had been in the same class as Judith and had avoided her as much as possible. Now that they were both eighteen, nearly nineteen, it seemed not much had changed.

Judith hated Kathy. When Kathy had been sneaking out to see her soldier, Judith had covered for her. But not out of friendliness. Oh no, she had demanded payment every time. Kathy would tell Mary that she was going next door to see Judith and help with old Mrs Lennox, Judith's aunt who had bouts of illness. Then she'd quickly pay her thruppence to Judith and rush off up the road to a street near the army barracks where he would meet her.

Although everyone was told that Dennis was Mary's child, the residents of Kiltie Street suspected the true story. Most were kind and didn't mention it. Old Mrs Lennox, however, had beaten Judith when she found out that her niece had been involved, even in a minor way. She had stopped Judith from taking any money out of her pay packet and forbidden her from going out in the evenings for months. Even Judith was scared of Irene Lennox. She had deflected all the resentment and anger that she couldn't express to her aunt onto Kathy. She blamed her.

It was hard to avoid Judith as she lived in the next tenement, even though Kathy tried. Sometimes Judith lay in wait for her, baiting her and calling her names. Kathy thought she'd get bored eventually and leave her alone but Judith was horribly persistent. In the nineteen months since Dennis's birth she had maintained her hatred, and it didn't seem to have faded, not one bit.

'What do you want?' Kathy said, making her tone confident although she was ready to make a run for home if necessary.

'What do you want?' Judith mimicked, a sneer on her unattractive face. She strolled down the steps onto the pavement so that she stood opposite Kathy, blocking her way. Kathy calculated how quickly she could dash to the side and swerve round the other young woman.

'I'll tell you what I want. I want you to suffer the way I've done. All because you couldn't keep your knickers on.'

'You're being ridiculous,' Kathy snapped. She began to walk round Judith.

Surprisingly, there was no thump to her back or a foot whipping out to make her fall. She felt a prickling between her shoulder blades but refused to turn or look scared. Her own anger began to rise up. How dare Judith Lennox pick on her like this. It had gone on long enough. Never one to back down and, at home, always the one to have the last word in an argument, Kathy spun on her heel.

'I'm fed up with this. What have I ever done to you? You were happy enough to take my money and cover for me back then with no qualms. Find someone else to pick on.'

Judith's meaty arms flexed but she didn't move. Instead she favoured Kathy with a smile that belied the glint in her eyes.

'I'm not picking on you. I've got better things to do. I've got a date.'

Kathy snorted. Judith's fists went up but she swung her arms loose and flashed her pretend smile again.

'Aren't you going to ask me who with?'

'No.'

'Well, I'll tell you anyway. A handsome airman.'

Kathy stared at her. Judith nodded as if satisfied with Kathy's reaction.

'You're not the only one he likes,' she said. 'I saw the both of youse this morning. What a gent, helping you pick up the scabby meat you dropped. I followed him to his house and we got chatting and he asked me out.'

'I don't believe you,' Kathy said.

Judith shrugged casually. 'I don't care if you do or not.'

'Have a lovely time on your imaginary date,' Kathy said sarcastically. She turned to walk towards home when Judith's next words stopped her dead.

'As I said, I know where he lives. How's about I pop over there and tell him that you're not the nice girl he thinks you are? I don't think he'll hang about when he hears you've got a baby. Do you?'

Kathy froze. Judith was quite capable of carrying out her threat. In fact, she would enjoy doing it. She tried to ignore the snickering laughter and ran up the steps to home. She could only hope that Judith was bluffing.

'Bill says he's got leave and he's coming up soon,' Jeannie said as they sat down for their meal that evening. 'He says he's looking forward to spoiling me, what with the baby on the way an' all. I keep telling him it's early days but he's that excited about it.'

The sun shone in through the big tenement window onto the kitchen table and glinted off the cutlery. Mary was piling the plates with mash to go with the small pork chops. On the side of the sink there was a heap of carrots with their feathery green leaves and the dark soil clinging to the roots. Harry had put them there proudly after a day tending his allotment.

'That's good news love,' Mary said, putting the plates in front of them.

Harry licked his lips and picked up his knife and fork to tuck in to the hot food. Kathy poured water into cups. It still felt strange, just the four of them and Dennis when Jimmy, Isa and Bob were all away. Without the other children it was much quieter, and they all missed the noise and bustle in the flat.

'I can't wait,' Jeannie said. She sighed and rested her chin on her cupped palms dreamily.

Kathy had always thought Jeannie was a wee bit soppy over Bill and invariably rolled her eyes when her sister was like this. But now she understood. What if it was her and Alisdair? Even thinking his name made her heart thump. She'd wait for him if he asked her. And, like Jeannie with her Bill, she'd be so utterly happy if he came to visit on his precious leave. Suddenly she knew she was in love with him.

'What are you sitting there for like a statue? Are you not feeling too good?' Mammy asked, concernedly.

'Is it Miss McGrory you're worried about?' Jeannie chipped in, dropping her hands and focussing on Kathy. 'Because you needn't, you know. She was quite relaxed today. She's given me a new knitting pattern. Hannah's so clever with a needle, she can sew and knit wonderfully.'

'Aye, it's fine for you being on first name terms and all,' Kathy said. 'But she hates me, so she does. I don't know why.'

'Och, you do too. If you're going to wander in late half the time, no wonder she gets upset and tells you off.'

'Girls, girls,' Harry chided softly. 'Your mammy would like to eat in peace. So would I. Give it a rest, will you?'

'Sorry, Harry,' Jeannie murmured, turning to her meal.

Kathy made a face at her but caught Mammy's gaze and blushed. Honestly, she and Jeannie couldn't help it. They bickered and sniped at each other but they were good friends too. It was just the way they had always been growing up. She loved Jeannie and knew it was returned.

'I'm glad Bill's coming,' she said now as a peace offering and was warmed by Jeannie's wide smile.

Later that night, they lay in the two beds in the back bedroom. It was so warm they had left the window open and through it the sounds of the city could be heard. There was the rumble of a late tram and a man's voice calling to someone in the street below. There was birdsong too even though Kathy reckoned all the birds should be asleep.

'Are you awake?' she whispered loudly.

'I was drifting off, but I'm awake now,' came the reply.

'Sorry.'

'No you're not. What's on your mind?'

Kathy saw Jeannie's shadowed outline as her sister propped up on one elbow and looked at her. She sat up in her bed.

'I've met someone. I think… I think I'm in love.'

'Goodness. When did this all happen? You never said anything yesterday.'

'I only met him today, he's called Alisdair. We went to Maggie's coffee shop and talked. He's so easy to chat to and we're meeting there again tomorrow. I can't wait to see him. Oh, Jeannie, I feel so odd. Like my stomach and chest are churning, you know? Only in a good way.'

'That sounds like either love or a tummy bug,' Jeannie agreed from the darkness. 'Does Mammy know?'

'I can't tell Mammy. She and Harry won't like it.' Kathy's sigh filled the bedroom.

'You can't blame them after what happened. But your life has to go on too. I tried to tell Mammy that but she blames herself for not noticing what was going on with you and that… that man. She's worried you'll get hurt again.'

'What should I do?'

The bed beside her creaked as Jeannie moved. Kathy waited. Jeannie must know. She had had her own experiences with being engaged to a man who wasn't right for her before she fell in love with Bill. It hadn't been a smooth journey for her love life.

'Will you tell this Alisdair about Dennis?' Jeannie asked.

'No, I won't. Even if it got serious and he asked me to marry him. There's no reason to. Dennis is Mammy's child. We all agreed that.'

'You'd keep it a secret from him forever?'

'Yes, I would. You sound horrified but I could lose him if I told him. I'm not risking that.'

Kathy sensed Jeannie lying back down on her bed. There was a rustle of the bedclothes as her sister pulled the sheet up to her shoulders.

'I couldn't do that to Bill, if it was me. Living a lie your whole married life, it's not right.'

'Anyway, it's only a second visit to Maggie's Café. He might not want to see me again after that.'

She was only saying that to get away from Jeannie's disapproval, which was obvious. Her instinct told her Alisdair liked her too. That this could turn into something serious. Oh, she really hoped so. As for Dennis, well, he was fine with Mammy and Harry. There was no reason to disrupt his wee life by telling Alisdair her secret. It could change everything.

'Kathy?' Jeannie's voice came sleepily through the thick, dark air in the bedroom.

Kathy grunted as she was sliding into sleep and only half heard her sister's voice.

'Be careful, won't you?'

—

Kathy hurried home from the factory, the sound of the machinery still ringing in her ears. She barely answered Mary's greeting, rushing into the bedroom to change her clothes so she could get to the café on time.

'What's the rush?' Mary said as Kathy shrugged on a light cardigan over her summer dress and grabbed her handbag.

'I'm away out. I'll be back for my tea,' she called over her shoulder as she rushed through the door and out into the close. She glimpsed Mammy shaking her head but her mind was full of the anticipation of seeing Alisdair again and she didn't care. The bus journey took forever. It felt like the driver waited for each passenger and blethered for ages. Kathy felt like taking over the driving herself. Eventually, there she was, dropped off in the city centre and striding towards Maggie's Café.

Oh, but it was busy. Luckily, her table was free. It was the smallest in the café so less popular than the tables that sat three or four. Kathy slid into the chair after squeezing past women's shopping bags and murmuring apologies. There was no sign of Alisdair yet but glancing at the clock above the counter, she saw she was early.

Maggie came across, pencil and pad in her hands. It was noisy with chatter in the café and the air was summer-warm.

'I'll not order yet,' Kathy said. 'I'm waiting on my friend.'

Maggie began to speak but a loud shattering of china from the back of the counter made her rush away with an apologetic wave of her hand. Someone had dropped a plate of cakes and Kathy saw Maggie's bent back as she helped the other waitress clean up the mess.

Never mind, she was in no hurry for tea or biscuits. She decided she'd have whatever Alisdair chose. Soon, however, she was tapping her fingers on the tabletop and glancing at the clock where the arms went round ever so slowly. It was a shock to see that he was a half hour late. Maggie had disappeared with the weeping waitress into the back of the café and not returned. A couple at a nearby table were affronted at the delay and huffily the gentleman helped his wife on with her coat and they swept out with loud mutterings of complaint.

After forty minutes, Kathy knew with a cold chill that he wasn't coming. She fumbled with her handbag, pretending to search for something inside it. It felt as if everyone in the café knew she'd been stood up. Her thoughts flew to Judith Lennox. Had she carried out her threat? Was that why Alisdair wasn't here?

That had to be it. There was no way he'd simply forgotten to meet her. Judith had told him Kathy's secret and he was disgusted by her. Humiliation flooded her. She picked up the handbag and with her head held high, stalked out of the café. Once outside, her bravado crumbled and she ran along the pavement, oblivious to passers-by until she was out of sight of the place. She was *never* going to Maggie's again. How could she? She bet they were all laughing at her. What a silly little fool she was, imagining she could be with such a lovely man as Alisdair Meikle. Not when she was soiled goods. The tears threatened and Kathy swiped them away angrily.

–

Back at the café, Maggie soothed the other waitress and listened to her sobbed story of an argument with her husband in the early morning and how the plate had slipped from her tired grip. She got back to the café floor just in time to hear the door chime and see Kathy's ramrod back going out. That twigged her memory and she went behind the counter to pick up an envelope the young man had left there that morning. She raced to the door and ran out onto the pavement but there was no sign of the girl. Maggie shrugged. Never mind, she'd give her the envelope next time she was in.

Sitting in the back of the truck, bumped up and down by its movement over the country roads as they drove south, Alisdair thought about Kathy. He hoped she'd got his letter by now. He'd scribbled it at speed that morning and had just had enough time to drop it in at the café and get back to the base before the squadron left. They had been given two hours' notice to get packed and ready to go. His friend had picked him up at Culmore Road at a horribly early hour, giving him the bad news. Nana Mackie was confused but gave him a fierce hug as he left.

The letter was, of necessity, short.

Dear Kathy, he had written.

> *I am so very sorry I can't meet you this afternoon but I received orders to leave at very short notice, and in a few minutes I'll be heading south for a new destination which, as you will understand, I can't share with you. I will be back as soon as I can and I hope very much that we can meet and have a meal together and get to know each other better.*
>
> *Will you wait for me, Kathy? I can't promise I'll be based in Glasgow anytime soon but I want to see you again. Can we write to each other? Please send me your address. In the meantime, my nana will pass on your letters to me if you will write and let me know everything about your everyday life. It is all fascinating to me, however dull you protest it is!*

He put Nana Mackie's address, and signed it 'Yours, Alisdair' and meant it.

Kathy walked along towards George Square in the centre of Glasgow. It was too early to go home, Mammy would only ask questions. She could stare in the shop windows for a while. She felt hollowed out when she imagined what Alisdair thought of her. He was probably counting his lucky stars that he'd found out about her before it got serious between them. That awful Judith Lennox. She was never going to let Kathy forget the grudge she held.

There was a poster on the wall of the brick bomb shelter in George Square. One corner had peeled off and flapped in the breeze and it caught her attention. She stared at it properly. It showed a picture of a young woman in a smart army uniform. The words were in bold black and white. 'YOU are wanted too!' it blazed. 'Join the A.T.S.'

Her emotions in turmoil and determined to get away from Judith and Alisdair and everybody else, Kathy headed in the direction of the recruiting hall.

Chapter Three

The tweed jacket was slightly too large for her but if she kept her shoulders back she could carry it off. Clothing coupons saved for such a long while had purchased a neat blue utility dress which fitted her nicely and suited the second-hand jacket bought at a local market stall. Kathy finished pinning her red hair into a victory roll and stepped back to admire herself. Her grey eyes, staring back at her from the mirror, flashed with excitement and her cheeks were flushed pink showing up a scattering of freckles which she hoped no one would notice. She had no more face powder to dust her face with and it was hard to come by in the shops.

She was finally going. Having enlisted in the Auxiliary Territorial Service at the recruiting hall, she had been sent for a medical and passed it with no problem. Two weeks later, a letter had arrived, telling her to report to army barracks in Yorkshire. The letter had enclosed a travel warrant for her journey. There were other papers, too, entitled 'General Instructions', about bringing her ration book and her gas mask, and a helpful pamphlet suggesting what else to bring with her, including a toothbrush, buttons, needle and thread and a woolly cardigan.

Outside in the street, she heard Mammy's voice and others chiming in. She took a deep breath. This was the hard part, leaving her family. Being in Kiltie Street and being with Mammy and her brothers and sisters was all she had ever known, and when she thought about leaving Dennis it felt like a part of her was being ripped out. And yet the thrill of excitement pulsing through her made it difficult to concentrate on saying goodbye. Instead, she was wondering about travelling south across the border. She had never left Glasgow, let alone gone to another country. She couldn't wait.

She held her head high as she clattered down the stone steps of number four, Kiltie Street, in case any of the neighbours were watching. Which of course they were. Housewives leaned out of the tenement windows to wave and shout their best wishes. Everyone knew everyone else's business around here but they were good people and had watched her grow up along with all the children in the street. Kathy grinned and waved back.

She looked at Mammy, who was wiping her eyes. She felt a flicker of impatience. There was no need for tears. This was an adventure, couldn't Mammy see that? Dennis broke free from Mary's arms and clung to Kathy's leg. She ruffled his hair and his hot little body warmed her skin before Jeannie picked him up. There was that tug again, that invisible cord that bound him to her even when she had to leave.

'Say bye bye to Kathy,' Jeannie said.

She was wearing her work dungarees, her hair covered by a white turban. Miss McGrory had given her an hour off from the factory to say goodbye to her sister. Dennis reached out grubby starfish hands to Kathy and wailed. Their neighbour, Annie, pushed a pram with her own baby boy over and began to ask Jeannie what was happening. Harry had his arm round Mary now, comforting her.

33

Suddenly Kathy wanted to go. It was plain embarrassing, all the attention and noise. If her family was like this now, what were they going to be like at the train station? She had to bite down on her lip when Mary asked Harry to bring Kathy's suitcase down and he took an age to do so. In the meantime, she could hardly bear Dennis's sobs. She was going to miss him so much, but she had to go.

'Do you want to carry him?' Jeannie said.

Kathy thought about her smart new dress and jacket and shook her head, not wanting her outfit to get crushed or dirty. 'Harry can take him until we get to the bus stop.'

'I need to get back to work,' Jeannie said. 'All the best, and don't do anything I wouldn't do.'

'That's not going to leave much left over,' Kathy laughed.

Jeannie put Dennis down and he toddled over to Mary. Jeannie hugged her and then held her at arm's length with a long stare.

'Have I got a smut on my nose?' Kathy asked.

'No, I'm just fixing you in my mind, that's all. I can't believe you're going.'

'Mammy neither. I almost backed out after telling her I'd signed up when she had that expression she gets when she's disappointed with one of us.'

'I don't think you can back out once you've signed the papers,' Jeannie smiled. 'But I know what you mean about Mammy. She's upset and she doesn't want you to go but she won't say it. She knows she can't stop you now.'

'I want to do this, Jeannie. I want… to play my part and to stop this war.' *And get away from here, all the mistakes I've made. Get away from Judith. And memories of Alisdair.*

'Will you take my advice?' Jeannie said slowly.

'Aye, you know I will, or at least I'll listen,' Kathy joked. She had had advice from her older sister her whole life and let it gloss over her while she did what she wanted. But Jeannie's serious face made her stop. 'What is it?'

'Wherever you go, don't tell them about Dennis. Do you hear me? It's a fresh start for you.'

Kathy nodded. Jeannie was right. She didn't want anyone judging her because she had a baby and wasn't married. There was enough of that around here and people like Judith Lennox were making sure she couldn't forget and move on.

'I won't. Jeannie...'

'Mmm?'

'Take care of yourself, ye hear? And the wee one.' Kathy placed her hand on Jeannie's flat stomach.

'You'll be back on leave and I'll be as big as a house. You'd better not laugh at me.'

Kathy grinned. 'I'm not promising anything.'

She squealed when Jeannie poked her in the side. She'd miss her sister, that was certain.

Jeannie gave her a last hug and went up the road, not looking back.

That's what I have to do, Kathy thought. I have to walk away from here and not look back.

The train station when they got there was bustling with young men and women in uniform, the air hot and muggy with the fumes from the engines and a taste of coal dust that caught in the back of her throat. There were plenty of other families saying tearful farewells so that the Woodleys and Dougals were just figures in a crowd and Kathy was relieved that she wouldn't be embarrassed by them.

She took Dennis from Harry for a final hug. He smelled of biscuits and the feel of his soft hair on her mouth as she kissed his head almost made her cry. Reluctantly she gave him back to her step-dad.

'See you Den-den. Be good for your mammy and daddy, won't you now?'

She leapt up onto the train and Harry swung her suitcase up after her. The commotion of other bodies and luggage squeezing past her meant Kathy's welling tears went unnoticed. By the time she'd straightened up and pushed down the window to wave, her eyes were dry again. This was her new beginning, her adventure. She had to look forward and forget the past.

She was glad when the train started and she waved furiously out of the carriage window, pressed by others beside her at the open window also waving and shouting to their families on the platform. There was a blast of the train's whistle and the carriage rattled and juddered, then they were on their way. Her cardboard suitcase was packed on the shelf above and she felt smart and important and purposeful.

She had packed a book and after staring out the window with interest as the city gave way to fields and farms, she took it down and read for a while. Alisdair Meikle stole into her thoughts, but it was too raw and hurtful, and she made herself concentrate on the blurring print in front of her as the train hurtled forward in a billowing cloud of steam.

After six cramped hours travelling, wedged between an elderly widow with a wide velvet hat and a Wren who wept all the way without making eye contact with anyone, Kathy's utility dress was creased and she felt sure her face powder had melted entirely away. She hoped her armpits didn't smell. Pushing the door open eagerly, she grabbed her suitcase and stepped onto the platform. There were other young women appearing from the other carriages and she was certain they were destined for the ATS camp too.

A bellowing male sergeant waved an arm at the advancing sea of young women. The widow, passing Kathy, managed an acknowledging smile and a frown of disapproval for the man's shouting all in one look. She saw the Wren slip past with a white face and red-rimmed eyes and felt a brief pang of sympathy. But her attention was soon focussed on the sergeant and the girls following him. Kathy hurried after, her suitcase banging painfully on her leg.

There was a huge army truck waiting for the gaggle of women. The back of it was down and girls were being pushed and hauled aboard with scant attention to modesty. Kathy was glad her skirt was below knee length as she took a proffered hand and scrambled up. They were crammed in and bobbed up and down as the truck drove off. There were nervous giggles and someone started singing 'It's a Long Way to Tipperary' until they all joined in.

Arriving at the barracks and spilling out of the truck, Kathy was struck by what a picture they must make. Like her, most of the women were dressed smartly in an assortment of colours and a few were wearing high heels. In front of her, a girl's hat feather bounced merrily as if they were on a Sunday walk. The babble of chatter was quickly subdued by the sergeant's shout.

'Quick march. Hurry, hurry. In threes now!'

It was a bunch of out-of-step and out-of-breath new recruits that reached the barracks block. It looked grim and uninviting but there was no time to dwell on that as they half marched inside their allocated hut and Kathy gazed in dismay at the rows of single iron beds placed head to head.

'Three biscuits each,' she heard someone say.

'Oh, thank goodness,' she said with relief. 'I'm that hungry I could eat a horse.'

There was a hoot of derision from a tall, lanky girl and Kathy flushed. What was wrong? She was desperate for a biscuit and a cup of tea.

A small girl with long black hair leaned in and whispered to her, 'They're not for eating. That's what they call the mattresses.'

She was right. When Kathy looked at her bed, there were three separate hard blocks to make up a mattress and three tightly folded blankets. Did everything in the army come in threes, she wondered. She was ready to sink down onto her bed, hard and uncomfortable or not, but they were being shouted at again. Following the others, she was issued with a knife, fork, large spoon and mug and warned not to lose them. Next they were marching again in threes towards the cookhouse.

'It's the mess,' the dark-haired girl told Kathy as she marched cheerfully beside her, not quite in step.

'A mess? Don't they clean it up?' Kathy was feeling hot and bothered and her lovely new dress was damp with sweat.

'That's just what they call it. I'm Bridie, by the way. My sister's in the ATS so I've learned a few things which are coming in handy now. I'm local so I'm hoping I can get home at the weekends to help on the farm.'

Bridie's accent was so thick that Kathy had to listen hard to understand what she said.

'Kathy Dougal,' she replied.

'They've sent you a long way from home,' Bridie remarked. 'Most of the other girls are from the Midlands judging by the way they speak.'

They were in the cookhouse by now, filing in obediently and sitting ten to a table while an orderly slung down plates of stew and potatoes and bread in front of them. Kathy tucked in hungrily, the laughter about the biscuits still stinging. She glanced along the table at the lanky girl but she was intent on her meal and chatting to the girl beside her. The biscuits and Kathy's ignorance seemed forgotten and no malice intended. In fact as she listened, the lanky girl's hoot of laughter rang out and others laughed too, seemingly not at all offended. Kathy breathed out and some of the tension left her. Not everyone was like Judith. Besides, no one here knew anything about her. She was just like them, a young, single girl here to do her bit for the war effort. All she had to do was keep her secret tucked away and forget all about Kiltie Street.

After scraping their plates, the girls were marched to the wash house where Kathy was horrified to find rows of wash basins with no screens or curtains to hide behind.

'They can't expect us to wash in… in front of each other?' she whispered to Bridie.

Bridie's mouth twisted. 'You get used to it, I suppose.'

Kathy reckoned she never would. Not meeting anyone's gaze, she tried to wash parts of herself under her clothing without exposing any skin. It was humiliating and awful and a terrible pang of longing for home shot through her, almost like a physical pain. Why hadn't she kissed Mammy at the railway platform? She'd been too embarrassed and now she wished she'd hadn't cared about all the other people standing there saying farewell to their families. And Dennis. She hadn't carried him to the bus stop because she was worried about creasing her outfit. She'd missed that chance for a wee bit longer hugging him just for a silly dress. She squeezed her eyes tightly shut. When she opened them, she wasn't the only one who was white-faced and a bit shivery. Quietly the girls sloped back to the barracks block, ignoring the sergeant's shouts to march properly and his threats of drill the following day.

Kathy found that Bridie had the bed on one side of hers and with a sinking heart saw the tall, lanky girl sit on the other side. For a blessed while there was no sergeant or other officer in the room and the girls began to chat and mix. Tall and lanky turned out to be called Jennifer and once they got talking, Kathy realised she was nice enough. Bridie seemed to make friends easily and was soon giggling with a group. Kathy wished she had that knack. When Bridie came back to her bed, she threw out names – Hilda, Geraldine, Letty, Sally, Joan, Bets – until Kathy's head was spinning.

'Everyone's so nice,' Bridie announced with a wide smile.

Kathy nodded and pretended to be busy sorting out the contents of her suitcase. Lying on the next bed, Jennifer let out a snore.

'There's a medical tomorrow and kit inspection,' Bridie yawned. 'Of course, we'll have to get our kit first.'

'I had a medical before I came here,' Kathy said.

Bridie shook her head pityingly. 'You'll have more than one. My sister warned me about the injections too. Never mind, we'll have to cope.'

Geraldine, thickset with dark, curly hair and more than a hint of moustache over her upper lip, came over to tell them that Hilda had been told they could get mugs of cocoa in the evenings between eight and nine p.m. They were all going, did Bridie and Kathy want to come too? She glanced at the snoring Jennifer.

'We can bring a cup back for her,' Kathy said quickly.

They went across to the cookhouse in a bunch, chatting and giggling. Kathy felt as if she was one of them, even if it was only for a short while. Here they were, still in their civilian clothes, treading on the muddy ground, soldiers shouting in the distance and ugly brick buildings around them. It was all so odd, as if she was in a dream. She might wake up in her bed in Kiltie Street and find none of this had happened. The sour stink of the mud sucking at her shoes made it only too real, however.

It turned out that they could get a slice of cake as well as a mug of cocoa from the cookhouse and the mood of their little group soared. Jennifer woke up at the noise as they all trooped back into their block and grinned when Hilda presented her with the sweet-smelling drink and a piece of sponge cake. Her hoot of grateful laughter made them all join in.

It was a shock the next day to be rudely woken by the regimental bugler playing 'Reveille' at six a.m. and then being marched to breakfast. The next hours were a blur of being issued with uniforms, being taught how to drill, marching for meals and another medical.

'What lovely red hair,' the sergeant said, as they marched round the barracks square in the early evening. Kathy's stomach was hollow with hunger and her toes hurt. His comment took her aback and she smiled at the compliment until he stood in front of her, his face right at hers and shouted. 'Get that chopped. Hair off the collar by two inches. What did I say?'

'Hair off the collar by two inches, Sergeant,' Kathy shouted back, her smile gone. There was no way she was cutting her hair. Not even for the army.

Sitting huffily on her hard bed after drill, she pulled off her cap and let her hair spill in all its coppery glory onto her shoulders. Bridie looked at her from where she was sitting with her feet in a bowl of warm water and mauve potash, sharing it with Geraldine.

'Do you want me to trim your hair?' she asked, sympathetically. 'Jennifer's cut mine and it's so much easier to keep it neat and off the uniform's collar.'

Kathy shook her head, her mouth pursed mutinously. 'No thanks. It's taken me ages to grow it this long. They can't force us to do that.'

'Let me help you roll it and pin it up then under your cap,' Bridie suggested.

When Kathy didn't reply, Bridie dried her feet, sighed and came to sit beside her on the bed. 'Do you want a bit of advice, hard won by my sister?'

Kathy sniffed. Bridie went on as if she hadn't noticed. 'Choose your battles carefully. That's what she advised. The army will win most times.'

Kathy was still too annoyed by Sergeant Burton to speak. She felt Bridie's gentle fingers on her hair, combing through it and twisting it up. She felt the pins pricking her scalp and the cool air on her neck as Bridie worked her magic.

'There. That should do it.' Bridie handed Kathy her cap, motioning for her to try it on.

With her cap on, and peering into Bridie's tiny hand mirror, Kathy saw that her collar was indeed clear of her hair and that she looked smart and neat.

'Thanks, Bridie.'

'My pleasure. Come along, that's the call for another march to the cookhouse. I hope my feet can make it. I've got blisters the size of dinner plates.'

They both groaned. Jennifer, coming to find them, linked her arm with Kathy's on one side and Bridie's on the other. 'In threes, girls. In threes.' She did a fair imitation of Sergeant Burton's booming voice, which had them snorting with laughter.

Kathy's hopes of an evening out enjoying herself and exploring the area were soon dashed. None of them were allowed off camp for the first two weeks of training. Instead they square-bashed and had kit inspections and learned to scrub the linoleum on the hut floor until it shone. They learned how to scrub it twice after the sergeant had walked his muddy boots all over it, inspecting them. Kathy found it hard to contain her frustration with the discipline demanded.

But she found herself almost enjoying the exams they sat. It was like being back at school. Nursing a sore arm from injections, she pored over papers on English and Maths and problem solving and felt very proud when she got good marks.

'Och, I wish we could escape from here just for an evening,' she complained one evening to the girls a fortnight later as they huddled round the stove, drinking cocoa.

'As it turns out, we can,' Bets, a glamorous girl with pale blonde hair and high cheekbones like Veronica Lake, said with a smile. 'There's a dance in the town that one of the soldiers told me about. He's asked me to go with him.'

'And are you?' Geraldine said, her eyes almost popping out at this news.

'Of course not. I said we'd all go.' Bets winked. 'You owe me, girls. I've got us all into the dance.'

'Oh, well done,' Hilda breathed, gazing adoringly at Bets.

Kathy grinned at Bridie behind Hilda's back. It was well known that Hilda, who was rather plain, had a crush on Bets. Bridie risked a quick smile back but then joined in the oohing and aahing that greeted Bets's news. Bridie was far too nice to make fun of Hilda.

'When is the dance?' Kathy asked when there was a small lull in the excited chatter.

'Tomorrow evening,' came the reply, and then some screams from the others as they realised how little time there was to organise dresses and hair and make-up.

'But we're not allowed out,' Jennifer said.

Bets slung a lazy arm around Jennifer's shoulders. 'As it happens, we are from tomorrow. I asked our lovely corporal and she's confirmed it.'

The next day, Kathy hardly noticed the bugler blasting away outside the window before dawn, the shoe polishing and the early morning kit inspection or the drilling. She was too excited by the thought of the dance.

In the evening after their meal in the mess and a quick dip of their eating irons into the usual bucket of water, they marched very quickly back to the hut. Kathy was very glad she'd packed her best dress in spite of Mammy telling her she'd have no reason to wear it. She had also taken Jeannie's sandals. After all, it wasn't as if Jeannie would be going out much now she was pregnant. She and Bill would spend all his leave cuddling and talking in the flat. They were saving for their future apparently, which in Kathy's view seemed to mean no fun.

The girls had discovered that the army biscuits had their uses. The night before they had put their dresses underneath them and now they came out just as well as if they had been ironed.

'That's a lovely shade of green,' Bridie remarked when Kathy put on her dress. 'It's nice with that bright hair of yours.'

'That red velvet you've got is nice with your black hair too,' Kathy smiled, happy to return a compliment.

In fact, when she glanced around, they all looked good in their finery. Some dresses were more worn than others and there were a few patches and darns in stockings but no one commented. They helped each other with their hair styles and shared make-up. Kathy was popular because she'd brought Jeannie's Tangee lipstick and let everyone take a tiny swipe to rub into their lips. *I'll buy Jeannie another one with my first pay and post it home*, she promised herself. But right now, my need is greater.

It was two miles into York and Bets's soldier had somehow managed to commandeer an army truck to take them to the dance. Some of the male soldiers were going too and there were whistles and cheers when the girls walked over to join them. It was a tight squeeze in the back of the truck but no one minded. There was an air of excitement and determination to have a good time. Kathy felt safe tucked in between Bridie and Jennifer, and ignored the stares and good-natured jokes from some of the soldiers, who were only showing off to the women.

The dance was in a hall that smelled of wood rot and ancient dust but someone had hung balloons from the rafters and there was a live band in the corner and a makeshift bar, which the soldiers rushed to. The girls followed more slowly. The violinist started up a country tune which Kathy didn't recognise, but she liked the lilting melody. There were other soldiers there from different barracks and a few local girls. People were dancing already and her feet itched to join in.

'May I?' A soldier with two stripes on his shoulder stepped in front of her.

'I don't think so,' she said, looking for Bridie and Jennifer but finding only thin air.

They were already on the dance floor and waved to her with smiles.

'Your friends are enjoying themselves. Shall we join them? I'm Gary. And you are?'

'Kathy.'

'A lovely name for a lovely girl,' Gary said, as he guided her to the crowded dance floor. 'Just enough room for two more small ones,' he said cheekily as he winked at her and elbowed his way into the throng.

Kathy wasn't sure about him but she let him take her hands and lead her in a foxtrot. She could do this dance. She felt the music lift her and take her and soon they were spinning and foot tapping with the rest. She laughed and let the mood take her. Gary was a good dancer. In quieter moments he told her about his girlfriend back at home in Northern Ireland and how he missed her dreadfully. Glad that he only wanted to dance and nothing more, Kathy let herself relax.

They had a break for drinks and Gary bought her a lemonade. She gazed about and saw Bridie and Jennifer still dancing. Geraldine was sneaking out of the door with a soldier, a guilty glance over her shoulder as she did so. Well, well. Who would have thought it. Kathy looked for Bets, who was quite the most beautiful of their group. She wasn't escaping with a handsome man at all. She and Hilda had their heads together, talking quietly at a corner table.

'Fancy another dance?' Gary asked, setting his empty beer glass down on the table.

'Why not,' she grinned.

'You're a good little dancer,' he complimented her as he swung her round expertly, managing to avoid the other couples as they did so.

'You're not too bad yourself,' Kathy said. 'Oh, I could do this all night.'

'Your wish is my command.' He gave a mock bow and she giggled.

It seemed only minutes later that Bridie was pulling at her arm and she leaned in to hear what her friend was saying.

'We have to go. The truck's ready and we have to be back in barracks before ten.'

'It can't be anywhere near that time.'

'It's still a bit early, but it's either that or walk back,' Bridie said. 'Me and Jennifer are going on the truck. You should too.'

Kathy shook her head. 'You go on. I'm staying for a wee while longer.' She ignored Bridie's worried frown, feeling impatient. Bridie wasn't her mother, for God's sake. She was a grown woman and could do what she liked. With determination, she put her head down and led Gary through the dance crowd away from her friend.

After a while her feet were getting sore from all the stamping up and down and the smart toe-tapping and she yawned. She was surprised to glance around and see that the dance floor was nearly empty and there were only a few soldiers propping up the bar.

'Time for me to go. Thanks for the dancing, Kathy. I won't forget you,' Gary grinned. 'I'd like to walk you home but I'd be late in barracks then myself. Do you want me to point you in the right direction for your own camp?'

They went outside, and although it was dark with the blackout being observed, there was a half moon and a few twinkling stars. It was enough for Gary to show her where to go and describe the way back. It wasn't a difficult route but it was going to be two miles alone in the black night. Kathy shrugged. So be it.

'I haven't had so much fun for ages. I hope your girlfriend writes to you soon,' Kathy said, waving him goodbye.

Outside the hall, she shivered. It wasn't the nice, warm evening they had started out with. There was a damp chilliness now and she regretted wearing Jeannie's sandals, which exposed her bare toes to the night air. It was a shame she'd missed the transport back but she reckoned she could find her way.

She stumbled her way down the road. There were a few people about; she could hear murmurs and some laughter in the near distance. She had a torch but didn't want to put it on. She followed some others she thought were from the dance but they soon turned off down a lane. Kathy turned her torch on then and thought that if an ARP warden shouted at her, she could ask him directions. Eventually, she saw the outlines of buildings looming up before her and she realised she had found the barracks.

'Halt!' a loud voice came out of nowhere, making her jump. 'Who goes there? Friend or foe?'

'Friend, of course,' Kathy yelled back, annoyed.

48

She was hardly going to be a German about to attack the barracks, was she now?

'Advance, friend, to be recognised.' The voice was cool.

Kathy rolled her eyes in the darkness and took a deliberate long step towards him.

'Pass, friend,' he said, with a more even tone.

Kathy tossed her hair and limped past him.

'You're late, so you'll be on a charge no doubt,' his snide voice came behind her as she went.

She tiptoed into their hut, hearing nothing but soft snores and sighs of sleep. Stripping off her dress and sandals she slid in under the scratchy sheet and blanket.

As it turned out, she wasn't put on a full charge the next day, which would have meant being hauled before the commanding officer. Instead she was reprimanded by the corporal, whose bed was placed nearest the door and who had heard her sneak in late.

'You will spend your free time this evening peeling potatoes for the mess cooks. If you're late back again you'll be on charge and confined to barracks. Do I make myself clear?'

Sitting that evening with a huge pyramid of brown, soil-clad tatties and a shiny metal bucket, Kathy wrinkled her nose at the orderly who grinned as he handed her a small, sharp knife.

'Cook wants them potatoes all lovely out of their dusty jackets. Gleaming white, is what he says. Off you go.'

She knew she ought to feel humiliated by the task and was sure that was what the corporal intended but instead she was still electric with the thrill of the evening before and memories of the dancing. She felt leaner and fitter after two weeks in the army than she'd ever been and she had made two good friends in Bridie and Jennifer. The ATS was suiting her very well. But whether she suited the ATS was another matter entirely.

Chapter Four

While Kathy was spending the evening peeling potatoes, Flight Lieutenant Alisdair Meikle was miles away to the north, pen in hand, tackling a stack of paperwork in the office he had been allocated after the sudden command to leave Bishopbriggs and relocate to Ayrshire.

If he looked out of his window, he could see Hawker Hurricanes and North American Mustangs, Bristol Blenheims and Westland Lysanders. They might not have many aircraft here but by God they had variety. He itched to be able to fly them. Damn his ears. An inner ear infection a couple of months ago had brought on spells of dizziness. None of the attacks lasted long but they were enough that he was grounded for now. Instead, because of his flying experience, he was being sent around different airfields training other pilots.

There were rumours that Fighter Command itself was to be restructured because of the expected invasion of Europe by Allied forces. Alisdair found that hard to believe, but he did know, despite all the hush hush, that this Ayrshire airfield was going to have a vital role to play if, and when, that second front came.

The resident No 516 Squadron was to assist the other armed services with realistic training for that eventual invasion of Europe. He had already seen for himself the practice attacks with live ammunition, the laying down of smokescreens and the dangerous low-level training flights across stretches of beaches and the sea. He expected to be here for a while as there was plenty to do training these brave pilots to fly across the Firth of Clyde and further away on tactical missions but he was wise enough to realise that Headquarters could intervene at any stage and send him anywhere across Britain.

His thoughts slid neatly from the war to a red-haired girl with big grey eyes, as they always did. Where was Kathy? And what a fool he was not to have asked for her address. He had no way of finding her again. Not unless he roamed the streets of Glasgow until he saw her. He was tempted. If he ever got sufficient leave, he'd be back to Nana Mackie's, walking around the streets by the river, the butcher's shop where he had run smack into her and the city centre café which she had told him was her favourite. There was a waitress there, the one he had left the letter with. She might know where Kathy lived.

But if Kathy was keen on him, why hadn't she written? It had been just over six weeks since they'd met and there had been no word. Beatrice Mackie knew to re-address any mail to him. He had written several letters to Nana and enquired but her replies said nothing had come from his 'highland lassie'. Don't let her break your heart, Beatrice warned in her spidery copperplate writing. Your work is important, concentrate on that. Another girl will come along. You'll see.

Alisdair was certain he didn't want another girl. It had taken only seconds for him to fall in love. The trouble was, it looked as if she hadn't fallen in love with him, if her silence was anything to go by. With a sigh that was as much annoyance as disappointment, Alisdair forced himself back to the task in hand. Signing off training modules was dull but vital and could mean, as with most of his work, the difference between life and death for the men he was working with.

–

Judith Lennox had also been peeling potatoes that September day. Unlike Kathy, she had finished preparing a mountain of them before midday so they were ready for the meal in the Maryhill Barracks where she served as one of the cooks. While the tatties boiled up in the large pots on the stove, she cut up tripe into strips and calf's liver into slices. She took a plate of sheep's kidneys over to the sink and washed them before removing the fat and cutting them into small pieces. Savoury tripe casserole was a regular dish at the barracks and the hungry soldiers polished it off in double-quick time whenever it was served up.

'Don't forget the dumplings,' the head cook shouted over to her.

Judith scowled. Of course she hadn't forgotten. That idiot seemed to think she had four hands instead of two to do all the work. She set the casserole in the hot oven and took her time getting the flour and dripping. Rubbing the dripping into the flour with a pinch of salt, she then moistened the mixture with water and rolled it into balls. She'd made them so often she reckoned she could do them in her sleep. She detested the job. She hated the way her hair reeked of fried meat at the end of her shift and her hands were reddened from the constant immersion in water.

It was all because of her Aunt Irene. Old Mrs Lennox, as she was known to the other inhabitants of Kiltie Street, was prone to bouts of illness and needed Judith to look after her, so there was never any question of Judith leaving home to join the services or undertake any other war work out of the city. It was Irene who had pushed Judith to apply for the cook's position when she saw it in the local newspaper early on in the war.

'It's no a proper cook, what they're wanting. Just a cook's assistant to chop the veg and whatnot. Even you could manage that,' Irene had told her. 'Stop sitting there like a fat lump and get yourself down there now to apply. Do ye hear me?'

Judith had heard her loud and clear. If she hadn't, a clout round her ear to make her head ring would have got her going. Aunt Irene wasn't shy about slapping and punching when Judith needed correcting. She often had a purpling bruise on her arm or leg where she'd been taught 'a wee lesson', as Irene would put it.

'Aye, you're slow for your age,' she'd say, shaking her head dolefully. 'I don't want to hit you, girl, but ye ask for it. I swore to your poor departed parents that I'd bring ye up proper. And that's what I'm doing. It's no ma fault if you cannae learn fast. But I'll learn ye. That's ma job. Your job is to be a good girl for me.'

Judith was a good girl. At least on the surface at home. She learned quickly enough as a child to duck some of the blows being handed out and to smile and be polite to her aunt. She had no memory of her parents to know if life with them would have been any easier. Her mother had died of influenza when Judith was a tiny baby and her father had died in a shipyard accident not long after. The anger that sat like a burning coal in her stomach was only reduced by lashing out at other children. She knew it was better to be a bully at school than be bullied herself.

Being large for her age and strong, it was easy to belt the few girls and boys who dared cross her. The rest kept out of her way. She had no friends at school but that hadn't bothered her.

Even though she hated her job cooking for the troops, until ten days ago she had hated going home after her shift even more. She would go wearily up the steps to number five Kiltie Street and the second-floor flat and as she stepped inside, the stink of urine would nip at her nostrils. She'd hardly be in the door before Irene was calling for her.

'I'm needing the cludgie now. Help me get there. Hurry up. My but you're as slow as a bloody cow!'

Irene's hand painfully clawed around her arm, Judith struggled to lift her aunt from the urine-soaked chair. They hobbled together out of the flat to the shared toilet on the landing. Judith managed to situate Irene over the toilet. She turned away. Once Irene was finished she helped her adjust her clothing and leaned over to flush the cludgie. There was blood in the water, as there had been for quite some while. Irene waddled back to their flat on swollen legs.

A year before, Judith had suggested that they get the doctor in because Irene was peeing so frequently. She'd got a slap on the face for that. Her aunt thought she was being cheeky. So Judith never mentioned the doctor again. Even when Irene began to have little accidents on a regular basis and the chair where she sat began to stink. It was Judith who had to mop it up with soap and hot water.

She ought to have been grateful for the neighbours coming in to help care for her aunt when the periodic bouts of illness got worse. But she felt their judgement on their smelly, shabby home even if they didn't say it out loud. She didn't want their pity. Especially not from that Kathy Dougal's ma. Aye, she might have a gentle voice and offer to make meals for Judith and to clean the flat, but Judith knew Mary Dougal blamed her partly for Kathy getting into trouble even if it was never mentioned.

Hadn't she paid twice over for her part in Kathy's shame? Irene had seen to that. She'd beaten Judith properly with a broom handle so that her ribs hurt and her skin was blue-black. She'd made sure Judith had no money to spend on herself and she wasn't allowed to go out except to work for months. And what punishment did Kathy Dougal get? As far as Judith could see it was none. She went away for a few months and came back acting like butter wouldn't melt in her mouth. Acting as a big sister to her brat and getting away with it. Well, not if Judith had anything to do with it. She enjoyed whispering comments and passing along a wee bit of chit chat when she could. There were several women working at the barracks who lived locally and liked to spread gossip.

And then, ten days ago, Irene Lennox had up and died. She'd been poorly all day, complaining of pain in her bones and her hips and screeching when Judith tried to lift her bloated legs up onto a stool to ease them. She looked so pale that Judith had been scared and had run to get Leila Connelly, who lived at number one and was a friend of Irene's. Mrs Connelly had taken one look and insisted on calling out Doctor Graham. Irene refused to go to hospital, declaring she'd rather die in her own home than in a place she didn't know. She had got her wish, Judith thought with a mixture of guilt and satisfaction. A few hours after the doctor and Leila Connelly had arrived, she took one big sigh from her prone position on the couch and flopped back dead.

Now Judith's back ached, not from one of her aunt's beatings but from sheer hard work cooking over huge pots and lifting heavy trays from the oven and hefting them over to the scarred wooden tables before they were taken out to the mess and the noisy soldiers waiting for their grub.

Wearily, she put on her navy blue coat, pulling another frayed thread from the left cuff. The elbows were shiny with age and the coat was tight against her chest, but it was the only coat she owned so it would have to do. Her mid-brown hair and chestnut eyes might have been better suited to a green-coloured coat, but at least the dark colour hid any stains. No one wished her good evening as she left the barracks. They might enjoy the titbits of gossip she provided but she knew they didn't like her.

At least she had the flat to herself. She'd scrubbed it clean after Irene's funeral to get rid of the disgusting ammonia smell. Some traces lingered but it wasn't too bad. She'd nicked a couple of slices of tripe and slipped two tatties into her pocket for her tea. As she went up to the flat she was looking forward to eating them and having peace and quiet on her own.

There was a man standing outside her door. Well, not what she would call a man exactly. It was her landlord's son, Frankie Bett. She'd been to school with him. He turned when he heard her behind him and his prominent Adam's apple bobbed under the skin of his throat. His buck teeth appeared in a nervous grin.

'What do you want, Frankie? It's been a long day.' Judith yawned.

'I... I need to come and see your flat. Ma dad says I must.'

She smelled the stale sweat wafting off his work shirt. It was probably no worse than her own smell of sheep's offal and boiled veggies.

'Why do you need to see my home?'

'It's just… with yer ma passing an' all…'

'She wasn't ma ma, Frankie. She was ma auld aunt. And I don't want ye comin' inside. I'm tired after a day's work and I want to rest.'

Judith pushed past him and he shied away. She'd forgotten how she used to bully him at school when he was a quiet wee laddie and make him give up his play-time piece to her. Sweet apple jeely on bread it was without fail, and she'd looked forward to it to each day.

'Why aren't you fighting for yer country anyhow?' she said, knowing full well he had failed his medical on account of flat feet and being a bit slow in the head.

She ignored his stuttered answer and went inside, letting him follow like an unwanted dog.

'…I'm taking over some of the business from my dad,' Frankie finished proudly. 'And yours is the first bit of *negotiation* what I've tae dae.'

'What's that?' Judith said sleepily, remembering to remove the potatoes from her pocket and the paper package of tripe, both of which she laid on the sideboard.

She sank down onto the cleaned couch. She had bought a red blanket to cover the urine stains which refused to come out of the material completely. It clashed with the purple cushions but it had been cheap at the market which was what mattered the most.

The newspaper lay open where she'd slung it that morning. She intended to use it to make tapers for the fire. There was much talk of Mr Churchill's Second Front. 'Army for the Second Front is Ready' shouted the headline with a photograph of Mr Churchill himself smiling. Even Judith knew that the Italian government had unconditionally surrendered a fortnight before and that the Allies were gathering a huge army to invade Western Europe.

But her gaze now was drawn to a smaller article entitled 'Rent Ramp' as Frankie fidgeted and went pink in the face. 'The rent ramp has been one of the most unpleasant features of that aspect of the war which is dominated by those who seek to draw profit from misfortune... about the extortionate nature of the rents charged in many of the larger cities there can be no doubt.' Aye, a lot of big, fancy words which she didn't understand but she got enough to know that she was, right now, the victim of that rent ramp.

There was an advertisement at the bottom right-hand corner of the newspaper page. There were sketch drawings of six young women in uniform, including a Wren, a soldier, a nurse and a bus conductor. 'Housewives to be... We, who owe our success to the housewives of peace-time Britain, record here our tribute to their daughters and grand-daughters in uniform.' Then in large bold letters: 'Salute! FROM HOOVER'. For some reason it seemed important. Judith puzzled over why it had caught her attention until Frankie's polite cough brought her back to the moment.

'My dad... that is myself... we need your flat back,' Frankie said. He looked at his feet rather than at Judith. 'This flat is too big for one person and Dad... I mean myself... we know you can't afford the rent. Which, by the way, is going up.'

'What?' Judith wasn't sleepy now. The shock had woken her right up. 'You can't throw me out.'

'Yes, we can. If you can't pay the rent.' Frankie sounded more confident now.

Judith knew he was right. Without Irene, there was no way she could pay the rent on a flat that included two bedrooms and a parlour as well as a kitchen. She had avoided thinking about that in the last ten days as she had enjoyed her aunt's absence. Now Frankie and that bloody rent ramp newspaper article were in her face, making it a reality.

'Where will I go?' she said, without thinking.

'That's no ma problem,' Frankie said, a slight swagger appearing in his gait.

If he thought he had the upper hand, he could think again. Judith's brain was working at a rapid rate. Aunt Irene might have called her slow, but she was wrong. Judith was quite capable of working things out. Besides, hadn't she bested Frankie as a child many times over?

'Have you got a smaller flat I could rent? A single end then, just the one room?' she asked, trying to keep the desperation out of her voice.

'There's none available,' Frankie replied.

Judith undid the top two buttons on her blouse. Her cleavage showed nicely.

'Are you sure about that?' she said, leaning forward from the couch so that Frankie could get an eyeful.

'I'm pretty sure,' Frankie said doubtfully. 'Dad said there was nothing to rent. We've got all our properties full up.'

Judith cursed him under her breath. She plumped up her breasts but other than staring and swallowing so hard his Adam's apple bobbed up and down like a fisherman's float, Frankie didn't say anything.

Judith stood up from the couch. Her throat was dry and she felt a pulse beat painfully in her temple but she could see no alternative to what she was about to do. She beckoned to Frankie and made her way to her bedroom. She didn't wait to see whether he followed. She sat down on the bed. The door was wide open and then he was there, staring at her.

'I need a small flat, Frankie. A single end. That's all I'm asking for.' She hated begging to this scrawny youth but managed a sickly smile as she patted the space beside her. A few kisses and cuddles would be worth the price if she had a place to stay. 'Can we at least chat about the payment?'

Chapter Five

After four weeks at the barracks in York, it was time for the new recruits to move on to different camps depending on what they were now being trained for. All the marching and physical exercises had toughened their bodies but it was the exam scores and personal traits that were important when it came to being assigned to further ATS duties.

'I wish I'd known why we were doing all those bloomin' tests,' Kathy said as the girls sat together in their hut on one of their last evenings together, sipping hot cocoa and nibbling the ginger cake that was Cook's latest offering.

'Why are you complaining? I'd be delighted to be going to anti-aircraft training,' Geraldine said miserably. She had been told she was going to be a general ATS orderly and was headed for a posting up in Aberdeenshire.

'I'm all right with it,' Kathy said, wrinkling her nose. 'But there's Hilda getting to drive trucks down south. I quite fancy that.'

Hilda raised a tear-stained face in astonishment at Kathy before her gaze flicked to Bets and her expression crumpled. Bets wasn't going to the same place as Hilda. She had been directed to office work, which she seemed happy about, and was staying at York doing secretarial duties for the senior officers.

'Well, I don't care about driving trucks,' Bridie said cheerfully. 'I'm glad that me, Kathy and Jennifer will all stay together when we go to Shropshire. Besides, we're all doing our bit whatever we end up being trained in. We're all helping to defeat Hitler and end the war.'

That sobered them up and made a few shoulders go back proudly. They weren't raw recruits any more. In fact, they had stared at the new arrivals fresh off the truck just the day before and grinned at each other. The light chatter and sight of fresh-faced girls in their dresses and coats dragging suitcases and releasing a lingering delicate scent of different fragrances wafting into the cold October air was odd when they were used to khaki and stinky mud and the sergeant bellowing.

'Don't be glum, chum,' Bets said in her rich, low voice that made them think of movie stars. 'Think on the bright side. We've all got forty-eight-hour passes before we move to our new abodes. How fabulous to be going home after all this time.'

'Do we?' Kathy squealed. 'Why did nobody tell me that?'

'Probably because you weren't listening as usual when the corporal announced it,' Bets laughed.

Oh, what a lovely thought, to be in Kiltie Street once more, and see Mammy, Harry, Jeannie and most of all her baby Dennis. She couldn't wait. Suddenly it didn't matter if she wasn't going to be a truck driver. Who cared if she was being sent to a mixed AA battery. The only thing she could think of was going home. She might have been desperate to leave a month ago but a couple of days with her family was just what she needed before her next adventure.

On the day of departure from the York barracks there were tears and hugs all round. Kathy didn't mind saying goodbye to Bridie and Jennifer because she knew they would meet soon enough at Oswestry, but it was sad to hug Bets and Hilda and Geraldine knowing they might never see each other again. With promises to write and keep in touch, they went their separate ways. Only Kathy was going to the railway station. There was an army truck taking some of the others south for part of the journey while a few weren't going home at all.

She felt a little lonely, lugging her suitcase into the railway station with its smell of coals and hot, damp steam. Her train had just arrived and passengers were coming off while others waited to get aboard and find a carriage. She sat in a middle compartment which was quiet, with only an elderly gentleman reading a newspaper and a woman who was knitting and who smiled at her as she came in. It would take most of the day to get home. She'd only have a few hours and overnight and then would have to get the train back before midday. It would be worth it though.

The train was delayed starting and seemed to chug along sluggishly while Kathy wished it forward with her mind. The elderly man shook his newspaper pages impatiently and grumbled to the woman, who nodded and kept knitting. The conductor came round when they'd been travelling a couple of hours.

'I say, when do you expect us to arrive in Berwick?' the gentleman said. 'If I'm not mistaken, we will be quite late in.'

'I do apologise, sir. There's a war on, of course, and that doesn't help. We'll be in Berwick-upon-Tweed soon

64

but I'm sorry to say we'll be sitting there for a good hour or so for various reasons I can't share with you before we journey further north.'

Kathy heard that with dismay. It was a long enough journey to get to Glasgow without delays. Perhaps she should've gone straight down to Shropshire the way Jennifer had decided to do.

'Oh dear,' the woman murmured, looking at Kathy. 'Is someone meeting you, dear? Will they be worried?'

'No, I'll be fine, thank you.' She'd written to Mammy to say she was coming but hadn't told her exactly when. She was glad of that now. She didn't want Mammy and Harry fretting at Glasgow Central Station when she didn't turn up.

The train eventually pulled into Berwick-upon-Tweed's red sandstone railway station in a great waft of steam and with a blast of the horn. Kathy could taste the coal dust in the back of her throat as she gingerly stepped down onto the platform. She had left her suitcase in the carriage and hoped to find a cup of tea somewhere as she was parched. Maybe a bite to eat too. They had been given fish paste sandwiches wrapped in paper to take with them, but she'd eaten those already.

The station was busy with troops. There was a young couple clasped together at the edge of the platform, the girl sobbing loudly as Kathy went past. She stared around and saw a tea room beside a waiting room. Marching with determination towards it, she was brought up short by the sight of a man in RAF blue uniform appearing in front of the tea room. He stared at her.

'Alisdair?' Kathy said in disbelief.

Her heart leapt at seeing him in spite of her memories of being stood up in Maggie's Café and her humiliation and shame at him finding out her secret. She felt her face heat up and her hands flew to her hair, hoping it was neat and tidy.

'Kathy, I can't believe it's you. What are you doing here?'

'I'm going home on leave before my next posting.' She was surprised to find her voice was steady despite the mixture of anger and uncertainty she felt. Was he going to explain why he had stood her up in the café? Would he shame her by telling her he knew she was unmarried with a baby and that she wasn't good enough for him?

But when he spoke he didn't mention either.

'You joined the army, that's marvellous.'

Did he remember that he was the one who had encouraged her to do so? She was about to ask when a tall man came out of the tea room and called to Alisdair. He had to be Alisdair's father – he had the same strong features, although his hair was grey instead of black.

Alisdair looked dismayed as he waved to the older man and glanced back to Kathy.

'I'm sorry, I have to go,' he said abruptly.

Kathy watched as he followed his father back inside the tea room and closed the door. He was ashamed to introduce her to his family. Her face was hot with embarrassment. There was no way she was going in there to get a cup of tea now. How could she face them?

She stumbled on her heel as she turned and went back towards the train. Sitting in the carriage, mercifully alone as her travelling companions were nowhere to be seen, she shook her head as she went back over what had just happened. Had he been pleased to see her? She'd thought for a moment that his eyes had lit up. But she must have been wrong. He thought she was a slut because of Dennis.

That was why he didn't want his father to know her. She'd made a fool of herself twice over for him. Never again, she promised. If she ever met him in the street she'd pretend they were strangers. After all, what was one pot of tea together in the grand scheme of life? Nothing at all.

–

Inside the railway station tea room, Alisdair followed his father back towards the small table where his mother was surreptitiously mopping her tears. If Donald Meikle had noticed Kathy, he didn't mention it. The tea room was busy, thick with cigarette smoke and a hubbub of chatter.

'Be a good chap and speak to your mother, will you? I won't have a scene in public, do you hear?'

Alisdair was still reeling from the shock of seeing Kathy. Had it been a dream? He was desperate to run out of the tea room onto the station concourse to find her but common sense prevailed. This was the worst possible time to introduce the girl he loved to his parents. He knew his dismay must have shown on his face and he cursed himself. She must think he didn't care for her when that was the absolute opposite of the truth. He would write to her, care of Maggie's Café, and explain.

Although it was hard to explain what was going on between his parents. His father's cold, sarcastic comments to his mother and her easy tears baffled him. And embarrassed him, if he was honest. There was no way he could have invited Kathy to join them for tea.

'Alisdair!' his father said quietly but with a steely tone that had him almost standing to attention. Years of being disciplined whenever he was home from boarding school saw to that. Donald was a 'spare the rod and spoil the child' sort of father.

'Sir?'

'Damn it, tell her to stop crying,' Donald whispered harshly.

They were almost at the table now. Mabel Meikle glanced up, her eyes red-rimmed, sniffing into a small handkerchief.

'Your father is being most unkind, Alisdair. I think we should go.'

'Mother, the train doesn't leave for another half hour. Please calm yourself, there's a dear. Another cup of tea, perhaps?'

'He doesn't care a jot for me, you know,' Mabel said, ignoring her son's suggestion. 'I only run the shops. He didn't ask me if I wanted to sell one of them.' Her face crumpled.

'Oh, for goodness' sake. Tell your mother it's for her own good. We can retire a little early on the proceeds.'

'I don't want to retire, Donald. That's what I keep telling you, but you're not listening,' Mabel hissed.

Alisdair wished he was anywhere but here. What a fool he was, not to have run after Kathy and got her address. She was in the army. He was impressed. She looked so beautiful in her khaki jacket and skirt and her neat cap with its ATS badge. He looked at his parents. Donald was sitting ramrod straight, his large hand clasped round the tea cup, his gaze fixed on the wall. Mabel was blowing her nose and darting nervous little glances at her husband.

'Excuse me just a moment,' Alisdair said suddenly.

He heard their murmured exclamations but didn't stop. He had to find Kathy. He hurried through the tea room as fast as a polite walk allowed. Outside, he stared about at the platforms. There were throngs of passengers, a luggage cart and porter, steam and so much khaki that unless he

68

caught sight of Kathy's bright red hair, she was going to be camouflaged from his view.

He brushed past a few folk. His RAF uniform gained him a way through but he couldn't see her.

'Train to Glasgow?' he called in desperation to the guard coming towards him.

The older man shook his head. 'You've missed it, son. It left about five minutes ago. Not another now till tomorrow.'

That was that, then. His own leave was coming to an end. He'd accompany his parents home from the disastrous visit to their accountant and then head north, back to Ayrshire. He might not see Kathy for a very long while. He refused to believe that it might be never. She'd said Maggie's was her favourite café, and Maggie had promised to pass on his letter. Even if Kathy had somehow missed that first letter with his nana's address, she couldn't miss his second. He'd put the address once more, in capital letters, and beg her to write to him.

–

It was very late when Kathy rapped on the door to number four Kiltie Street. Inside, she heard Mammy's voice and Harry's deep tones. The door opened and their expressions of surprise and delight were worth the long journey. Suddenly she was enfolded in their arms and Mammy was kissing her cheek and rubbing her back and asking so many questions that Kathy didn't bother to answer.

'Mary, let your daughter breathe for a minute,' Harry laughed.

'I cannae believe she's home, so I can't. How long are you staying for?'

'I've to go again tomorrow midday,' Kathy said. 'Where's Dennis?'

'Och, he's in his bed as you might well imagine. Don't you go waking him up,' Mary warned.

Kathy ignored that and sneaked into the back bedroom. In the darkness as her eyes adjusted she could make out the small lump under the covers. Only tufty hair and one outflung arm was visible. She kissed her son's soft hair, breathing in the smell of him.

'I'll see you in the morning,' she whispered.

Dennis mumbled in his sleep and rolled over. Kathy tiptoed out. She longed to give him a cuddle but Mammy was right. She'd have to be patient and wait for tomorrow. She realised Mary and Harry were in their nightclothes. It was later than she knew. They stood there yawning and Kathy yawned too.

'I'll catch you up on it all tomorrow. I need a sleep,' she said.

Lying in bed, with Jeannie breathing evenly in the bed beside hers, it was as if she'd never been away. Images of York and sleeping in the hut with Bridie, Jennifer and the other girls drifted into her mind but they seemed unreal. She snuggled down with a sigh. It was good to be home.

–

'It was a long way to come just to be going again after a very early lunch,' Jeannie remarked as they sat at the kitchen table the next morning.

Kathy was cuddling Dennis. He pulled at her hair and grinned up at her. She blew a raspberry into the soft curve of his neck and he shrieked happily. She bounced him on her knee and looked at Jeannie.

'The army only gave me forty-eight hours,' she said. 'Let's make the most of it by eating breakfast.'

Jeannie shuddered. 'None for me. The thought of it makes me want to boak.'

She did look pale. Kathy hadn't suffered much with morning sickness during her own pregnancy but Jeannie was clearly having a different experience. Kathy knew she'd have to make the porridge but, reluctant to get up, jiggled Dennis. Before she knew it, he had slipped off her knees and hit the floor. He lay there and cried, great sobs that made her feel terrible.

'Come here, wee man. Come and Kaa will make it better,' she said, grabbing for him.

He squealed and wriggled away. Mary came into the kitchen, no doubt wondering what was going on. Dennis crawled to her and she picked him up. He burrowed his head into her neck.

'For the love of God, what a din youse are making. Can you no boil the porridge without any nonsense,' Mary snapped.

Without another word, she took the sobbing Dennis out of the room. Kathy got up and took the blackened pot from the side, filled it with oatmeal and water and put it on the range. She hardly saw the porridge as she stirred it. Dennis had never rejected her before. She had kissed his hurts and fears away since he was born.

'What did you expect?' Jeannie said gently from behind her.

'I don't understand.'

'You've been away a whole month. That's a very long time when you're a toddler. He's got used to you not being here.'

'But I'm his mammy.'

'You're not though. You gave him up. Our mammy's his mammy.'

Jeannie stood up, cradling her belly. Kathy smelled the porridge burning, an acrid stink rising from the range.

'How dare you judge me?' she cried. 'It's easy for you. You've got Bill and you're married. It was different for me.'

She turned away from her sister and took the pot and flung it into the sink. A loud hiss of steam spat up and water splashed onto the front of her dress. She was livid with Jeannie. *She* would never give her baby up. Miss Goody Two Shoes. She'd never have got pregnant like Kathy did, in a back lane up against a wall. The shame burned her cheeks.

'What's wrong with Mammy anyway? She's never grumpy like that,' she flung out.

'She's exhausted. She's been napping afternoons.'

'Why? Is she ill?'

'She's got too much work looking after the house, and Dennis is lively. I help where I can but I've been sick myself mornings and I'm at the factory all day.'

There was reproach in Jeannie's soft voice, even if she didn't come right out and blame Kathy for leaving them. Fear for Mammy and anger with Jeannie made her stalk out of the kitchen. She wished she'd never come home.

–

She and Jeannie still hadn't made up by midday. Kathy told them she didn't need an escort to the train station, she'd make her own way. Was it her imagination or did Mammy look relieved at that? Hurt, Kathy was bright and brittle in her conversation with Mary and Harry. She tickled

Dennis under his chin. He seemed to have forgiven her for his fall and chuckled his lovely, deep little boy's laugh at her touch. She noticed he turned to Mary though as he got sleepy.

She slipped on her smart ATS jacket and army cap, tucking her hair in neatly. She picked up her suitcase from the hallway.

'See youse all sometime. I don't know when I'll next get leave or whether I'll get home again. I'm based way down south now.'

With a bright, fixed smile, she clattered down the steps and onto Kiltie Street. She glanced back once at the end of the road. Mary and Harry were standing watching her. They waved. Kathy waved back briefly, hoisted her suitcase and walked with determination towards the bus stop. She felt very alone. She'd fallen out with Jeannie, Mammy had been annoyed with her and Dennis didn't need her. As for Alisdair Meikle, he had made it very plain that he didn't want her.

Chapter Six

'Kathy!' Bridie cried. 'There you are. Me and Jennifer have been watching out for you. We've kept you a bunk. It's next to mine.'

'This place is enormous. I wasn't sure which hut to go to.' Kathy's suitcase bumped against her leg as she fell into Bridie's walking pace.

Bridie seemed very much at home already as she took Kathy to their accommodation block and showed her the bed. She put her suitcase on it and sat down gratefully. It was evening now and there were thirty or so other young women sitting in the large room, drinking cocoa, darning socks, mending uniforms or sewing.

'Good journey?' Bridie asked, sitting beside her.

'Aye, it was all right. Bit slow as usual.'

'Training starts tomorrow. Was it nice seeing your family?'

'Aye.' She wasn't going to tell Bridie about falling out with everyone. She still didn't feel she knew either her or Jennifer well enough for that. 'Did you not want to go home?'

Bridie shook her head. 'Better to come straight here. My dad's not the easiest to be around.'

There was so much she didn't know about her new friends. Kathy didn't like to pry further; Bridie's expression said she didn't want to elaborate. Jennifer arrived at that moment, bringing mugs of cocoa, and the three girls chatted and caught up with one another.

'Oh, I forgot, Bets sent you this.' Bridie jumped up and rummaged in the box beside her bunk. She waved a lipstick triumphantly.

'That's for me?' Kathy said, feeling ridiculously pleased that Bets had given her a gift.

Bridie smiled. 'They came in the post. Bets is missing us all. She's met a generous American. Actually she's his personal secretary. So there was chocolate and a pair of stockings and a piece of soap too. Jennifer got the stockings and I got the soap and we'll give you a bit of the chocolate but Bets remembered you sharing your lipstick with us the night we went out dancing, so this one's for you.'

Kathy took the top off and the creamy orange-red colour of the lipstick and its sweet scent reminded her so vividly of Jeannie that guilt flooded through her. She hastily put it in her bag.

'Don't you like it?' Jennifer asked with puzzled brows.

Kathy nodded. 'It's kind of Bets.'

'She's so loved up, she wants the world to share it with her,' Jennifer laughed.

'And she's not the only one,' Bridie said snidely, poking Jennifer in the side until that familiar hooting laugh rang out and heads all turned briefly in the busy hut before conversations continued.

'Ooh, do tell,' Kathy said, putting Jeannie and their argument firmly out of her head. Here she was back in her new life and she was determined to enjoy it.

'Jennifer here has met the handsome Sergeant Kenny. He's about six foot four so is actually taller than Jen.'

'It makes a nice change to look up to a man and not down on the crown of his head,' Jennifer agreed, looking somewhat smug as Bridie described the sergeant to Kathy.

'I think I'm in love,' she added with a dreamy look that had the other two glancing at each other and grinning.

'Do you believe in love at first sight?' Jennifer asked them.

A shaft of pain shot through Kathy's midriff. Yes, she did. Wasn't that just what had happened to her when she bumped into Alisdair Meikle? She had been smitten immediately. His dimple, the intense green eyes, his cultured accent and those broad shoulders. He was surely every girl's dream. But it was more than that. She couldn't describe it. Something about how he held himself, his confidence in himself which had rubbed off on her when she was with him, the faint aroma of hair cream and woodbines and soap…

'Kathy Dougal, you've gone all soppy. You're in love too, aren't you?' Bridie cried.

'No! Not at all,' she snapped.

There was an awkward pause and Bridie looked uncomfortable.

'Sorry, I didn't mean to… I'm happy for you, Jennifer, but it's not for me. I'm not looking for love.' Kathy sniffed and rubbed her nose.

It was true. Alisdair had put her off the whole notion when he'd rejected her. She tried not to blame him. After all, no man was going to want her when she had a child. Oh, if she hadn't been such a wee fool, going with that soldier. She'd thought they were getting married and he had duped her. Now she seemed a long way from her sixteen-year-old self.

'What about you, Bridie? Any men on the horizon?' She forced herself to be cheerful.

Bridie gazed at her shrewdly for a moment as if she'd say something, then shook her head.

'I've never met anyone that I fancied yet.'

'Oh, but you will,' Jennifer said, enthusiastically. 'There's lots of men here. Stands to reason there's one for you. And if you don't fancy the men here, someone told me there's an RAF base close by at Rednal.'

'I don't know. It's like there's something missing in me. I like men, but as friends, not lovers.'

Jennifer was having none of that and the conversation proceeded with her arguing the case of sheer numbers while Bridie protested and the three of them ended up giggling. Listening to Jennifer recounting Sergeant Kenny's many wonderful virtues, Kathy hoped that, in time, she could forget Alisdair and the pain of thinking about him. Maybe she'd be like Bridie and never get a man. Even if she found someone, there was no getting away from the fact that Dennis existed. That had to remain her secret forever.

Before long, the bugle sounded and the lights went out. Kathy lay there in the dark, the sounds of rustling blankets and other women's breathing all around her. She shut her eyes and thoughts of home and of Dennis and then of Alisdair swirled up, even though she had decided to forget him. With a deep breath, she turned over. It felt now as if she was ready for camp life again.

–

Park Hall Royal Artillery Training Centre was stretched out across the Shropshire countryside. Beyond the camp was a gentle carpet of fields and hedgerows with undulating small hills in the distance which Kathy glimpsed as they marched the next morning. It felt good to swing her arms and pump her legs in time with Bridie and Jennifer on either side of her, managing a quick grin to them before the sergeant noticed, then head straight forward, face solemn, all energy focussed on the repetitive movements until he was satisfied.

In the afternoon, they were trained in aircraft recognition, using scale models and charts showing black silhouettes of the planes.

'It would be awful if we shot down one of our own,' Bridie whispered, leaning over to Kathy in the hall.

'If I had to shoot right now, it's a distinct possibility,' Kathy whispered back. 'I had no idea there were so many different sorts of aircraft.'

'They sound different, I'm told,' Jennifer chipped in and then blushed when the instructor paused in his lecture to stare at them.

It was like being in school again. Kathy felt a bubble of laughter rise in her chest and stifled it. Besides, Jennifer was mainly blushing because the instructor was none other than her lovely Howard Kenny. His stern glare had softened as it landed on Jennifer's face.

After that, they had a class in vocal training. They were hoarse afterwards as they had to do a lot of shouting, or 'voice projection' as the instructor called it.

'What was that all about?' Kathy coughed, stroking her neck.

'It's because we'll have to call the firing orders to the men on the guns when we get posted to the mixed batteries. We have to make ourselves heard. It could be life or death.'

Kathy shivered. It was hard to imagine that in a few short weeks they would be doing this for real. They were training to be gunner girls with the Royal Artillery. It made her feel proud, and for a moment she wondered if Alisdair would be proud of her too. She squashed that traitorous thought. She was over him. Of course she was!

That evening, she sat on her bed and decided to write a letter to Jeannie. Around her, the other girls were talking in small groups or writing. A few girls were preparing different coloured silk threads to begin embroidering a plain white tablecloth that one of them had brought with her to the camp. They invited Kathy, Bridie and Jennifer to join them. Kathy said she would once she'd written her letter.

She felt bad about arguing with Jeannie. She knew that her sister was worried about Mammy and that was why she blamed Kathy for leaving. She picked up her pen and it hovered over the blank page of precious paper. She sighed and put it down. She glanced over to where the sewing circle were giggling together. It was tempting to forget about writing and join them. She picked up the pen.

> *Dear Jeannie*
> *I'm sorry I took your lipstick but here's a new one. I hope you get to wear it on a night out dancing with Bill. How is Dennis? How's Mammy and Harry?*
> *Love from Kathy xxx*

She popped Bets's lipstick into the envelope and sealed it. She'd post it tomorrow after her duties were done. With relief, she slipped into a chair next to Bridie. A girl with very curly brown hair gave her a needle threaded with scarlet thread and pointed at the outline of a rose. Kathy shook her head.

'I'll only spoil it. I'm terrible at sewing. But I'll sit with youse lot and watch, if that's all right.'

Heads nodded as the girls sewed and Kathy was content to sit with them.

As it turned out, her letter and Jeannie's crossed in the post. After a day of more marching and shouting and exhausting physical training, she came back from the post-box to discover a letter from home.

> *Dear Kathy*
>
> *I'm so sorry we argued. I know we squabble a lot but that was a proper argument and I feel terrible about it. I should have made it up with you before you left. I kept thinking what if something happened to you before I had a chance to make it up? I hope you get this letter quickly. I know the trains are so awful these days and post doesn't always make it.*
>
> *Please don't worry about Mammy. She's tired but I'm here and so's Harry. We'll look after her. She says herself that it's the weather and the war grinding on. She promises she'll be better by spring when it's brighter days. Harry doesn't want you to worry.*
>
> *Dennis misses you too. He's been calling for his Kaa. I'm that sorry I said you gave him up. I know you had to. It wasn't easy for you the way it is for me. You were right. I've got Bill and I'm married so it's respectable. But you're strong, Kathy Dougal. You'll be all right. You'll find a man who loves you and will love Dennis too. I know it.*

*Until then, you take care, do you hear me? I
love you, wee sister. I always will.
Your loving sister Jeannie*

She felt better after reading it. It was like a weight had
lifted from her. Which was odd because she hadn't realised
that their argument had affected her. She was used to bick-
ering with Jeannie, but this had been different. Harsher,
somehow. Reading it again, she was annoyed with Harry.
He was too over-protective. Of course she was going to
fret about Mammy. He couldn't stop her doing that. She
wasn't a child to be sheltered from whatever was going on.
If only she wasn't so far away. If she was able to nip home
every few weeks, what a difference that might make. That,
however, was unlikely now. Especially since the rumour
was that after Oswestry, they'd be going to Wales to a
practice firing camp, directing gunfire for real at targets.

In the meantime, their training continued. They had
to learn about the different guns used in the batteries and
were introduced to the spotter telescopes, the height-and-
range finder and predictor instruments. Kathy huddled
with the other girls in the slimy ankle-deep mud on chilly
October days, their steel helmets on, peering into the
height-and-range finder and trying not to slip on all the
muddy cables. This was accompanied by the constant,
tiresome noise of the generator and lots of voice projection as they practised shouting numbers to the men at the
guns. It took five operators to work the predictor which,
as far as Kathy could see, was a magic box giving answers
to where the enemy aeroplane would be, when combined
with distances to the target, and how long it would take
for the round to arrive at that future position.

Soon, any pangs for Alisdair were lost in the gruelling
long days of training. In the evenings, the girls continued

to embroider the tablecloth. They drank mugs of cocoa and huddled round the stoves as cold draughts blew in from the window frames and under the door. Kathy and Bridie took walks in the country lanes on their evenings off while Jennifer spent her free time with Howard Kenny when possible. Thursday evening, however, was camp night, when they were expected to clean their uniforms and kit, sweep and wash the floor of the room and perform other tasks.

'We're getting a new corporal,' Jennifer announced, draining her mug and giving herself a cocoa moustache. She wiped it away with the back of her hand.

'That's not surprising,' Bridie said wryly.

Their corporal had left abruptly the day before and the rumour was that she had been having an affair with a senior officer and had been sent home.

'But the new one's a Scotty, like our Kathy here,' Jennifer said.

'How do you…? Oh, Howard told you, I suppose. Hot off the press.' Bridie grinned.

'And, here she is now,' Kathy murmured and shot the other two a warning stare, as a slim, fair-haired girl came into the room and looked around with a smile.

'Hello, everybody. I'm Violet Stewart, and I'm your new body in charge. Anyone has any problems at all, come and see me and I'll sort it out.'

She sounded cheerful and the atmosphere in the room went in an instant from alert to relaxed, as the girls all looked at the arrival and realised their new corporal was a good sort. She had a Scottish accent, Kathy thought, but not a Glasgow one like hers.

Her questions were answered when Violet came to introduce herself to them all.

'Where are you from?' Violet asked when Kathy spoke. 'That sounds like a voice from home.'

She was being nice, of course. There was no way Violet's posh accent placed her home in the same area as Kathy's.

'Maryhill in Glasgow.'

'Gosh, what a coincidence. I was based in Glasgow until I was given this posting. I'm from Helensburgh. You must know it?'

Kathy did know it. Helensburgh was a seaside town about thirty miles north of the city. It was a traditional holiday destination for Glaswegians who went 'doon the watter' (down the water) on their two weeks off work in the summer by boat or train. Or had done before the war. The Dougals had gone there once for a day out and Kathy remembered donkey rides on the sandy beach, building sandcastles for a competition and eating ice cream.

'It's a beautiful place,' Kathy said politely. 'Must be nice to live beside the sea.'

For a moment Violet's bright smile slipped, but then it widened again and she agreed that it was indeed jolly nice. She excused herself from them and circulated round the other young women, chatting and putting them all at ease.

'I think she'll do just fine,' Bridie remarked as she picked up her sewing kit and her shirt, which had a tear in it.

'Aye, it'll be good to hear about homely things,' Kathy agreed. 'I love youse lot but it is nice to hear a west coast voice, even if Violet's as posh as they come.'

But over the next few days, whenever they had free time in the evenings and during that weekend, Violet was never about. She seemed to vanish mysteriously only to reappear when on duty.

-

Violet slipped out of camp, glad that it was Saturday and she had a whole day off. Her new bunch of recruits were a lovely lot and she had worked them hard with physical training the last few days while also keeping an eye on their wellbeing. It helped having her bunk in the same room as theirs so she could check on them discreetly, and at least as corporal she had the privacy of a curtain to draw across her tiny section of sleeping space.

Now she was glad to escape from the army camp, if only for a few hours. It was hard to forget the war completely when she had to wear her khaki skirt and jacket and army cap along with the obligatory clumpy shoes. But still. She had a parcel wrapped in brown paper under her arm as she hurried through the village. The cottage was a mile on from the village, down a winding lane fringed with hawthorn and hazel. At this time of year the hedges were covered in bright red berries and birds flitted up with a trill of song as she passed. The leaves were turning to gold. She loved autumn, with its crisp, cold sunshine and misty mornings. She glimpsed a red toadstool with white dots as she picked up her pace. She grinned, thinking of fairies. Evie would love a story about that.

The cottage also looked as if it was out of a fairy story. It had a thatched roof over solid honey-coloured stone walls and a climbing rose adorned the blue front door. Violet shivered slightly. It might look gorgeous, but she knew from brief experience that it was hard to heat and that things rustled in the rafters.

A small face appeared at the window.

'Auntie Violet's here,' Evie shrieked, tearing open the door and flinging herself at Violet's legs.

She staggered, almost losing the parcel, but managed to stay upright and bent to hug her niece.

'Happy Birthday, Evie. This is for you.' She gave the little girl the parcel and Evie ran back into the cottage.

'Mama! Auntie Violet's here.'

'So I gathered. Hallo, Violet dear.'

Felicity leaned against the door frame looking slight but beautiful, a cigarette held lazily between two slim fingers. She had the same fair colouring as Violet and they were of similar height and build, but Violet knew she wasn't as pretty as her older sister. It didn't bother her. It had been nothing but a curse to Felicity, she thought privately.

'Wipe your feet on the mat, dearest, and then come and tell me all. What excitement have you had this week with your children?'

'They're hardly children, Felicity. They're gunner girls. But they are in my charge and I do feel an awful lot of responsibility for them. You'll never guess, there's a girl who's from Glasgow. It made me feel quite homesick, hearing her speak.'

'Oh yes. Anyone we know?'

'Not quite. She's a working-class girl from Maryhill, but jolly nice.'

'Jolly nice,' Felicity mimicked her and chuckled. 'God, Violet, *you're* jolly nice. You see the best in everyone, don't you?'

'Well, most people are nice, aren't they?'

'You're not counting our mother in that, I take it,' Felicity remarked.

'Shhh,' Violet said, glancing around for Evie. 'She'll hear you. Whatever the circumstances, Mummy is Evie's grandmother.'

But her niece had bounced happily into the living room with her birthday present and was singing to herself. Felicity coughed. Violet went towards her but her sister waved her away with a plume of blue-grey smoke.

'Don't. Let's enjoy the day, shall we. Come and have a seat and I'll make a pot of tea. Evie and I baked some scones and we've got some WI jam from the village which is just the ticket.'

Violet bit her lip to stop the reproach that threatened. Honestly, Felicity was the end. She never listened nor did what she was told. Ian Regan being a case in point. Their parents had opposed the match as the Regans were not social equals. Felicity, in high dudgeon, had run off and married him and been cast off by their parents. She and Ian had lived together in a tiny fisherman's cottage on a rundown highland estate until he was conscripted when the war came and lost his life at Dunkirk. Felicity had stayed on at the cottage until Violet persuaded her to move with her down to Shropshire.

Felicity never spoke about Ian but gave no indication that she regretted marrying him or losing out on Mummy's attention and financial support. Their own father had died the same year as Ian from a heart attack brought on by drinking too much whisky. As he had been a distant father, neither of them had been devastated. Still, it had to be hard on Felicity, being a single mother, and Violet liked to help when she could.

'Milk, darling?' came the call from the tiny kitchen at the back of the cottage.

'You know I take milk.'

'I was hoping you'd say no, because there's only a drop left. We put some in the scone mix. Evie, are you going to open your gift or carry the parcel about all day?'

'Happy birthday, sweet girl,' Violet whispered, kissing Evie and cuddling her.

'Thank you, Auntie Violet.' Evie wriggled, head to one side as she gazed up at Violet with big, dark brown eyes.

'You can't thank her until you see what it is. Might be a jar of worms,' Felicity said, reappearing and taking a deep draw of her cigarette to blow out another stream of smoke.

'Honestly, Felicity, you'll give her nightmares. Open it up, sweetie. Be careful with the paper. We'll fold it up and keep it to use again. And the string. That's it. Well done, Evie. Do you like it?'

Evie let out a muffled shriek as she buried her nose into the soft fur of the teddy bear.

'She likes it,' Felicity smiled. 'Well done. Wherever did you find it? Toys are so hard to come by these days.'

'I got it in a little shop in Glasgow when I was posted there. The chap I was seeing at the time knew the shop keeper who had a few treasures put by. This little bear was one of them.'

'Ah, the handsome Roy. What happened? I thought you really liked him.'

Violet shook her head and took a sip of her black tea to give herself a moment. Its bitter taste helped.

'I did like him. Quite a lot actually. But Roy was in love with someone else, even if he didn't realise it for a long while. Doris was the girl next door. She's good for him and I don't mind as much as I thought I would. Still, I was glad when I got this posting. A fresh start is what I needed.'

'Did you mind, dragging me with you?'

'Don't be silly. I'm hardly dragging you about. It makes sense for you and Evie to travel where I go. That way we can look after each other, can't we.'

Felicity's mouth twisted wryly. Violet kept her gaze on Evie and the teddy bear. It wasn't that she needed looking after. But Felicity certainly did, even if she was in denial.

'Let's have scones,' she said brightly. 'I'll be mother.'

She pulled the plate over and concentrated on spreading jam on the scones. There was no butter but the thick blackberry jam would give enough moisture and flavour. A draught rattled down the chimney and blew a small cloud of soot out into the room. Felicity coughed. It had a painful, rasping quality that made Violet wince.

'Bloody fireplace. Needs the chimney sweep to clean it out,' Felicity spluttered.

'Language,' Violet said automatically.

She knew her sister didn't want sympathy or comments so she poured another cup of the bitter tea for them both and pushed the cup towards Felicity. Evie chatted to her teddy. On the floor beside her, there were crayons and a newspaper that had been coloured on. Felicity's birthday present to her daughter. She had very little money. Mummy wouldn't budge on that, despite Violet's pleas via letters. An army widow's pension didn't go far and Ian had only been a private. Felicity never complained so Violet didn't either. They simply had to make the best of things.

'That fire doesn't give out much heat. It's a poor show when we have to wrap up inside as if we're outside,' Felicity said with a laugh.

'Any more creatures in the thatching?'

'Only at night. When I'm lying in bed, I can hear something moving about. Evie and I make up stories about a family of mice called the Squeakies.'

'Oh dear. It's not for long. I suspect we'll be moving on again soon.'

'I won't miss this place. I'd quite like some warmth for the winter.'

Violet looked at her. There were smudges under Felicity's eyes that she didn't like the look of. Her face had a fragility to it, the cheekbones accentuated. It deepened her natural beauty but frightened Violet.

'Evie, come here. I've got one more birthday present for you. Put your hand in my pocket and see what's in there.'

Evie came over, teddy dangling in one hand while the other small hand dug into Violet's jacket pocket and came away with a small paper bag of sweets.

'Thank you, Auntie Violet. Do you want one?'

'You are a very generous little girl. I'm stuffed after all the scones so I won't have one, thanks ever so much.'

Felicity also declined and Violet suggested that Evie take her sweeties into the kitchen and get a plate to set them out so she could see all the shapes and colours. It was an excuse, of course, to have Felicity to herself without Evie hearing.

She waited until she heard the clatter of crockery and the screech of wooden chair leg on flagstone floor.

'Please, Felicity. For Evie's sake, if not for mine. Please say you'll see a doctor. That cough hasn't gone away.'

'I do love you, sister, but you're quite mistaken. The cough is nothing to worry about and I do not need a quack telling me horror stories and costing me a fortune.

89

Now come along and let's enjoy Evie's birthday tea without fussing over me. Promise?'

Violet could do nothing but nod and then smile and exclaim over the plate of prettily coloured sweets that Evie showed her. But Felicity was wrong if she thought the subject was closed. Violet would be keeping a watch over her. Felicity and Evie were so very precious, and apart from their distant mother, they were the only family she had.

Chapter Seven

She might have moved away from Glasgow, but Judith was still elbow deep in vegetables needing peeling. She was in an ATS camp in the borders and learning to march and drill and keep her kit in order just like all the other new recruits. Only she had been daft enough to complain about the food and boast of her cooking skills. Before she knew it, she was on the cooking roster and had already been told she was likely to remain a cook when she moved on to the next camp. They were short of girls who could run up meals and cater for large numbers, the corporal had told her, and it was just as important a role as the gunners, the truck drivers and the kinetheodolite operators.

It was all her own fault for gazing at the advertisement in the newspaper the day that Frankie had come to throw her out of the flat. The sketch drawings of six young women in uniform, including a Wren, a soldier, a nurse and a bus conductor, had given her an idea that sat in her head until it was needed.

At first, Frankie had been satisfied with a few kisses. He had moved her into a single end flat not far from Kiltie Street but had begun visiting her rather too often. She'd come home exhausted from her shift and there he'd be, waiting in her home, having let himself in with the landlord's spare key.

She realised it wasn't going to work almost as soon as she'd moved into the single end but it took her brain another two weeks to work out her escape. That was when she remembered the newspaper article and decided to join the ATS. More fool her! The work was hard and she didn't like any of the other girls. They were a soppy bunch, wittering on about doing their bit for the war effort and sharing hair curlers and books. None of them had escaped Frankie Bett and lost their home in the process. Judith didn't care about them. She also didn't care for peeling mountains of vegetables but at this moment in time there was nothing she could do about it.

Where was Kathy Dougal? Judith had bumped into Mary Dougal and heard that Kathy had joined the ATS too. There had been real pride in Mary's voice when she told Judith. She'd asked carefully after Judith's health and said once again how sorry she was that Irene had passed away. But Judith wasn't fooled. Mary Dougal didn't care a toss about her. She simply wanted to boast about her daughter.

Judith flicked a carrot top into the bowl beside her. She felt a little cheered by the thought that her path might yet cross with Kathy's. And if it did, well, Judith would make Kathy's life hell in any way she could.

—

'You'll never guess what,' Bridie said, plonking herself down on Kathy's bed and tossing her cap onto her own bed. She loosened her black hair with a sigh.

'All right, tell me then,' Kathy replied with a yawn. 'It'll save time.'

'Spoilsport. There's a dance at RAF Rednal in the NAAFI tonight. Some of the girls were talking about it. Shall we go?'

'Try and stop me.' Kathy grinned brightly, all yawns vanished. 'That's the best news we've had all week. I thought we were doomed to spend all our days in the mud, shouting at each other and being deafened by the generators.'

'A chance to dress up, put on our make-up and style our hair.' Jennifer sighed with pleasure, joining them.

'There's a truck leaving at seven and it'll bring us back at ten. No staying any later,' Bridie said, with a pointed look at Kathy.

Kathy shook her head. 'I won't this time. It's a bit of a longer hike to get back if I miss the truck. I hope it's as good a dance as the York one was. I wonder where Gary is now.'

–

The dance was in full swing at the RAF base NAAFI when the ATS girls arrived that Saturday evening. The air was thick with cigarette smoke and there were tables of boys in blue with beer bottles in front of them. A few local girls were much in demand, being swirled around the dance floor. Kathy reckoned they were in the Women's Land Army.

'They've got fresh faces and brawny arms,' she told Bridie as she glanced in the doorway and they took off their coats to hang them up in the cloakroom. Behind them, another twenty ATS girls waited impatiently for their turn to get their coats off and dive in to the dancing. The laughter and chat boomed.

'There are plenty of partners to go round anyway,' Bridie said, having a look too.

'I'm not dancing tonight. Howard wouldn't like it,' Jennifer said, loyally. 'I'll watch you two though.'

They sat at a small table and Jennifer went up to buy them lemonade.

'Where's Violet?' Bridie asked. 'Most of our lot are here but I don't see her.'

'I asked her if she was coming but she said not,' Kathy said. 'She's a funny one, our corporal. Keeps herself to herself.'

'But she's very kind and thoughtful to us lot. You can't fault her there.'

'It's a bit odd the way she disappears off camp when she's allowed. Wonder if she's got a fancy man somewhere?'

'Kathy!' Bridie said. 'Don't go spreading rumours like that.'

Kathy shrugged with a laugh. 'Don't be so stuffy. What's wrong with Violet having a fancy man?'

'I don't think it's that, really. Do you? When she comes back, she always looks… worried. Not happy. If she'd been seeing someone, she'd be glowing, wouldn't she?'

'Aye, right enough.' Kathy nodded. 'She's a mystery, Violet Stewart, so she is.'

At that moment a couple of the RAF officers approached their table and asked Kathy and Bridie to dance, and Violet's behaviour was forgotten. Kathy's feet flew nicely to the gramophone music in a foxtrot and she noticed that her partner was a very good dancer, keeping time and guiding her round the dance floor with a firm hand. She managed a glance. She hadn't really bothered to look at him properly, she was so excited to be dancing again. He had fair hair and dark brown eyes, a strange combination. Shouldn't he have blue eyes to match such blond hair? He also had a moustache, which gave him a dashing appearance.

He met her stare boldly and gave her a wink as he swept her round expertly.

'Like what you see?' he said.

'I beg your pardon?' Kathy's tone was haughty.

'You heard me. I like what I see, in any case. What's your name? I'm Don Whitworth.'

'Kathy,' she said, feeling it rude not to answer but slightly annoyed at his cheek.

'A Scottish Kathy. How marvellous. And do you like our fair country?'

He spun her so fast she hadn't the breath to answer him. The music changed to a slower beat and without asking her if she wanted another dance, Don's embrace tightened and they waltzed gently across the scuffed wooden floor.

'Well, do you?'

'Aye, it's fine. I've only been here a wee while.'

She shut up. Loose lips and all that. She shouldn't be telling him anything. But he had a way with him that made her want to talk. As if he expected her to answer him and to dance with him without quibbling.

'You must let me show you the countryside. Shropshire is quite delightful. We have beautiful villages and towns.'

'I don't get much time off,' Kathy said.

'They must let you girls out sometimes. You're here tonight, aren't you?'

He was persistent, she'd give him that. So why was she reluctant? He was a good-looking man, a fantastic dancer and seemingly a reasonable conversationalist. It was Alisdair. That was why. Despite swearing that she never wanted to see him again, she was still in love with him. She might always be. Her love for him was a hard knot deep inside surrounded by hurt and pride. She had to face facts though. Alisdair had made it plain he didn't want her.

She made a sudden decision. Just because Alisdair didn't love her didn't mean she couldn't enjoy life. She loved dancing, and Don was a great dancer. Why not enjoy the evening? She didn't owe Alisdair Meikle anything!

'Shall we dance another?' she said, gripping his arms as the music stopped and the gramophone was cranked up for the next tune.

Don's eyebrows rose lazily and he grinned, showing her even, white teeth under his fascinating moustache.

'Why not, indeed,' he said. 'If you have the stamina, my lovely Kathy, then I certainly do too.'

They returned to the table after a couple of dances, Kathy's energy undiminished but Don pleading that she'd tired him out and he needed a rest. Bridie and her partner followed them.

'These are my friends, Kathy and Jennifer,' Bridie said. 'And this is Neil Smythe.'

Neil smiled at them all in a friendly fashion. 'More drinks, ladies?'

He was a tall, thin man with brown, curly hair and grey eyes that twinkled when he smiled. He and Don went to fetch beers and lemonades. Jennifer leaned over to Bridie.

'Is he the one?' she whispered, nudging Bridie with her elbow. 'Do you like him?'

'He seems nice enough,' Bridie said. 'But Jennifer, you can stop with your cupid's arrow. I don't fancy him.'

'There are plenty more in here,' Jennifer laughed. 'Take your pick.'

Don and Neil came back balancing bottles and glasses and they all drank gratefully. It was warm in the NAAFI despite the cold autumnal evening outside. There were enough bodies energetically dancing to keep the heat high. Kathy took a long sip of her lemonade. It tasted particularly nice and sweet so she took another gulp. Soon she felt warm and a bit fuzzy, but in a pleasant way.

'How was the drink?' Don asked, taking her arm and leading her onto the dance floor once more.

'Sweet.'

'Just like you,' Don murmured, drawing her into his arms and waltzing them both.

Kathy's head swam a little but she was enjoying herself.

'It was a lemonade and port. Have you had that before?'

'I didn't ask for that,' she said, moving her face back to see him properly.

'I knew you'd like it. You girls need to live a little. Away from home and all that. Why not?'

She wasn't sure whether to be annoyed with him or to agree. In the end, she found herself laughing and Don along with her. There was a devil-may-care edge to him she was beginning to find fascinating. They danced some more until Jennifer came rushing over to her, pushing through the crammed couples to grab her arm.

'Kathy, where's Bridie?'

Kathy glanced around, not seeing her friend or Neil anywhere. She shrugged, wanting to get back to dancing with Don.

'I can't see her. Maybe she's gone outside for some fresh air?'

'Oh, I need to tell her…'

Kathy felt Don's arms slip from her shoulders and felt a brief, abrupt sense of loss. He winked at her.

'I'll be back in a jiffy. Look after your friend.'

Kathy watched his broad, straight back disappear between the dancing couples. With a silent sigh, she turned to Jennifer.

'What is it? What's wrong?'

Jennifer pulled her off the dance floor and into two empty chairs at a table.

'It's Howard. He's here. He wants to take me back with him.'

'Why, what's happened? Is something wrong at camp?' Kathy felt alarmed. If they all had to leave now… she had to find Don and tell him.

Jennifer shook her head. 'He's waiting outside. He says when we left for the RAF base tonight, he realised how much he missed me. He cadged a lift on a tractor to get here. He says he's in love with me and he… Oh, Kathy, he's asked me to marry him.'

Jennifer's face was glowing. In the soft light of the NAAFI, she looked quite lovely.

'I'm so happy for you,' Kathy said, hugging her friend. 'How romantic.'

'I'm in love with him too. I've loved him ever since I met him.'

Lucky Jennifer. It was all so simple for her. She and Howard felt the same way about each other. They'd get married and live happily ever after, if the war let them. Why wasn't life like that for her? Kathy stifled that thought. She jumped up and took Jennifer with her.

'Why are you still here? Howard's waiting for you.'

'I wanted to let Bridie know. Howard wants us to go back to camp together. Will you tell Bridie for me? Where can she be?'

'I'll find her and tell her,' Kathy promised. 'Now, go and find your Howard. Congratulations, Jennifer. I'm very happy for the both of youse. I really am.'

Jennifer practically ran to the exit of the room. She turned and waved at Kathy and then disappeared. Kathy drained her glass of lemonade and port. Don was nowhere to be seen, and neither was Bridie or Neil. There was another young pilot heading towards her but Kathy hastily got up and walked to the door, not wanting to dance with someone other than Don. She hadn't reached the cloakroom when Bridie appeared.

'There you are. Where have you been?' Kathy cried.

Bridie blushed a fiery red. 'Neil and I stepped outside for a bit.'

'Quite a long bit,' Kathy remarked, her mind full of Jennifer, Howard and Don so that she didn't think much on why Bridie looked so embarrassed. 'Did you see Jennifer?'

'No, why? Shall we go and find our table? It's cold out there.' Bridie shivered and walked into the room.

'Jennifer has only gone and got engaged to Howard Kenny,' Kathy said excitedly, as they sat down.

Bridie's face fell before she managed a smile.

'What's the matter? You should be happy for her. It's so romantic. He came to fetch her back tonight as he missed her so much.'

'The irony is that he will miss her if he marries her. And so will we.'

'You're not making any sense,' Kathy told her.

'Don't you see,' Bridie said impatiently. 'The army won't let married couples serve at the same camp. Howard's a sergeant, so it'll be Jennifer that they send away somewhere else. We won't be together, the three of us, any more. We might not see Jennifer again until the war is over.'

They sat glumly, clutching their glasses. Kathy's was empty but she held it anyway for something to do. She couldn't stay sad for long though. The music had started up after a band break and she tapped her foot to the rhythm. Looking up, she saw Don and Neil coming towards them.

'We can't do anything about Jennifer except wish her luck,' she said to Bridie. 'She deserves to win her man. Even if she leaves, we can write, can't we? Come on, there's another good hour of dancing before the truck leaves. I want to dance with Don again. And Neil's not too shabby on the dance floor either. Up you get, Bridie. The night isn't done yet.'

–

Rural Shropshire was very, very dark. There were no village lights near Felicity's cottage and, even if there had been, blackout meant they'd be covered up. Some creature outside shrieked and Violet jumped. The windows were black squares behind the faded velvet curtains drawn against the night. They rattled every so often in the wind.

'I bet you wish you'd gone to the dance now,' Felicity said, lighting a cigarette and smothering a cough as she sat on the edge of the armchair in the tiny living room. There was a small fire in the hearth, flickering and radiating just enough warmth for an illusion of comfort. On the table was an empty bottle of wine and two glasses. Upstairs, Evie was fast asleep, her teddy tucked in beside her under the blanket. Violet had put her coat and gloves on and rammed a knitted beret over her fair hair.

'I don't care about dancing. I'd rather be here with you and Evie.'

'Look, forget what I said. You don't have to do this.'

Violet took in a deep breath. What Felicity had said, almost as soon as Violet had arrived that evening, was that there were rats in the outhouse. She was certain of it. Evie was scared and refused to go out. She was using the chamber pot and it was all getting rather difficult. Felicity wasn't too keen to use the outhouse either. She had pointed at the coal shovel, leaning against the wall in the hall.

'That's my weapon. I'll bonk the rats over the head and it'll be done.'

She had then proceeded to have such a coughing fit that Violet had been alarmed and ready to call for a doctor. Felicity's frantic arm-waving had stopped her.

'I'm quite all right, darling, as I keep telling you. I had a horrid cold some weeks ago and the cough is lingering. That's all. Now, stop trying to change the topic of conversation, which was all about our rat problem. I'm plucking up the courage to face them down in their lair in my outhouse. One more ciggie and a glass of wine and let me at them.'

But of course Violet couldn't let her sister do that. Felicity, whatever her protests, mustn't be allowed out into the cold, damp October air to scrabble about in the bleak outhouse. Her face was quite pale except for a rosy circle high up on each cheekbone.

'Don't be silly. I'll go and sort it out,' Violet said firmly. 'After all, I'm in the army now. What's killing a couple of rats compared to that?'

'Kill a lot of things, do you, on a daily basis? Well, that's all right then. Carry on, please be my guest.'

'Right then. I will.' Violet picked up the coal shovel, ignoring her rising heart rate. Sometimes, Felicity could be very annoying. 'Put the kettle on, won't you. I'll need a cuppa when I get back.'

She went outside before Felicity could answer and shut the door behind her. No point letting what little heat there was in the cottage escape. Her breath puffed white in the icy air. The handle of the coal shovel felt cold through her woollen glove. She gripped it tightly. She could barely see the outline of the outhouse. It was tucked away under a grove of cherry trees. In spring, no doubt, the cherries were beautiful with their pink, frothy blossom, but now they loomed out at her with twiggy arms as if they'd snatch her up.

'Oh, for goodness' sake, get a grip,' she whispered angrily. 'Are you woman or mouse? Great, that's got me onto rats again. Please, God, let Evie and Felicity be imagining things.'

The outhouse was right in front of her now. Looking back, it was hard to see the cottage in the gloom. A branch hooked her beret. With a gasp, Violet put it back on her head. She stretched out a hand and pulled the outhouse door open. Inside, it was just as dark as everywhere else. As her eyes adjusted, she saw the privy, the stone floor and the boxes of who knew what stacked against the wall. It was a large outhouse, not just for the necessities but also for storage. Probably back to the Middle Ages, Violet thought grimly, remembering the endless dusty cobwebs from a previous visit in the daylight.

There was a squeak and a rustling from behind the boxes. Now wasn't the time to be scared. Violet thought about Felicity and Evie. It was up to her to sort out the rat problem. To keep her family safe.

She needed a stick. She stepped backwards and turned to the cherries. Hunting on the ground, she found a stout branch. Shovel in one hand and branch in the other she advanced to the outhouse again. With a trembling hand, she poked at the boxes. With more vigour, she tried to move them to the side. As they slowly toppled, a shape darted out past her and through the open door and Violet screamed and dropped the coal shovel.

When she'd stopped shaking, she glanced about to see if there were any others. She felt sick. There was still rustling. Feeling even sicker, Violet took a step over to the scattered boxes and stared. There was a nest of six wriggling baby rats. One of the boxes had been chewed into ribbons for nesting material. The nest was lined with bird feathers. Such care from their mother. And she had scared it away. What would happen to the babies? She found an empty box and, taking the shovel, gently scooped up the nest and its occupants and slid them into it. Then she took the box outside and tucked it under a shrub, hoping the mother rat would find it.

Afterwards, she was violently sick. The moon chose that moment to come out from behind the dark clouds. She saw her shadow cast onto the grass, looking monstrous. Violet wiped her mouth on her glove. She looked over towards Felicity's rented cottage. Inside were her sister and niece. Her only true family. Mummy didn't really count, as she had cast them off so carelessly. And it was up to Violet to keep Felicity and little Evie safe. There was no one else.

Violet felt suddenly and very powerfully alone.

Chapter Eight

At the end of October, they left Park Hall for a firing practice camp in Wales. Here they used real ammunition and tried to hit billowing targets streaming out behind small planes. It was exciting and unnerving and brought it home to Kathy that soon they would be doing this for real somewhere around Britain.

Jennifer and Howard got married by special licence at the Kennys' family church in a tiny village across the border in England. Howard was being sent overseas, to Jennifer's dismay, hence the need for a quick wedding. While the girls hoped that meant Jennifer would stay with them, it wasn't to be. She had orders to present herself to barracks in Aberdeenshire. The only bright spot was that she might see Geraldine up there.

Much to their relief, Kathy and Bridie were given passes to attend the wedding. It was a crisp November day and a pale sun glittered brightly as the guests walked the short distance from the church to the church hall for the wedding feast.

Jennifer's mother and aunts and Howard's two sisters had gathered enough clothing coupons at short notice for the bride to wear a white velvet dress, knee-length, with a borrowed bridal veil. She was wearing her mother's Sunday-best shoes.

'You look lovely, Mrs Kenny,' Bridie cried when she and Kathy managed to get a second with the new bride.

'Mrs Kenny. It sounds so fine,' Jennifer giggled. 'I can't believe Howard and I have tied the knot. It's all gone so fast. Look, did you see what all the girls have given us?'

She spread out the embroidered tablecloth, which had been folded on a table with other gifts. They had worked every evening to get it finished in time and it had been handed to Kathy and Bridie with strict promises to get it to Jennifer on her wedding day.

'Don't I know it,' Bridie said with feeling, showing them her thumb. 'Can you see that purple bruise? That's where the embroidery needle went in. Yes, there's a hole in my flesh as well. But I have to say it was worth it. I hope you'll remember us whenever you sit down to dinner with Howard.'

'Of course I will,' Jennifer said.

'Open our other gift,' Kathy urged her, lifting a soft oblong parcel wrapped in brown paper but with a pink ribbon instead of string. 'Me and Bridie wanted to get you something just from ourselves.'

'Oooh, I'll be keeping the ribbon for a start. Oh, these are gorgeous. Thank you.'

Inside the parcel was a cotton nightie. It had been one of Bridie's but she had made it special by sewing on bows made of the rest of the pink ribbon that she'd found in a shop on her day off camp. Nestled in the folds of the material was a bar of precious soap. That was Kathy's contribution. Mary had sent it to her in the post. She'd been tempted to keep it, as soap was so hard to come by, but after all it was Jennifer's wedding day, so she had tucked it into the nightie with a small sigh.

Now she was glad she'd done so, to see the delight on her friend's face.

'Did you get a piece of our wedding cake?' Jennifer asked. 'Cardboard cover, of course, which will look lovely in the photos, but my mum's neighbour made us a real fruit cake.'

'The food is delicious,' Kathy smiled. There hadn't been enough cake for her and Bridie to get a slice but she wasn't going to tell Jennifer that.

'Everyone's been so kind, giving us dishes and mucking in to make it a real feast,' Jennifer said. 'I'm sorry your two beaus couldn't make it today. They would have been very welcome.'

The practice camp wasn't too far from RAF Rednal and Kathy had seen Don on several occasions since the dance. He had made it plain that he liked her, although he hadn't kissed her yet. For a large part, she was relieved at that. She wasn't sure how she'd react. The last man she'd kissed was Dennis's father. The memory of those kisses was blended with shame and guilt.

'Neil's not my beau,' Bridie was saying as Kathy zoned back in to the conversation.

'Anyone can see that he'd love to be,' Jennifer insisted. 'Why not give him a chance?'

'I told you. I don't like him that way. He's a friend, that's all. If you want love birds, ask Kathy and Don.'

'Hardly love birds,' Kathy protested. 'He's not even kissed me.'

'He's a gentleman, that's why. He's taking things slowly because he respects you. But we've seen the way he looks at you. He definitely fancies you.'

He wouldn't respect her if he knew she had a baby. That was something he was never going to find out. She felt a flicker of excitement at Jennifer's comment. Don fancied her. And she quite fancied him. She wasn't sure how physical she wanted it to become, though. Mammy's warnings and Harry's protectiveness had made her wary.

'Here comes Howard,' the bride said, her face lighting up as he approached the three of them. 'Let's get the dancing started. You two will have to dance together. There aren't enough men, unless you want to dance with Howard's great-uncle Roland.'

—

'I can't believe that Jennifer and Howard only got one honeymoon night together before they had to leave camp and go their separate ways,' Kathy said the next evening as the two of them sat by the stove in the otherwise empty room warming the front of their shins. Two mugs of tea balanced precariously on the stove top.

It was Friday night and most of the girls in the hut had gone to a dance in the nearby village, but Kathy and Bridie had stayed on camp. A description of a previous dance in the village hadn't enticed them. Lukewarm tea to drink, stale biscuits and a few elderly farmers to dance with didn't sound like much fun. Besides, Bridie had announced she was tired.

Bridie rubbed her face before answering. 'There's a war on, don't you know.'

'No need to be snippy,' Kathy said, staring at her friend.

It was most unlike Bridie to be so. She was the kindest, gentlest girl in their hut. Now, Kathy noticed the mauve shadows under Bridie's dark eyes and how pale her face was.

'Are you all right, hen?'

'No, I'm not. Oh, Kathy, I've made a terrible mistake. I didn't want to say anything, what with Jennifer being so happy and the wedding and everything but…' Bridie's breath caught on a sob and she shook her head.

'What's the matter?' Kathy said, taking her friend's hand and holding it tightly. 'Tell me, Bridie. I'll help you sort it out, so I will.'

'No one can sort this out,' Bridie said. 'I'm pregnant.'

There was a ringing in Kathy's ears. She clutched Bridie's fingers and couldn't think what to say for a moment.

'You hate me, don't you?' Bridie cried. 'I hate myself even more. The shame of it.'

'But how… when…'

'It was that RAF dance. You and me dancing with Don and Neil and then that port and lemonade. It made me feel… bold, you know. And fed up. You and Jennifer find it easy to fall in love. What's the matter with me? I've never felt like that about a man. And then I thought, to hell with waiting to fall in love. It might never happen, and I wanted to feel like a proper woman, so I went outside with Neil and… well, things happened and here I am. In a proper pickle, as my gran would say.'

Kathy wasn't sure what shocked her more, Bridie swearing or what she and Neil had done outside the NAAFI building. The irony being that she had done the same herself in an alley way in Glasgow, leading to her having Dennis. Bridie's confession was bringing it all back vividly and Kathy pressed her hand to her mouth, trying not to shiver.

'Are you sure?' she stuttered.

'I'm sick every morning, everything tastes metallic and my breasts hurt. What else can it be?' Bridie stood up.

'I don't blame you for hating me. No decent girl would want to be near me.'

Kathy almost let her go, she was so frozen. It was as if Bridie came back into focus and she saw her friend's bowed shoulders and black hair.

'Wait, Bridie! Of course I don't hate you. We need to talk. Come and sit with me. Here, take a wee sip of tea for the shock.'

'Tea isn't going to get rid of the baby.'

'What will you do? Will you go home?' Kathy said.

Bridie's laugh was bleak. 'My father would throw me out if he knew. And my mum won't stand up to him. There's no going home for me.'

Kathy thought about how her own family had rallied round her. She'd been so lucky. At the time she'd huffed and complained about being sent away to Miss Main's cottage in Perthshire until the baby came. She had almost gone mad from boredom during those long months in the countryside and that had changed to fear when her contractions began. Mammy had arrived at that very moment and she and Miss Main and the midwife had all helped her deliver her wee Dennis. She hadn't been grateful enough by a long chalk to those strong women.

'There's something I need to tell you,' she said, taking Bridie's hand again, more for her own comfort than for her friend's. 'I… I got pregnant when I was sixteen. I was sent away to have the baby and then my mammy took him on as hers. He's a lovely wee boy called Dennis and he thinks I'm his big sister.'

'Didn't you want to marry the father?' Bridie's other hand flew to her mouth.

Kathy shook her head. 'He was married. He hadn't told me. He said we were engaged, gave me a cheap ring and I believed him.'

'Oh, Kathy, that's awful. What a brute he was.' Bridie hugged her.

'Aye, well. I got my Dennis and I love him. I wouldn't change that. But I wish I hadn't been a daft wee lassie, fooled by a handsome face and sweet talk.'

'He should have been whipped for what he did to you.'

'That's a bit fierce for you, Bridie. You're such a gentle soul.' Kathy smiled.

'He took advantage of you. You were just a child. It makes me angry. And you've kept that secret all this while. Poor you. What a burden.'

'I couldn't tell you all. People do judge and I wanted a fresh start in the army.' Kathy realised what she'd said as the words spilled out. Bridie would be judged too. 'What will you do?'

'Neil's asked me to marry him.'

'Och, Bridie. What are you worrying about, then? Get married soon and it'll be an early baby. No one need know otherwise.'

'But I don't love him,' Bridie wailed. 'Now I'll never know if I could've fallen in love. I'll be stuck with a man that I surely don't love.'

'Maybe love will come, in time.'

'He's a nice man, but I'm not attracted to him at all. Chatting to him is like chatting to you and Jennifer.'

'He must be all right if you like talking to him as much as us,' Kathy joked feebly.

'I haven't given him my answer yet. But I will have to soon,' Bridie said.

'Make sure it's the right decision,' Kathy said, feeling older than her nineteen years. 'It's a harsh world for a woman with a wean on her own and no ring on her finger.'

–

There was another reason why Kathy hadn't gone to the village dance that evening, but she hadn't had time to share it with Bridie and now it didn't feel right to. A soldier had passed her a note earlier which had come from Don Whitworth.

'He wants an answer, so I'll wait for you to scribble one,' the soldier had winked.

Kathy pretended not to notice the wink. She didn't want to read Don's short letter while the man watched but there was no alternative. Curious, she opened it.

> *My dear Kathy*
>
> *I have managed to wangle a pass for the weekend at great personal expense, now I owe a chum quite a few favours! I remember you saying you also had a pass so I very much hope you'll take pity on a poor 'boy in blue' and spend it with me?*
>
> *I know of a charming little country hotel on the Shropshire side of the border. It isn't far to get to for either of us. You'll love it. Bring a pretty dress for dinner.*
>
> *Ever yours*
> *Don*

He knew she had a pass because she'd told him a few days before during a snatched meet-up one evening. She couldn't help admiring his boldness in working out a way of getting the same days off as her.

She hesitated, conscious of the soldier tapping his foot, watching her. Should she go? If she didn't, there was very little else to do. She'd probably stay on camp, improving her sewing by helping embroider the next tablecloth the girls were working on. While it was fun to have a giggle with the others, it would be more exciting by far to spend the weekend with Don. Besides, she'd never been to a hotel before. That wasn't something folk from Kiltie Street did.

With Jennifer married and up in Aberdeenshire and Bridie being quieter than usual, Kathy was at a loss on her own. Being with Don was fun. He flirted with her and made her feel beautiful and interesting. She didn't love him, but she did find him attractive. There was no harm in it. More than that, it could be an adventure.

She took the pencil offered by the bored soldier and wrote 'yes'. Memorising the hotel address, she gave the paper back and found herself humming 'Don't Sit Under the Apple Tree' under her breath as she returned to duties.

On Saturday morning, she was glad she had agreed. Bridie was pasty-faced and listless and the other girls were either on physical training or cleaning the hut. Stepping past one girl on her knees scrubbing the linoleum, Kathy grinned. She had washed her hair and now it gleamed where it was visible under her army cap. She had packed her blue utility dress and tweed jacket in a small case borrowed from Bridie. They were the only smart clothes she owned, her green dress having acquired a rip which she'd mended poorly. Her face was made up and she had her tiny store of lipstick and powder in her case too, along with fresh underwear and a spare pair of lisle stockings, also borrowed from her friend.

'Be careful,' Bridie said, catching up with her at the hut exit.

'I'll be fine. We'll have walks in the countryside and nice meals. That's all.'

'Just as long as Don knows that's what you came for and nothing else,' Bridie warned.

Kathy shook her head impatiently. Why was Bridie trying to spoil things?

'What about you? Will you see Neil today?' she asked, deciding attack was better than defence.

'Yes, we've agreed to meet this evening. He's going to pick me up in his motor car.'

'Fancy that,' Kathy said, impressed. 'He must be rich then, if he's got a car.'

Bridie sniffed as if it didn't interest her. Kathy waved quickly and headed out to find a lift. She felt for Bridie, she really did, but all that moping about brought everyone down. Now, somewhere, there had to be an army truck going in the right direction. Glancing around hopefully, Kathy forgot about Bridie and began to feel excited for the weekend ahead.

There were plenty of trucks driving up and down the roads near the camp and she found it easy to get a ride in one that was going quite close to the hotel that Don had described. It was a pity that Don didn't have his own motor car like Neil, she mused as the truck jolted over the ruts, jarring her spine. He had such a posh accent, she imagined he must come from a wealthy family.

The truck driver left her at a crossroads with a friendly wave and a toot of the horn. Kathy stood and shivered. It was really very cold. Glancing about, she saw a thicket of bushes, their leaves still clinging to the branches. Nipping behind it, she swapped her uniform for her civilian clothes, praying no one would drive by. She stuffed the uniform into the case. Never mind the creases, she'd iron them later. She shook her hair loose so it spilled out across her shoulders.

Her dress and jacket were too thin to stop the cutting wind blowing across the roads from biting at her skin. At least her shoes were stout. She still had a couple of miles to walk to the hotel. She hoped the route wasn't muddy. She wanted to look her best when Don saw her.

The hotel came into sight after a draughty walk along country lanes fringed with bare-branched trees. There was no sign of Don outside so she went up the stone steps and into the hotel foyer. It was a pleasant space with a red carpet and a dark walnut reception desk. Behind the desk, a middle-aged woman peered at her. Kathy was suddenly nervous. She was conscious of her second-hand tweed jacket and how it didn't fit properly. She smoothed her hair and brightened her smile.

'How can I help you?' the woman said, looking as if she didn't want to help Kathy at all.

Kathy was suddenly annoyed with Don. He wasn't here to deal with this and she didn't know how. She was out of her depth.

'It's Mr and Mrs Whitworth checking in,' Don said from behind her.

Kathy spun round with relief. Don flashed her a grin and then politely gave the hotel manager some details. The woman's pursed mouth and suspicious gaze made Kathy feel dirty. She held her chin high. She had as much right to be here as anyone else. Don took the key and offered the crook of his arm. She took it gracefully. Let the old bag see how handsome Don was. She was obviously jealous of their youth and good looks.

'Here's your key, Mr Whitworth. I'll show you up,' the woman said.

'We can find our own way, thank you,' he said, and touched his finger to his cap.

She looked mollified by his polite charm and RAF uniform. It made Kathy want to giggle.

She kept step with Don's stride as they went upstairs. He had a small suitcase. She had all her belongings stuffed into Bridie's small case, which now looked scuffed with age and wear compared to Don's. She had a swift thought that he was used to staying at hotels. He unlocked the door to their room and motioned her to go in.

'How about a drink at the bar before we have a slap-up meal and an evening stroll?' he was saying.

But Kathy was staring in horror at the double bed that seemed to dwarf all the other furniture in the hotel room. No wonder the woman downstairs had given her a contemptuous look. She knew they weren't married. Kathy hadn't missed the glance at the fingers on her left hand. She just hadn't understood.

'What is it, darling?' Don asked, when she didn't advance further into the room.

In fact, she felt rooted to the spot. There was an anger building like a tornado inside her. How dare he assume she wanted this! Heat flooded her face, but it wasn't embarrassment. It was pure rage.

'How could you?' she cried, turning to him. 'Do you think I'm a cheap little tart? Is that how you see me?'

'Now, steady on, poppet.' His easy charm slipped and he looked distinctly uneasy. 'I thought you knew. I asked you to come away with me for a weekend. It's bloody obvious what that means, heh?'

'Don't ye call me poppet. Do ye hear me?' Kathy's Glasgow accent thickened in her outrage. 'I'm no yer poppet or anyone else's. Get out ma way.'

She pushed past him and rushed headlong down the stairs, hot tears almost blinding her. The woman behind the desk looked fascinated as Kathy ran past and out the front door. She kept going. She wanted nothing more than to be away from that room. Horrible memories of her seduction by the soldier in Glasgow rose up. He'd taken advantage of her. But she was older now. And wiser. It was just… she sobbed… she'd thought Don was a decent sort. But she was wrong. He wanted what all men wanted. Except Alisdair. He didn't want her at all. Och, it was all so confusing.

She flung herself against the trunk of a large oak in the hotel gardens, hoping Don wouldn't find her. She heard him calling her and shrank against the bark. He circled the gardens and the entrance. She knew she was being foolish. She couldn't hide from him forever. She stepped away from the tree. Perhaps if she started walking, she might make it back to camp before the end of the day.

'Kathy! There you are. Be a sensible girl and listen, will you?'

Don caught her up easily and grabbed her arm. She flung him off. Wisely, he didn't try again but matched his stride to hers.

'Where are we going?' he asked calmly, as if they were at a tea party, taking the air, like fancy folk do.

'I don't care where you go, but I'm going back to ma camp.'

'Hear me out, please. Then if you still want to go, I'll fix us some transport. I promise. Will you stop for a minute?'

She felt like marching on. Like running away from him. But it was foolish. He was taller and more athletic than her. He could outrun her if he wished. Besides, how daft they'd look, the pair of them haring down the road. She smiled at that.

'That's better, you look a damn sight prettier when you smile than when you're angry with me,' Don said, smiling back and showing those perfect white teeth. 'Let's sit there, shall we?'

He pointed to a wooden bench in the grounds. In the summer the roses planted nearby would smell divine, but now they were black thorny twigs. Kathy took a seat, feeling the cold seep into her legs from the wooden slats.

'Let me apologise,' Don said. 'I think we have had a communications mix-up.'

'It's a wee bit more than that, don't you think? This isn't one of your RAF sorties, you know. It's not a *communications mix-up*,' – she mimicked his words – 'it's about you not respecting me. You think I'm not good enough for you.'

'That's not true. You're a beautiful girl and I admire you greatly. But a chap's got red blood. You can't blame me for trying.'

'I'm not that sort of girl,' Kathy said firmly.

'Of course not. I made a terrible mistake. Will you forgive me?'

She looked at him. 'I can't go back in there.'

'We can take a walk first. There's a jolly nice pub about half a mile away. I'll get the hotel to change us to two single rooms.'

Kathy stood up. She was torn between wanting to believe in him and a desire to fly from there to the safety of the ATS camp.

'I don't know...' she murmured.

'Marry me then,' Don said, taking her hand in a firm grip. She felt the heat and strength of his fingers. 'I've never felt like this for any woman. You do something to me, Kathy, with your flaming red hair, and I must have you.'

She didn't know what to say. A handsome RAF pilot had asked her to marry him and here she was hesitating. She knew why. Alisdair Meikle was never far from her thoughts, however much she tried to banish him. But he was lost to her. He didn't want her. Don might be second-best but he was here and he loved her. She'd be well off and have the status of a married woman. Mammy and Harry would be pleased.

For a fleeting second, she imagined her and Don as Dennis's parents. She knew though that Dennis would remain her secret forever if she married Don. She imagined meeting Alisdair one day. She'd be cool and polite, being a married woman. She wouldn't be ashamed to be seen by anyone and that included Alisdair and his parents.

'Yes, I'll marry you,' she said.

Don gave a boyish whoop and lifted her to her feet. He leaned down and kissed her. The touch of his lips was warm and thrilling. As she responded, the kiss deepened. Kathy was relieved. She liked his kisses. There was nothing to worry about. All that business when she was sixteen, she could put behind her. She was engaged. There was the fun of planning the wedding. Don thought she was good enough to marry. Alisdair Meikle didn't matter one whit!

Chapter Nine

Kathy didn't have time to see Don before the women were posted to what was going to be their permanent location, a heavy anti-aircraft battery on a farm outside Glasgow. She managed to write him a short letter but knew the censor would cut out her words if she told him where she was going. She could only hint by saying she was going home and she'd miss him but she'd write as often as she could. His letters could reach her courtesy of the army postal service.

'Are you excited to be here?' Bridie asked.

'I'm excited they gave us trousers finally,' Kathy joked. 'It's freezing.'

They stood at the door of their new accommodation block, a brick and wooden slat construction, and stared out at the other concrete and brick buildings and, beyond the four gun emplacements, miles of farmland. Muirhead Farm, pronounced in the Glasgow way as Muir*heid*, was bleak and colourless in the dim November light. The battery was in a potato field on a hill. It was busy with personnel; nearly two hundred soldiers, men and women, were stationed there. Apart from the large accommodation blocks and the anti-aircraft guns, there was a command post and air-raid shelters with earth piled up against the walls for protection against bomb blast damage. Kathy shivered. She hoped they never had to use them. There were giant bomb craters in the fields outside the battery from the Clydebank blitz in 1941. They were a horrible reminder of the dangers of the war.

The girls all knew the importance of their posting. Violet had given them a pep talk after they learned where they were going and a ripple of dismay had gone through the room. Only Kathy was pleased to be going to Glasgow, it seemed. She wondered how Violet felt about it.

Violet had reminded them that the Clyde was of vital importance in the west of Scotland and one of the most significant assets of the entire country. This was due to its vital role in the shipbuilding industry. There were also many munitions factories that the Germans wanted to attack, and the Atlantic convoys bringing vital supplies and troops from the United States came to the Clyde too.

'We have to defend the Clyde and keep the harbours and the factories running,' Violet told them, her clear voice ringing out in the hut. 'I don't want to see disappointed faces, do you understand? You're being asked to do your duty. Whether that's in a field in Scotland or on the beaches of the south coast of England, it doesn't matter.'

There were sheepish glances and nods. Violet got them all standing for kit inspection and Kathy was sure she wasn't the only one to feel inspired and energised, ready to do her bit.

Now, standing in the mud in her calf-length black army boots and her new, rather stiff army trousers, she wished she had a greatcoat against the harsh weather.

'You missing him?' Bridie asked, mistaking Kathy's silence.

'Don? I suppose I should be, but the journey up here was exhausting, and now this… well it's all new, isn't it, and mebbe I'm a wee bit distracted. I'll probably miss him later when we're in our beds alone with our thoughts.'

'Is he posting your engagement ring?'

Kathy laughed and splayed her ringless fingers. 'I told him not to be so daft. I can wait until we meet up to choose a ring. We're engaged anyhow.'

'I'm surprised you haven't set a date,' Bridie said, glancing at her.

'Och, there's plenty of time to get married. I want to enjoy being a fiancée,' Kathy replied.

Which was sort of true. It felt glamorous to be engaged, although it would be nice to be able to flash a ring at the other girls. But she wasn't desperate to get married. Don had written back asking her to set a date but she hadn't answered him yet. Sure, there was no hurry, she told herself. It wasn't as if she and Don were going to see each other for a long while, what with him down in Wales and her back up in Glasgow, or close to it at any rate, in a potato field in the back of beyond.

'Don't you want to wear your ring?' she asked in return.

'Not in this mucky place. It was Neil's grandmother's ring so it's precious to him. I keep it in its little box and I'm terrified I'll lose it.'

Precious to Neil, but no mention of it being precious to Bridie, Kathy noted.

'Have you got everything ready for your wedding?'

Bridie shrugged. 'My mam and auntie are sorting it for us. I told Neil I don't want a big do and he's agreed. There's a war on and folk have more on their minds than watching us two tie the knot.'

'A wedding cheers everyone up though,' Kathy said with determined brightness.

'Not everyone.' Bridie sighed and turned back into the accommodation block.

Kathy followed her in, exasperated with her friend's attitude. 'You can't stay miserable for the rest of your life. You've made the right decision, marrying Neil.'

'Have I?' Bridie swung round, her face white. 'I don't love him, and he doesn't love me either. That's an awful start to a marriage, I'd say.'

'Aye, it's no the best,' Kathy admitted. 'But there's plenty of folk start out that way for the same reasons. I can think of a few in Kiltie Street, where I'm from. But they muddle along all right in the end.'

'No one knows what goes on inside four walls,' Bridie said darkly. 'People put a face on for neighbours.'

Kathy left her to it, making an excuse of finding the canteen. She didn't know what to say to Bridie to make things better. She wasn't sure she was in love with Don either but she was still looking forward to being his wife at some point. It was nice being engaged and having the other girls asking her all about it. Gladys, the girl who had started the tablecloth embroidery, had promised to begin new tablecloths, one for her and one for Bridie, for their bottom drawers.

She'd written home and told Mammy, Harry and Jeannie that she was engaged. Their letters back were full of astonishment and happiness for her. Mammy insisted that Don come to visit as soon as he could. Harry wanted to meet him properly, she had written. Dear Harry. He was doing his best as step-father, since her own dad had died when she was young.

On her way to the canteen, she met Violet hurrying in the opposite direction. Violet almost slipped in the mud and Kathy stopped her falling.

'Crikey, thanks. I nearly did myself a mischief. You'd think army boots would have a good grip, wouldn't you?' Violet laughed.

'You're in an awful rush. Mebbe you should walk and no run,' Kathy said.

'You're probably right, but I'm late already. I've got to meet my sister at the railway station and my lift is waiting. Must go. See you later.'

She waved at Kathy and hurried on. Kathy half-waved in response but Violet was gone, hidden by the nearest ugly concrete building. It was the first she'd heard that Violet had a sister, but then as corporal, she hadn't shared much that was personal with the girls under her command. They all liked her because she was fair and approachable. She didn't have to share anything. It did make Kathy curious about her corporal though.

–

'I'm not taking you out of your way, am I?' Violet puffed as she climbed up into the truck.

'I've got a load for the stores in Dumbarton, but we can manage a small detour,' the soldier winked. 'Railway station in Helensburgh, was it?'

Violet nodded and settled in for what was a good hour's drive on country roads. The soldier chatted and told her humorous tales of his life before the war as a travelling salesman. She didn't have to contribute much as he was a man who enjoyed sharing a yarn and laughed at his own jokes. Just as well, as it gave her time to wonder how

Mummy was going to react to Felicity and Evie coming home. Unfortunately, even when he dropped her off in the west coast town, Violet hadn't come up with an answer on how to deal with her mother.

Felicity was in the waiting room, calmly smoking while Evie ran round in small circles making engine noises. Luckily there were no other travellers to be disturbed by Evie's calls.

'Ah, darling, there you are. You're late,' Felicity said when Violet came trotting across the platform and into the warmth of the waiting room.

Violet thought how like Mummy Felicity could be sometimes. She had the same shade of critical blue eyes and off-hand put-downs. She chided herself immediately. She was being unfair. Felicity had her good side too. The same could not be said of their mother.

She lifted Felicity's heavy suitcase. 'Sorry, I got a lift on a supply truck and the driver stopped for a conversation with a farmer. There was a tractor blocking the road and… well, never mind, I'm here now. Shall we go?'

Felicity took Evie's small case. Evie took Violet's other hand and beamed up at her auntie. Violet glanced at Felicity with concern.

'It's a steep walk up to the house. Will you manage?'

'Goodness, I haven't forgotten the way, Violet. I may not have been home in six years but I do remember that Sinclair Street is on a hill. That's why Mummy and Daddy bought the house. For the view.'

Violet had to pretend not to notice how breathless Felicity was as they made their slow way up the street to the mansions at the top. They stopped once, halfway up, to catch their breath and look back down. There was a magnificent view of the sea, the Firth of Clyde, at the bottom of the town and across to Greenock and Gourock on the other side. The church tower gave a comforting feel to the town in contrast to the flotillas of military ships on the water. As they watched, a seaplane flew over, headed for its base at the nearby village of Rhu.

Violet pointed in the direction of the barely visible Rosneath headland which jutted out into the Firth. 'Can you imagine, all that from the Gareloch round to the Peninsula is a restricted area these days? It's impossible to go there without a travel permit and a jolly good reason. No more Sunday jaunts to the little tea shop at Kilcreggan. Do you remember those?'

'We went once as children and you got excited and were sick from too much ice cream. Mummy never took us again,' Felicity said drily.

'I have a lovely memory of it,' Violet said. She smiled down at Evie, who still held her hand with her mittened paw. 'One day, we'll take you there. When the war's over. You'll be able to choose any flavour of ice cream you like.'

'Will Granny come too?' Evie asked.

'Not if she hears you calling her that,' Felicity said. 'Come along, you two. I could do with a seat and a pot of tea. I do hope Mummy hasn't drunk her entire weekly ration. She was never one for budgeting.'

From a distance, the Stewarts' mansion looked rather grand. The red sandstone exterior seemed to glow in the low winter light and Violet felt a flush of love for the old place. She and Felicity had enjoyed many adventures as children, playing hide and seek in its many rooms and climbing the trees in the large garden.

'Do you remember Spooky?' she asked impulsively, turning to Felicity, who was also staring at the house. Her expression was unreadable.

Felicity's eyes widened. 'Gosh, I haven't thought about him in years.'

'Who's Spooky? Are there ghosts, Mama?' Evie said in an excited whisper.

'There probably are, dearest. Spooky, however, wasn't a ghost but Auntie Violet's pet cat. An enormous brute of a thing which scratched anyone who tried to stroke him. I can't say I was too upset when he...'

'Felicity,' Violet warned. 'Let's keep that story for when Evie's a little older, shall we. Come along, you two. Let's get inside.'

Felicity pulled at Violet's arm. 'You did tell Mummy that we were coming?'

'I didn't get a chance. I'm sorry. It will have to be all right, there's a war on. People have to make do.'

'People might have to make do, but not our mother,' Felicity murmured. Her jaw was set and Violet felt awful that she hadn't written to warn of their arrival. There had been too much to organise and she had a responsibility for the women under her command. For a start, she had spent hours begging for uniform trousers for them all from the stores. Warm coats were still to be found and on her to-do list.

'Come along,' she repeated brightly. 'Evie, this is where your mama grew up. Let's go and meet Grandmother.'

On the gravel path there was a broken roof slate. Felicity kicked it aside. Violet plucked away bushy strands of ivy to clear an area round the doorbell. She rang it but no one came. Evie clutched her hand. She stood there frowning until Felicity, with a deep sigh, pushed the front door and it opened slowly with a creak.

'Where is Mrs Lafferty?' Violet wondered out loud.

The housekeeper had been with the family forever. It was unthinkable that she wasn't there to greet guests at the door. There had been two maids too, but of course they had left for jobs in the munitions factories where they could earn much more and not have to deal with Mrs Stewart's uncertain temper. The gardener and gardener's boy had also gone, into the navy.

'Who's there?' came a querulous voice from beyond the staircase. 'Is that you, Mavis?'

Felicity nudged Violet and then gave her a little shove in the small of the back. Violet staggered forward with the momentum, breaking Evie's grip. She glanced back at her sister and niece and Felicity made a small waving motion with her hand. Go on, it said. Into the lion's den.

This was ridiculous. She was a corporal in the ATS. She had battled a nest of rats. Violet swallowed and pushed that memory deep down. The point was, she was brave and coped with all sorts of things.

'Hello, Mummy. It's me,' she said as she advanced into the drawing room at the back of the house.

It had once been a beautiful room. There were traces of its grandeur in the quality of the furniture and the original paintings by well-known artists that hung on the walls. However, the Chinese silk wallpaper was stippled with black mould and, in places, bulged with damp. In one corner, a strip of it had peeled off. A sharp, musty smell of mould and dust lingered in the chilly air. Their mother sat in an armchair next to a small, smoky fire, wrapped in a fur coat with a crumpled felt hat perched on her grey curls.

'Violet. Whatever are you doing here?'

'I'm stationed near Glasgow.' Violet was about to explain that she had only arrived back in Scotland recently but her mother cut across her.

'Where is Mavis? It's most inconvenient. I need my luncheon. And I have one of my dreadful headaches. Fetch my pills, Violet.'

'Mummy, Felicity is here too.'

'She wouldn't have the nerve,' Camilla Stewart said.

'Actually, I would,' Felicity said, advancing into the room with Evie. 'There's a bloody war on, Mummy, in case you haven't noticed, so we all have to make sacrifices. Yours, I'm afraid, is having Evie and me to stay with you.'

It was almost funny the way Mummy's eyes bulged with surprise. Under other circumstances, Violet might have laughed. Except this was so important. There really was nowhere else for her sister and niece to go except to some tiny rented flat in Glasgow. It was vital that Felicity had fresh air. Violet felt that instinctively. Surely that must clear Felicity's cough.

'Your father cut you off when you married that rogue. You made your bed and now you must lie in it,' Camilla snapped. The felt hat wobbled.

'My bed tonight is here, and yes please, I would quite like to lie in it. I'm exhausted. Please don't get up, Mummy. I'll find Mrs Lafferty and ask her to make up the beds.'

The mention of Mrs Lafferty distracted their mother. She groaned and clutched her head.

'I need my pills. You have no idea how I suffer with these migraines.'

'I'll fetch them,' Violet said kindly. 'Where are they?'

'How should I know? Mavis deals with that.'

Since when had Mummy been on first name terms with Mrs Lafferty? Perhaps it was because the two older women were alone together in the house now the rest of the staff and family were gone. Violet found the box of pills easily on an occasional table in the corner where there was also a glass of water and gave these to her mother.

'In any case the rooms upstairs are uninhabitable,' Camilla sniffed.

'I'm sure we can manage,' Felicity shrugged carelessly.

There was a chilly silence in which Camilla stared at Evie, who was jumping up and down with boredom and tugging at Felicity's hand.

'This is Evie,' Felicity said. 'Evie, say hello to your grandmother.'

Evie stopped jumping and leaned against her mother's leg. Camilla looked away at the fire.

'I'll find Mrs Lafferty and see if we can rustle up some food,' Violet said with forced cheerfulness.

There wasn't a sound behind her as she navigated to the kitchen, which was empty. She let out a breath she hadn't known she was holding. Goodness, but Mummy was hard work. She had almost forgotten. Still, at least she hadn't outright forbidden Felicity to stay. The headaches must have weakened her. Violet went along the faded corridor carpet to the housekeeper's private sitting room and knocked gently on the closed door.

'Just a moment,' Mrs Lafferty's muffled voice called.

Violet waited and the door opened slowly to show the housekeeper's reddened eyes, a handkerchief mopping her nose.

'Are you ill, Mrs Lafferty? Can I help?' Violet gasped.

'Violet, dear. You're home. Come away in. I thought it was Mrs Stewart... luncheon hasn't yet been prepared...

You see…' Mavis Lafferty sank down into a well-worn chair and her shoulders drooped.

'What is it?' Violet knelt beside her, her hand covering the other woman's, which was icy cold.

'It's my son William, you see. I've had a telegram… he's missing at sea.'

'I'm so sorry. You mustn't give up hope. He could be picked up by another ship,' Violet said.

'Yes, yes. Never mind me. I haven't peeled the carrots. I must get on. Time's a-wasting. Mrs Stewart must be wondering where her luncheon has got to.'

'Mummy is fine,' Violet lied. 'You rest here and I'll sort out the meal. Do rest, Mrs Lafferty, and please, please don't give up hope. I'll pray for William to come home and you must do the same.'

She hugged the housekeeper. How awful. William was her only son. As she headed to the kitchen she heard her mother complaining about Mavis and tardiness. Shaking her head, Violet went in. The carrots were in a small pile on the wooden table, earth clinging to them. A tea towel lay on the stone-flagged floor. Dropped in shock, she imagined, when the telegram boy arrived at the back door. The telegram, with its blue band and 'priority' written on it, lay on the table.

There was a plate of scones beside the range. Violet found a tray and put the scones on it along with a tiny pat of butter from the pantry and a jar of blackberry jam, which looked from the label to be part of a pre-war stash. She boiled the kettle on the range and made a pot of tea. Before taking it through to her family, she put a teaspoon of sugar into one of the cups and poured in the tea. Sugar was good for shock. She took it to Mrs Lafferty along with a scone.

Taking the tray, she went back to the main sitting room. Her mother hadn't moved but Felicity was kneeling at the miserable fire, moving pieces of coal with the brass tongs but failing to generate any flames. Evie was standing on a small stool, staring out the window, elbows on the windowsill and her chin resting on her cupped palms.

'Well?' Camilla said.

'Poor Mrs Lafferty has had some bad news. William's missing in action,' Violet said, putting the tray on the low table in front of the fire.

'Gosh, what bad luck,' Felicity said. 'Makes me quite glad we don't have a brother to lose to this ghastly war.'

'What about luncheon?' Camilla's voice was shrill.

'Today, it's scones with jam. Felicity can make dinner tonight. I have to head back to camp soon.'

Two faces looked aghast at her but Violet ignored them. She busied herself with coaxing the fire into producing a few tentative tongues of flame until there was actually some heat coming from it.

After their meal, eaten mostly in silence with even Evie subdued, Violet suggested that she help Felicity air the beds. They trudged upstairs. Evie stayed in the sitting room, shaking her head when asked if she wanted to come too. She had discovered she could kick the wall under the window and no one scolded her. They left her kicking and sneaking glances at her grandmother.

'Make the dinner?' Felicity said, at the top of the stairs. 'I had hoped for a bit of a rest on coming home. I'm capable of cooking, I had to learn quickly when Ian and I lived in the cottage, but…'

'It's only until Mrs Lafferty feels better,' Violet said.

'Don't you mean Mavis? Whatever is that all about? Mummy's gone quite mad. That hat is frightful.'

'Not as frightful as this bedroom,' Violet sighed, pushing open the nearest door and peering inside.

'The whole house smells of damp. I might as well be back in the cottage in Shropshire.'

'I worry about your chest. Maybe this was all a mistake. Perhaps we should try and rent a flat in Glasgow instead?'

Felicity shook her head. 'We can't really afford it, can we. Besides, the smog in the city is far worse.'

'If only Daddy hadn't run up all those debts with his bad investments. This was such a lovely home when we were growing up. Now it's falling down.'

'Chin up, sweetie,' Felicity said. 'Remember it's my role to bring us down. You're the cheerful Stewart.'

Violet didn't feel cheerful right at that moment. She pulled the dust covers off the antique wardrobe and the chest of drawers and the dressing table with its age-spotted mirror. When she pressed her fingers on the bed, the bedspread was damp. A grey mould was growing on its edge. She pulled off the bedspread, blanket and sheets and draped them over the furniture.

'I'll find coal for this fireplace, see if we can dry out the bedding. Then I have to go. I mustn't be late back.'

Evie ran in and clambered up onto the stripped bed. She began to jump up and down. It reminded Violet of doing exactly the same with Felicity as children and Mummy screaming at them to stop. She grinned at her sister. Felicity grinned back. It was a shared happy memory that warmed her more than a tiny fire in the fireplace could. They both scrambled onto the bed and joined hands with Evie and jumped with her.

Their laughter filtered through the cold house. Downstairs, Mrs Lafferty smiled at the sound and forgot, for a brief second, her terrible news. In the sitting room,

Camilla Stewart grimaced, eyes to the ceiling, and struck her fist on the arm of the chair. Her box of pills flew off and landed on the floor where they would stay until someone else came to pick them up for her.

Chapter Ten

'I can't believe we've been here a month already,' Bridie shivered.

'Shut that door. There's a gale blowing through here,' someone cried from the back of their hut.

The door slammed and a sheepish girl slunk past Kathy and Bridie and hurried to the pot-bellied stove to warm her hands.

'So much mud being tracked in,' Violet sighed. 'We'll have to have another scrub of the linoleum after kit inspection.'

There was a collective groan but no one argued with their corporal. Gladys and her sewing pals were huddled round the other stove in the long room. One tablecloth, for Bridie's wedding, was complete. It had been much admired with its decorations of roses and thistles representing Bridie's home and where she was posted.

'It's only a week before Christmas,' Kathy said gleefully. 'I can't wait.'

'I think we gathered that,' Bridie smiled. 'What are your family celebrations like?'

Kathy was so glad to see Bridie returned to her sweet, amiable self that she'd have gladly chatted on any subject. Some colour had returned to Bridie's cheeks in the last couple of weeks and she'd confided in Kathy that she didn't feel so sick. She refused to discuss Neil and the wedding but Kathy was still hopeful that her friend would gradually fall in love with her tall RAF pilot.

'We have a big meal on New Year's Day and a party and all the neighbours come. Mammy pushes the boat out and makes a smashing roast chicken, tatties and vegetables and a boiled pudding. We exchange gifts, and Mr O'Leary, who lives in the same tenement close as us, is the traditional Scottish "first foot". He brings coal wrapped in newspaper, a paper twist of salt and black bun for luck for the whole year ahead.'

'What about Christmas Day?' Bridie asked. 'You missed it out.'

Kathy laughed. 'It's a working day up here. Last year I was on a twelve-hour shift at the factory with workers' playtime on the wireless blasting out Christmas carols.'

'A working day?' Bridie turned to Violet in horror.

Violet nodded. 'Kathy's telling the truth. Although in our family, because Daddy was from Oxfordshire, we always celebrated on the day with a lovely big tree covered in pretty decorations and candles and lots of presents colourfully wrapped under it.'

They all sighed, remembering the pre-war festivities.

'There may not be so much food or so many gifts but we can still have fun,' Kathy said, holding up strips of paper. 'These have been donated and I volunteered us to make them into paper chains to decorate the canteen.'

'I'll cut them up if someone else glues,' Violet offered.

'Nice of Cook to give us the flour.' Bridie lifted a jar of flour and water paste on the metal cabinet next to Kathy's bunk and stirred the spoon. 'It has the consistency of that porridge you're so fond of, Kathy.'

'Perfect for sticking the loops together then.'

There was a feeling of optimism, not only between the three friends but throughout the camp, and in the newspapers too, that perhaps this might be the last wartime Christmas.

Although Mr Churchill was ill with pneumonia, which had been reported on in the *Daily Record* the day before, the paper now stated that 'The prime minister has had a good night. There is some improvement in his general condition.'

Not only that, but the British and their allies were doing well at pushing back the Nazis all over the world. The paper lying on Bridie's bed had articles on the front page. 'Allied troops have landed on New Britain, only 270 miles from the great Japanese base of Rabaul, and after taking their initial objectives are pushing inland with tanks,' one reported. Another declared in bold print: 'Heavy Raid on Berlin, Germans Say'. That article went on: 'The German overseas news service said last night that "British bombers tonight again attacked the capital of the Reich." The attack is described in Berlin as a terror attack on a considerable scale.'

'Ooh, I've had a great idea,' Kathy cried, almost spilling the jar of paste in her excitement.

'Watch out or Violet will have us all cleaning the blankets to get the glue out of them,' Bridie said, grabbing the jar to save the contents.

'We'll put on a Christmas show,' Kathy said, her eyes gleaming. 'In the canteen. There's plenty of room and there's a piano in there. The boys can make a stage somehow and we can have different acts.'

'There's only a week to go,' Violet said. 'That's hardly enough time to prepare.'

'Och, you're right.' Kathy deflated.

'Maybe not a whole show, but surely we can have a sing-song and someone dressing up as Father Christmas?' Bridie said quickly with a glance at Kathy and Violet.

'Aye, and we could set up tables for card games.' Kathy perked up again. 'And ask Cook to make mince pies.'

'That sounds lovely,' Violet agreed with a smile. 'And don't forget that there's a party in Glasgow next Friday, Christmas Eve, which we are all invited to, organised by the Americans. There'll be a couple of trucks to take us there and back.'

'I wish Jennifer was here to join in the fun,' Bridie sighed. 'Her letters are always cheerful but Aberdeenshire is miles from here. I wonder if we'll ever meet again. She and Howard have been apart since their honeymoon weekend. What this war does to couples isn't bearable. Oh, sorry, Kathy. How awful of me. You're missing Don too. Did you get a letter this morning?'

Kathy had received a letter from Don that morning. It hadn't told her much. Just that he was busier than ever. Having seen the article about the repeated raids on Berlin, Kathy guessed he was involved, although obviously he couldn't write about it. He wrote that he loved her and couldn't wait to see her again. Had she thought some more on setting a date? He wanted to send her ring. Yes, he knew it was safer without it going through the vagaries of the post, but he wanted to send it in any case. Would Kathy be a darling and accept it?

The letter had made her uncomfortable, but she didn't understand why. It was as if… as if she was being boxed in somehow. She had folded it and stuck it under her pillow to read again later.

'Aye, I did,' she nodded. 'He's fine the now. There's couples all along the country having the same problems.

There's a war on and that's the way it is.' She said the words automatically and found she wasn't missing Don as much as she should.

'What about your young man?' Violet asked Bridie.

Kathy glanced at Bridie. Of course Violet didn't know about the baby on the way, or how Bridie really felt about Neil.

But Bridie said mildly, 'I can't complain. I'll see Neil for our wedding in January so there's not long to wait.'

'Have you got someone special?' Kathy asked Violet curiously.

Violet shook her head. 'I met a chap a while ago whom I thought was special, but it turned out he was in love with someone else. I was quite cut up about it to start with but I got over him quickly, which made me realise I wasn't as much in love with him as I had thought. There's no one now. Anyway, I have enough on my plate looking after my sister and niece.'

Kathy was about to ask why Violet's sister and niece needed looking after when the door to the hut was flung open and a figure stood there. Kathy's jaw dropped as the other girls in the room all glanced up to see who was letting in the cold night air. She couldn't believe her eyes. It was Judith Lennox.

It was hard to say who was more surprised, Kathy or Judith. Then Judith's eyes glinted maliciously.

'Hallo, how can we help you?' Violet asked.

'I've tae bunk down here.'

Kathy saw that Judith had her full kit, a gas mask slung over her shoulder, steel helmet and army rucksack. She had obviously just arrived. What awful luck that Judith Lennox should end up here of all places.

'Are you on the guns? Only I'm not expecting an addition to my squad.'

'I'm a cook, so I am.'

'You're in the next accommodation block. Come along and I'll show you where to go,' Violet smiled.

Judith's sturdy legs didn't move. She stood square to the door frame and shook her head. 'Naw, there's a lassie in there been as sick as a dug. I've tae report here.'

Her gaze flickered from Violet to Kathy and Kathy had a horrible feeling that Judith was enjoying this. She *wanted* to be in the same sleeping quarters as Kathy. The only reason that might be was to make trouble. Judith was always trouble.

'Oh dear. I did hear there was a bout of the lurgy on the go. Very well, there's a spare bunk at the back. Make yourself comfortable and we'll sort it out tomorrow.'

Kathy could scarcely breathe. She was very conscious of Judith lumbering past and the squeak of the bedsprings and murmur of greetings from the girls at the back of the room. Her joy in the paper decorations was gone. Bridie frowned in concern but Kathy couldn't say anything. How was she to explain her history with Judith? Not without bringing up Dennis, and that was impossible with Violet there.

She pasted paper chains numbly. Violet went away to carry out her corporal duties and Bridie leaned over.

'Whatever it is, I've got your back,' she whispered.

Kathy's whole body relaxed. She had forgotten. She wasn't alone. She had Bridie and Gladys and the other girls as friends. Violet too was beginning to be a friend. It wasn't the same as dodging Judith's sly foot in the roads around Kiltie Street and hearing the women's whispers in the shops. She was stronger here. And yet… if Judith told

them about Dennis, what would happen? Bridie understood, but then she was in the same situation. What about
the others? She might lose all her new friends. Judith had
power over her and knew it.

Mammy's letter arrived the next day. As part of her
regular update on the doings of their wee street, she wrote
that after Mrs Lennox's death, Judith had moved out and
disappeared. No one knew where she had gone. The letter
went on to say that Dennis had learned to dress himself.
Mammy's pride burst out from the paper and Kathy smiled
and felt a sudden terrible longing for home and her wee
boy. She was missing out on him growing up. But she
loved being in the army too and couldn't imagine being
back in the munitions factory on dull shifts. Oh, it was all
so complicated.

Over the next few days she tried her best to avoid
Judith. It wasn't too difficult as they trained on the
predictor and practised on the height and range finder,
marched, undertook physical training and readied themselves for the ever-present kit inspections. The promised
army greatcoats arrived, but even better there were a few
of the much-desired 'teddy bear' fur coats with hoods and
Kathy managed to get one.

She was very glad of it when called to do night-sentry
duty. In her teddy bear coat with her khaki trousers and
long boots, she stood with a pitchfork outside the ablutions hut in the dark night. Her breath formed little puffs
of white. Her gloves didn't stop the cold seeping into her
fingers as she gripped the pitchfork handle. Was she really
to stop the enemy with it? Around her were sounds of
the camp and the countryside. Some noises were easily
identified and others mysterious. Above the potato field,
the searchlights beamed bright shafts into the sky.

A day later she was on spotter duty. She wore her coat and her steel helmet. Armed with a pair of binoculars, she lay on a wooden reclining chair in the muddy grass, sweeping the sky slowly for enemy aircraft. She wondered what she'd do if she saw one. Hopefully her training would kick in immediately. In the fields beyond, when she sat up, she saw sheep grazing. They looked incongruous in among the bomb craters and set against a foreground of gun emplacements and the busy camp of khaki-clad men and women.

–

Judith was also busy. Boxes of herring, freshly caught from the River Clyde, arrived at camp. The head cook was a bossy woman. Judith gritted her teeth at the barked orders. She cut the heads off the herring and gutted them. The stink of fish was nauseating. She put the roe, lumps of egg masses, to one side. They were to be washed, dipped in flour and fried in a little hot fat until golden brown to be served at dinner with carrots and cabbage.

She took the back of her knife and scaled the fish, holding them by their tails and scraping firmly towards the head end. Briskly she cut off the tails and rinsed the fish in a bucket of cold water. The pile of slippery bodies didn't seem to diminish, no matter how she chopped, scraped, split and plucked at them.

But she wasn't thinking about herring. Her thoughts were on Kathy. What a coincidence that she was here. Looking cosy too with all her pals. While Judith hadn't found any friends yet. Aye, they were friendly enough to begin with, but they hadn't approached her after that first evening. Too snooty, that lot, by half. And cheeky too.

One girl had asked to borrow Judith's hairbrush. She'd soon put her right. If you lent things, you lost things. They had brought in mugs of cocoa and balanced them on the stove. When they weren't looking, Judith finished hers and drained the dregs of the mug next to it. The look of surprise on the girl's face was hilarious when she went to drink and found it empty.

She hadn't seen much of Kathy, what with the cook keeping her and the other assistant cook slaving, but she'd overheard there was a party off camp that evening which was an opportunity too good to miss. She'd bring that girl down a peg or two, she vowed.

It snowed on Christmas Eve and Kathy was worried that it might prevent them travelling into the city for the party, which was to be held in a hall near the city centre. She and Violet peered out into the black night from their hut. The flakes were pale and soft, floating down in the moonlight.

'Look, the snow is only a thin layer on the ground,' Violet said. 'The trucks will be fine.'

'Let's hurry and get ready then,' Kathy replied.

'I'll be back in a jiffy, some things to settle with the sergeant,' Violet said, ramming her cap onto her fair hair and rushing out into the freezing air.

Once she'd gone, Kathy spun round to the others who were in various stages of getting ready. There were curlers in hair, lipstick being applied and stockings being rolled up legs.

'Quick, dresses on and greatcoats!'

Kathy slipped into her green dress and put on her teddy bear coat. It might not be the height of fashion but it was warm and hid the fact she wasn't wearing her uniform. She stuffed her make-up into her gas mask box and ran her fingers through her hair, glad that it was thick and shiny and sat well without a fancy hair style.

'Violet's a good sport,' Bridie said, coming up to her, wrapped in her own greatcoat and with her gas mask slung over her shoulder crossways. Behind her there was a buzz of excitement as the other girls beautified themselves.

'What do you mean?'

'You don't actually believe the sergeant called her over to the communications room? Violet's giving us space to dress up so she can't put us on a warning for lack of uniform or leaving our gas masks.'

'Och, I never thought of that.'

Gladys pranced around, her red skirt flaring, pleased with her appearance. She came to a sudden stop and there were hoots of laughter from her friends. Her knickers were round her ankles.

'Oh, me knicker elastic's finally gone.' Gladys joined in the laughter.

By the time Violet returned, they were ready to troop out to the waiting trucks. Kathy found herself sitting next to Judith. The other girl's leg bumped against hers all the way into the city and Kathy was sure it wasn't accidental. Kathy joined in the lively chatter and tried to pretend she didn't care about Judith. The other girl's presence cast a shadow over her evening, though.

–

The dancing was held in a large, draughty room down a dingy hallway from a public bar. It was the sort of place that nice girls wouldn't have gone to before the war. A few of Kathy's companions hesitated at the door but she took an eager step over the threshold and waved them on. Mammy would be horrified but Kathy was curious to see what it was like.

The bar smelled of spilled beer, fresh sweat and cigarettes. There was an eager huddle of uniformed men who whooped when they saw the new arrivals. It was clear that the party had started early. Violet pulled at Kathy's arm, shook her head and steered her charges away from the bar, along the corridor and to the cloakroom.

Kathy took off her teddy bear coat and gave it to the young woman who was hanging coats onto hangers. The others piled theirs on top. Violet pretended not to notice all the dresses and glamour. She was wearing her ATS uniform. There was a sweet fragrance in the air because Gladys had shared her precious White Lilac perfume with them.

'Let's grab a table together.' Bridie had to shout to make herself heard above the live band and the noise of people talking and laughing. There were plenty of uniforms but also women and a few men in civilian clothes. Kathy thought their wee group brought colour to the room.

She walked quickly to sit at an empty table and the others followed suit. They glanced about, smiling. Soon men arrived with offers to dance, and only Kathy, Bridie, Gladys, Judith, Violet and a few others were left. Kathy wanted to soak up the atmosphere before dancing. She was surprised when Judith leaned on the table and smiled at Bridie.

'I hear congratulations are in order,' Judith said.

'Thank you,' Bridie replied.

No one knew about Kathy and Judith's history together and Kathy had decided not to share it even with Bridie.

It wasn't fair. Besides, maybe Judith had changed. In spite of that she felt tense now.

'I suppose you'll be planning on a family once you're married,' Judith went on pleasantly.

Kathy's skin prickled.

'We... that is...' Bridie stammered, clearly worried that Judith had guessed she was pregnant.

'Aye, you're lucky. Where I come from, there's many a lassie who has a wean without the wedding.' Judith flicked a glance in Kathy's direction.

Kathy shot up out of her chair. 'I need a wee bit of fresh air. I'll be back soon.'

She pushed into the crowd on the dance floor, never minding who she hit with her elbows or trod on with her heels. Judith was bent on destroying her. She wasn't going to stay around while Judith turned the others against her. She pushed on blindly, intent only on reaching a door on the far side of the room that she'd noticed when they entered. Surely it must lead to the world outside. Away from Judith Lennox.

As she pushed and swayed in the mix of bodies, she thought for a crazy moment that she saw Alisdair Meikle's dark, coppery head above the RAF blue uniforms. She blinked and wafted away the smoky air which was stinging her eyes. A tall American, ruddy-faced and stinking of beer, was standing in front of her asking her to dance. By the time she'd shaken her head and protested no, so much so that she had to push him away, any signs of the man who looked like Alisdair had gone.

She reached the door and lurched outside. The cold was a shock to her skin. The two army trucks were parked there and she ran to the nearest one, hauled herself up into its cabin and shut the door. She slunk down in the seat, shivering.

'I'll wait a wee bit and then go back in,' she told herself.

–

Alisdair was only up in Glasgow for a fortnight. He was working twelve-hour shifts and this was the first night he'd been persuaded by the chaps to come out. He had been able to visit Nana Mackie briefly but hadn't managed to get to the city centre coffee shop and doubted he would.

Just as he was thinking about Kathy, he glimpsed a girl with flaming red hair, in the midst of the dancing couples. It couldn't be her, could it? Had he conjured her up with his longings?

Even while he shook his head at his imagination, Alisdair's feet turned to follow.

'Excuse me,' he murmured politely, trying to find a way through.

'Blast it!' He used his shoulder to barge a way in when everyone ignored his polite words.

The girl with the gorgeous hair had been heading for the door, he thought. He barrelled his way there and flung the door open.

'Kathy?' he called, hopefully.

It was a bitterly cold night with fresh snow beginning to fall. No one was foolish enough to be outside. Still, he stared into the darkness, his heart rate heightened. There were two large army trucks, badly parked at an angle as if the driver had left them in a rush. The snow there was churned up and tainted with mud where many shoes had trodden.

Alisdair walked over to them. There was no sign of life. Of course there wasn't. Everyone was inside having a jolly time. And that was where he ought to be too. He sighed and turned back and went into the building again.

'Ah, there you are, Ally old boy.' One of his squadron rushed up. 'Have to go, I'm afraid. Orders from high command. We're needed back in Ayrshire, toot sweet.'

–

Kathy slipped from the truck's cabin. She knew she couldn't hide forever. Whatever damage Judith had inflicted, she had to deal with. But when she rejoined her group of friends, there was no sign that anything was different.

'Are you all right?' Bridie asked. 'You were gone quite a while. Violet wanted to go and find you but I said you'd be back soon. I was on the verge of coming to get you myself.'

'I'm fine, so I am. Did… did Judith say anything?'

'Not much. She started drinking after you left. Violet had to have a word with her. Most of us are on the lemonade. Judith's drinking beer.'

Judith hadn't told them. Kathy felt a rush of relief. She was simply tormenting her. Kathy's secret was safe.

'Are you no dancin'?' she asked Bridie.

Bridie shook her head. 'I'm too tired. But there's a couple of likely lads approaching so I'm betting you'll be dancing soon.'

Kathy resolved not to let Judith worry her for the rest of the evening. She smiled when the first soldier arrived and asked her for a dance. It was time to enjoy herself.

–

The next day was Christmas Day and the heavy anti-aircraft mixed battery at Muirhead Farm was blanketed in a white covering of snow along with the rest of the bleak fields surrounding it. After a long, tiring day of drills and practice, the girls were glad when evening came and, with it, the anticipated celebrations in the recreation room.

It was crammed with bodies as everyone who was not on duty was determined to enjoy themselves. A soldier at the piano played favourites such as 'Jingle Bells' and 'We Three Kings' and they all joined in the singing, remembering previous Christmases and loved ones. Cook had outdone herself, providing trays of hot mince pies, which Judith brought in with a scowl on her face.

Kathy and Bridie had draped the paper chains round the room. Those that hung from the piano shook with the soldier's enthusiastic bashing of the keys.

'I'm worried about that girl,' Violet said, joining Kathy and Bridie and nodding towards Judith. 'She isn't fitting in with the team spirit. I must find a way to help her.'

'Didn't you say she was a neighbour of yours?' Bridie asked Kathy.

'Aye, she is, but she's...' Kathy searched for the right words.

It was odd, but she felt disloyal telling her friends what Judith was really like. After all, Kiltie Street was a close-knit community and Judith, for all her faults, was part of it.

Bridie groaned and clutched her stomach.

'What's the matter?' Kathy asked, alarmed at her friend's suddenly white face.

'Nothing, I'm fine.' But Bridie groaned again and bent double.

'You are very much not fine,' Violet said, moving swiftly to her side and supporting her. 'Kathy, take Bridie's other arm and let's get her back to her bed.'

With Kathy and Violet taking most of her weight, Bridie allowed them to half-carry her from the noisy room to the quiet accommodation block. They helped her sit on the side of the bed but when Kathy went to lift Bridie's legs to help her lie down she stopped.

'What is it?' Violet said, slightly impatiently.

'I'm bleeding,' Bridie whispered. Her eyes were dark holes as they stared at Kathy.

There was a thick smear of red on the blanket. Bridie stumbled from the bed and ran to the door. They followed her to the ablutions block and stood outside to give her privacy. The toilets had no segregations and no doors. Kathy thought it was lucky no one else was in there.

'It's more than a heavy period, isn't it?' Violet said.

There was no way of keeping Bridie's secret now so Kathy nodded. Was Violet going to be shocked? Or worse, condemning of their friend? But Violet's glance at Kathy was full of compassion and understanding.

'Goodness, how awful for her. Does Neil know about the baby?'

Of course Violet was a good sort. She was kind to a fault. Kathy shouldn't have doubted her.

'Yes, it's why they're getting married. Bridie didn't want to marry him but she felt she had to. Will she be all right?'

'I think she may have lost her baby. She'll need medical attention and possibly bed rest, but I'm not a doctor so I can't say for certain. You stay with her and see if you can keep her spirits up while I organise some help. Try not to fret, we'll make sure she's right as rain.'

Violet sped away. Kathy took a deep breath and went in to help Bridie.

Oh God, what should she say? What would Mammy or Jeannie say in such a situation?

'Bridie?' she said, cautiously, not sure whether to approach the toilet where her friend was.

'I've lost it, haven't I?'

Bridie's tear-choked voice had Kathy rushing to her impulsively, all worries on how to deal with the situation flown from her mind.

'I'm so sorry, I really am but… yes, I think so.'

'I know it. I'm cramping. It's so sore in my tummy and back and I've passed lumps that look like liver.'

Swallowing her nausea, Kathy crouched down and took Bridie's hands in hers.

'What can I do?'

'There's nothing anyone can do.' Bridie lifted her head and looked at Kathy. Her eyes were red with crying and strands of her black hair were plastered to her pale face. 'I prayed to God not to be pregnant and he listened. It's all my fault. I killed my own baby.'

'No, that's not true. These things sometimes happen to women. It's no one's fault. Where I grew up, there were times when Mammy had to go to a neighbour's to help when a woman lost a pregnancy. It's not God judging you, Bridie.'

'I didn't want it but now it's gone and I do want him or her. My own little baby. How could I have wished it away?'

Violet had told her to keep Bridie's spirits up but Kathy was at a loss how to do so. Instead, she kept hold of Bridie's cold hands until she heard Violet and the doctor outside.

Chapter Eleven

It was March and daffodils had sprung up to quiver in the fresh spring breeze in the field margins and around the barracks huts. Kathy and the others had marched and drilled until midday and now sat in the mess eating Irish stew with dumplings which had been served up by a sour-faced Judith. Kathy swore Judith had slopped the serving of her portion on purpose so that it left flecks of brown gravy on her uniform front. She'd have to dab it off after with cold water and hope it didn't stain.

'Wullie Campbell's been down again to ask for some help to cut logs in the woods,' Violet told the exhausted group.

'Is that Auld Wullie or Young Wullie?' someone asked.

Auld Wullie was the amiable farmer of Muirhead Farm who often visited the battery, bringing vegetables or a rabbit or two for the pot. He was in his fifties but called 'auld' to distinguish him from his son. They all agreed that Young Wullie was attractive enough but his taciturn personality was somewhat off-putting. The two Wullie Campbells found tasks for the army stationed at the HAA battery that the captain didn't quite have the heart to refuse. Especially after a difficult winter in which the Muirhead Farm tractor had come in very handy for helping to pull army trucks out of deep, muddy ruts.

'It's Auld Willie.'

The girls visibly brightened. Gathering logs and branches in the woods made a nice change from cleaning the ablutions block and practising yet again on the predictor or fixing the generator, which conked out every so often until its parts were tightened or oiled or replaced.

'I'll go,' Kathy said quickly.

She'd felt quite dull since Bridie left after Christmas. Violet and their commanding officer, along with the doctor, had seen to it that no one else knew the real reason for Bridie's illness and everyone had waved her off sympathetically on long-term sick. Only Kathy and Violet knew that Bridie wasn't likely to come back.

'Me too,' Gladys piped up, along with several other girls.

The walk to the woods wasn't a long one but it meant a good stride uphill with the breeze sharpening to redden their cheeks and pinch their nostrils. There were more daffodils, wild garlic and the last of the snowdrops in drifts under the trees and they all exclaimed at the wild beauty of the woodlands. After the mud, the dull colours of the barracks and other buildings and their own drab uniforms, a bit of colour was welcome.

Violet shared a saw with Kathy as they all spread out to find branches or fallen trees to drag back.

'Have you heard from Bridie?'

Kathy nodded. 'I got a letter this morning but haven't opened it yet. Here, let's sit on this log and read it together.'

Bridie's first few letters had been full of grief, guilt and regret about her baby. The wedding was off, of course, and she had gone home to Yorkshire. All that her parents had been told was that she had suffered from 'women's troubles' and anaemia. Mam suspects, she wrote in her first letter, but she won't say to my dad. She knows what he's like. He doesn't ask after me and that suits me fine.

Kathy unfolded the letter with some trepidation. How was poor Bridie doing now?

Dear Kathy

It's been a few weeks since I wrote you. Neil came to visit me and I didn't feel like writing while he was here and afterwards. He asked me to marry him again but said he understood when I said no. I think he was relieved. He's a good person at heart. I don't love him that way but we'll always be friends.

I miss you and the other girls. I even miss the drills first thing in the morning! I put away Gladys's tablecloth today even though I don't need a bottom drawer now and I'll always remember you all when I use it.

I'm not over my baby and I don't think I'll ever be, but life goes on as Mam says. That's the closest she got to letting me know that she knows. My dad, he'd have forty fits if he knew and Mam can't stand up to him. If he threw me out, I'd have nowhere to go.

Anyway, I'm getting better bit by bit. I'm going to make something of myself, Kathy. I don't think I'll ever marry. I don't want to now. If I ever lost another baby, I wouldn't survive it. So, when I'm healthy again, I'll rejoin the army or try something else, maybe nursing, and make a real go of it.

Let's not lose touch. When this awful war is done, can we get together? As the song goes, 'We'll meet again, don't know where, don't know when,

but I know we'll meet again.' That Vera Lynn knows a thing or two, doesn't she!
Love from Bridie

Kathy and Violet sat on the damp log, re-reading Bridie's letter. Overhead in the branches, birds chirped.

'She's more cheerful in this letter at any rate,' Kathy said. 'Jennifer's been writing to her too, keeping her spirits up.'

'That's good. Bridie deserves a good outcome. I know she'll do well whatever she sets her mind to,' Violet replied.

A blackbird flew past with a twig in its beak.

'Silly bird. It cannae eat that. Thinks it's a worm, does it?' Kathy remarked.

Violet giggled. She glanced at Kathy's puzzled expression and her giggling turned to loud chortles of laughter.

'What?' Kathy didn't know whether to be offended or not.

'Oh, goodness. I'd forgotten what a city girl you are. He isn't eating, he's nest building. It's spring after all.'

'Och, how was I to know that. There's no blackbirds or other wee birdies in Kiltie Street. Nearest we've got is a few daft ducks on the canal.' Kathy grinned. 'It's a bit uncanny being on a farm for me.'

'Especially when that farm is also home to a hilltop heavy anti-aircraft mixed battery,' Violet agreed.

'Aye. Fancy us being in the Royal Artillery. That's something, isn't it. Poor Bridie.' Kathy sighed. 'She's missing out on all this.'

'Don't worry about Bridie. I suspect she'll find her way all right. Tragic though this is, it might be the making of her path in life,' Violet said wisely.

Kathy tucked the letter into her pocket and they picked up the saw and found a likely branch. Around them, there was the laughter of the other girls as they picked up the sawn logs and collected brash. Most of the haul would go to Auld Wullie for the farmhouse but some of the smaller wood they would siphon off for the barracks stoves. It might be spring but it was still cold at nights.

'Phew, I'm jolly well melting from sawing,' Violet said after a while, wiping her brow.

'Have we enough for Wullie's satisfaction, do you think?' Kathy said.

They dragged the cut logs down the slope, following in the others' footsteps back towards the huts.

'I say, Kathy, I haven't asked you about Don. Has he written?'

'Aye, he writes regular. Too regular for my liking…'

'What do you mean?'

Violet stopped so abruptly that Kathy stubbed her toe on the log and it was a minute before she could speak. The problem was that Don's letters were becoming more frequent and fervent in tone. She was finding it harder to write back.

'He wants to get married and he won't let up. The last letter, he decided on a date for the wedding all by himself. Tells me he'll apply for leave and come up north and I've tae sort the banns. He sent the engagement ring too, even though I told him not to. I was scared it'd get lost in the post.'

'He does sound awfully keen,' Violet said carefully, with a glance at Kathy. 'Don't you want to set a date? Most girls would be delighted to have a chap so keen to tie the knot.'

Kathy's sigh came from a deep well within her. Violet had hit the proverbial nail on the head. She didn't want to set a date at all. In fact, she was beginning to realise she had made a terrible mistake in agreeing to marry Don. She didn't love him enough. She fancied him, and she was flattered that he seemed besotted by her. But the night she thought she'd seen Alisdair, she'd felt a jolt of love and desire so intense it had floored her. She was in love with Alisdair Meikle whether she wanted to be or not. There it was.

She stood stock still. Violet was in front of her, her brows drawn together in a frown as she stared back at Kathy. The others were a small group in the distance, almost back at the huts by now. There was a fresh scent to the air, some delicate fragrance coming from the spring flowers mingling with the odour of clay soil. Kathy felt as if she'd remember this instant forever.

'I'm still in love with him,' she whispered.

'That's good then, isn't it?'

Kathy groaned. 'Not him. I mean, not Don. I'm in love with Alisdair. Seems like I'm doomed to love him whether he wants me or not. It's not fair, so it isn't.'

'Who's Alisdair?' Violet sounded bewildered.

'I met him in Glasgow back in August last year. He bumped into me, nearly threw me to the ground. When I looked up, our eyes met… he has such lovely eyes. I fell in love with him right there and then.'

'I take it there wasn't a happy ending?'

'He was ashamed of me. He didn't want to introduce me to his parents. I'm no from the same class. Alisdair's posh. It could never work.'

'Oh dear,' Violet said. 'What a pity. And then you met Don?'

'Aye, on the rebound, as I now realise. I was swept along by his enthusiasm for me. Well, we're not from the same class either but somehow it doesn't matter. He tells me how beautiful and amazing I am. Which girl doesn't want to hear that from a man? But I can't get Alisdair out of my head. Oh, Violet, what am I to do?'

'Gosh, it's a tricky one.' Violet shook her head.

'No, it's not,' Kathy said suddenly. 'I know what I have to do. I have to break it off with him. I'll write tonight.'

She stooped to pick up her end of the log when Violet's hand clamped down hard on her shoulder, making her squeak with surprise.

'You mustn't do that,' Violet said. 'Don's fighting for his country. The RAF are out there every day battling the enemy and many don't come home again in the evening. You can't break it off in a letter. You simply can't.'

Kathy knew Violet was right. But if she let Don keep on believing they'd get married, wasn't that wrong?

'Let's get this log down into camp before it roots and becomes a tree again,' Violet said. 'You've got yourself in a pickle, but we'll sort it out. Somehow.'

'It's my problem.'

'Possibly, but that's what friends are for. Two heads and all that sort of thing. Come along. It'll all look better after Cook's sausage casserole and mash.'

–

The sausage and mash was delicious, even if Judith was serving it up, but Kathy still hadn't come up with a solution by late evening as they prepared to go to bed in their barracks. The stoves' warmth was dying down and Gladys had taken the dirty mugs back to the mess. Kathy got into bed and pulled the sheet and blanket up to her neck. She thought of Jeannie. Her sister had been engaged to one man but ended up marrying another. But that was different, she argued to herself. Jeannie's fiancé had hit her. He was an unpleasant man and no one thought she should stay with him. Don, on the other hand, was every mother's dream for their daughter. He was handsome, an RAF pilot and from a wealthy background. Not only that, he was dashing and bold. And he worshipped Kathy. She fell into an uneasy sleep.

–

For the next few days, Kathy was too busy to ponder her love life. She marched and did her share of plane spotting and guard duty. Coming back from working on the predictor one day she saw Gladys waving and shouting that letters had arrived. Kathy ran into the barracks, hoping for a letter from home. There were two letters. One in Mammy's distinctive looping writing and one in a hand she didn't recognise. She put Mammy's under her pillow to read later. She'd savour all the news of Dennis, because she was missing him. Curiously, she slit the other one open.

> *Dear Kathy*
>
> *We haven't met. I am Don's mother. He wrote to us often about you and your plans to marry and we would have welcomed you into our family with open arms. I am so sorry to have to write this letter instead.*
>
> *Don crashed his plane during a training flight last week. He didn't survive. We comfort ourselves with the knowledge that he died doing what he*

*loved. He will have told you that even as a small
boy he knew he wanted to fly.*

*Don was our only son. We had looked forward
to you being our daughter.*

Please come to visit us if you are ever in Dorset.
Yours
Esmee Whitworth

With a cry, Kathy sprang up and ran. She made it to the
ablutions block and the nearest toilet where she threw up
until it was only thin, acid fluid that stung her throat as
she spat it out.

She was blinded by hot tears. She barely saw the others
crowding in, or felt Violet guiding her back to the hut and
into a chair. Someone put a blanket round her shoulders.
She sobbed until a mug of hot tea was thrust under her
nose.

'Drink up, it's got a large dose of sugar ration in it.
That's an order.'

Violet's voice brooked no argument. The tea scalded
Kathy's throat but oddly helped. Gradually her sobs
lessened although she shivered despite the scratchy
blanket. She felt Violet take the crumpled letter from her
numb fingers.

'Oh dear, I'm so sorry for your loss,' Violet said quietly.

Kathy barely heard her or the others murmuring their
condolences. Don was dead. How was it possible? He had
written to her only days ago. His letter was packed with
the energy he brought to everything. She hadn't known
he wanted to fly from when he was a wee boy. He hadn't
shared that. Hadn't had time. There was so much they
hadn't discovered about each other. And now he was gone.

She felt sick all over again. She hadn't loved him
enough. She'd wanted to be free of him. Now she was,

but how terrible it felt. His poor mother, having to write and believing Kathy to be Don's devoted fiancée when all she was… was a sham!

'Let's get you into bed, shall we,' came Violet's gentle voice.

Kathy crawled under the covers, shut her eyes and let the darkness take over.

–

That wee bitch. It had to be all about her, didn't it. Judith's mouth twisted in anger. She glared over at the shape in the bunk that was Kathy. She was getting all the attention as usual. It didn't matter what went on, she came out smelling of roses. There they were, all crowded round her while Judith had no friends at all. Oh, they were polite enough, but they avoided her all the same. She wasn't one of them. So what, she told herself. I don't care.

Kathy had invited her out once, some months after she came home from having her wean. They'd gone to see Dorothy Lamour in *Moon over Burma* one evening. Judith had to sneak out while her Aunt Irene slept in her armchair in front of the fire. She was still banned from going out of an evening. Judith had accepted out of curiosity. She soon understood why she'd been invited. Kathy had acted as if nothing was wrong. She bored Judith with descriptions of her sister's wedding that had taken place that day. She laughed and chattered until she did Judith's head in. Aye, what she wanted was forgiveness, and to pretend nothing had happened.

Judith had a rib that still pained her from Irene's beating with the broom handle. If she breathed in too hard, it jabbed her like a fork prong. So she sat and fumed while

Kathy giggled and sighed over the movie and acted like they were the greatest of pals. She let Kathy pay for the tickets and let her buy them both a cup of tea from the wee café that stayed open all hours in the city centre. And she knew she hadn't forgiven or forgotten and never would.

After that, she'd made it clear they weren't pals at all. It felt good to see Kathy's wariness. A wee flick of a wrist or a foot stuck out as the other girl went by was fun. Any bruises were nothing compared to what Judith had endured.

After a few days of the sympathy in the barracks and with Kathy listless and pale, Judith had had enough. She sidled up the wee skinny lass called... Glenda... no, Gladys, and put on a sympathetic smile.

'She's no too good, is she now?'

Gladys frowned at her. Judith held her smile.

'It's a cryin' shame, what happened to her man, so it is. She's had an awfy lot to deal with, our Kathy, over the past while, never mind this happening.'

'What do you mean?' Gladys asked.

Some of the other girls were listening in. They were in the middle of their endless sewing that they did in the evenings. Kathy and Violet were nowhere to be seen.

'Och, she must've told ye. Her wean?' Judith said innocently. 'Her wee boy, Dennis, that her mother looks after for her. He's no Don's wean of course. His father's some other soldier Kathy went with. Oh, sorry, did youse not know?'

She was pleased to see a ring of shocked faces looking back at her. The barrack door opened and they all stared as Violet came in with her arm around Kathy's shoulder, the two of them talking in low murmurs.

'I don't believe you,' Gladys said loudly.

Judith was taken aback. Firstly that Gladys had the cheek to argue with her, and secondly that she had a piercing voice for such a thin girl. The other girls stood behind her, clearly on Gladys's side.

'Don't believe what?' Violet's cut glass accent rang out as she and Kathy approached.

The lilac shadows under Kathy's eyes looked like bruises and for a brief second Judith felt a pang of something approaching sympathy, but she quelled it.

'I can't tell you, it's so disgusting,' Gladys said indignantly.

'She says Kathy's got a baby what's not 'er fiancé's but another bloke's,' one of the other girls chipped in. 'We know it ain't true though. Judith's just a bloody liar and a troublemaker. It ain't true, is it Kathy?'

Now all the heads turned towards Kathy, who looked as if she might faint. Judith waited for the satisfaction of hearing her say that actually Judith was right, she was no better than the girls you saw at night in the east end of Glasgow in their thin coats and gaudy make-up calling to the punters. She couldn't wait to see all their faces when they heard it.

Instead, Kathy hesitated, and then shook her head. She didn't meet Judith's hard stare.

'There,' Gladys said and turned her back on Judith.

The others did likewise and Judith found herself at the back of the barrack room on her own while they crowded round Kathy and someone volunteered to go to the mess and bring back cocoa and biscuits.

–

'That's it. You've been moping too long. You're coming home with me,' Violet said. 'I've wangled a day pass for each of us.'

'Thanks, Violet, but I've got to sew my button back on my tunic and polish my boots.'

Violet snorted in a most unladylike way. 'Now I've heard everything. Kathy Dougal sewing and polishing voluntarily. No, pick up your jacket and cap and let's go. The trains are rather unreliable so we'd better hurry.'

It was two weeks since the awful news of Don's death and Kathy couldn't shift the listlessness that invaded her body. Her mind was a fog too. At night she had awful nightmares where she saw Don's plane crashing into the ground over and over. In other dreams, he proposed to her and she took his ring but it crumbled to dust and Don shouted, blaming her for destroying it and him with it.

The last thing she wanted was to leave camp. It had become a refuge where daily tasks and drill meant she didn't have to think about it all. Then there was Judith. She had told the truth about Dennis and Kathy had lied and denied she had a baby. She hadn't been able to bear the thought that they'd all turn away from her if they knew. Instead it was Judith that was shunned. No one spoke to her and she wasn't included in any of the communal embroidery, letter-writing and gossip that went on in the evenings.

Violet thrust her uniform jacket at her and stood there, arms folded, with a pursed lip. Kathy sighed. Violet clearly wasn't going to take no for an answer. Strangely, once they were on the train, going past the coast, she felt a small spark of interest in the stunning view of the sea and the ships with the mountains dusty grey in the background.

'I remember this,' she told Violet. 'When Mammy took us as weans for a day out to the beach in Helensburgh. The sea was all blue and sparkly. There weren't the navy ships of course. We built sandcastles and Mammy paid for me and Jeannie to have donkey rides. Oh, it was lovely.'

'There we go, it's doing you good already,' Violet said with a wide smile. 'You've had us all worried, you know.'

'It's only been a fortnight.'

'I know, dear, but you're not the only one to have lost a loved one recently and life must go on. We have to look after each other in our grief – in our little group, someone's lost a brother and someone else a cousin in the last week too.'

'I didn't realise,' Kathy said in dismay.

'How could you realise?' Violet said gently. 'You've been lost in your own world. That's understandable, but these days, well, we don't have the luxury of mourning for too long without also functioning in our daily tasks. I'm telling you that as your corporal as well as being your friend.'

'I'm sorry.'

'Don't be sorry. You've been through hell and everyone understands that. Today, I hope, is a change of scene to start your healing. Actually, once you've met Mummy and Felicity, you'll be only too glad to get back to camp and work hard again.'

'Are you sure they'll want you to bring me visiting?'

'It'll do them good to see a new face,' Violet said. 'Besides, I haven't been down in a while. I need to check they haven't murdered each other.'

Kathy wasn't sure if Violet was joking. Her mother and sister sounded terrifying. She looked out at the sea and felt a flicker of joy at its vast shining surface with wee flecks of foam licking the edges where it met the stony beaches. What a pity there was all that barbed wire and keep-out signs. She bet the donkeys were long gone from the promenade.

–

Violet's home was enormous. It was bigger than the houses on the hill above Kiltie Street where the better-off lived. Kathy shut her mouth to stop it gaping. They crunched on the gravel to the front door. There was an air of shabbiness that was at odds with the grandeur of the surroundings. She noticed roof tiles in a pile in a flowerbed next to the door as if hastily gathered and flung there.

An older woman answered their press of the doorbell and hugged Violet, who asked after her health and how she was coping. Kathy stood awkwardly until Violet motioned her to come in.

'This is Mrs Lafferty, Kathy. She keeps the whole place running.'

'They're in the drawing room, Miss Violet. You go on in and I'll bring a tray of tea. I've made a steamed ginger pudding for tea but we'll have it early unless you're staying the night?'

'Only day passes sadly, and given the state of the trains we'll have to leave by five, but ginger pud would be splendid please.'

Kathy sniffed. The house reeked of damp and coal smoke as if someone hadn't cleaned the chimneys for years. Unlike her cosy home in Kiltie Street where Mammy kept it clean and warm and very tidy, here it was cold and a bit smelly and there were odd mismatching items untidily scattered about. There was an elephant's foot umbrella stand near the door with two umbrellas, a long stick and a peacock's feather stuck in it. A brass trumpet lay near it, covered in a fine layer of dust. On the walls were far too many paintings of dull landscapes or portraits of po-faced men and women in their finery. Who'd want those to look on every day?

Violet led the way into a large room beyond the stairs.

'Hello Mummy, Felicity. I've brought a friend home to visit. This is Kathy.'

'Auntie Violet!' A small girl rushed across the room into Violet's arms.

The two women seated by the fire gazed at Kathy. She was struck by how similar they looked. The younger of the two also had a passing resemblance to Violet but was prettier.

'I'm pleased to meet the both of youse,' she said, trying not to sound nervous.

'Are you here about the job? Do go and see Mavis in the kitchen.'

'Mummy, don't be awful,' Felicity drawled. 'She isn't a servant girl. She's one of Violet's gunner girls. Isn't that right?'

'Have a seat, Kathy, and don't mind either of them. Their manners are quite appalling, and that's after an expensive education,' Violet said, guiding Kathy to a place on the couch.

Mrs Lafferty bustled in and Kathy was glad of the fuss of serving the tea and the passing around of the ginger pudding. There were murmurs of delight and praise from Violet and Felicity and a grumble from Violet's mother over the distinct lack of any ginger taste. Had Mavis actually added any ginger? Mrs Lafferty smiled at Kathy and gave her an extra slice.

'You look a bit peely-wally. A bit of sugar will bring back the blossom in your cheeks.'

'Thank you,' Kathy managed to say.

'Mrs Lafferty's only son is missing at sea,' Violet whispered once the housekeeper had left.

'I'm sorry,' Kathy said automatically.

She knew Violet was right. She wasn't the only one to have lost someone to the war. The trouble was that Don's death was wrapped up with her guilt. She had been on the verge of dumping him. She might have written to break off their engagement had not Violet stopped her. It wasn't as simple as loving him and losing him.

'You don't want the job?' Camilla Stewart said, peering at her.

'Oh, for goodness' sake, Mummy. Do shut up,' Felicity snapped, and then had a coughing fit that made her stumble from the room. She waved her hand furiously at Violet, who got up and followed her.

The small child jumped up onto the couch beside Kathy and stared at the second slice of ginger pudding.

'Do you want it? I'm full up,' Kathy said. Her appetite, usually so hearty, had been missing for the last two weeks.

'I'm Evie,' Evie told her as she sprayed ginger crumbs from her mouth and rubbed them from her checked dress. 'Do you want to see my teddy?'

'Aye, that'd be grand. I've got a wee brother who's not much older than you. His name's Bob.' Kathy felt relief. She was relaxed with children, having two younger siblings as well as Dennis. Anything to avoid the old woman's uncomfortable stare.

'How old is Bob?'

'He's nine. I haven't seen him for ages because him and my wee sister got evacuated to the countryside when the war started. I've been to visit them.'

'Mama won't let me go. She says she needs me, but we lived in a cottage in a field so Hitler couldn't see us to drop a bomb. Now we live with Granny and Hitler won't come here either,' Evie said, matter-of-factly.

'You're definitely safe here,' Kathy reassured her. 'Do you know, I've got another wee brother. He's called Dennis. He's only two years old and he's got red hair, just like mine.'

Evie beamed up at her. Kathy's longing for Dennis was a physical hurt. Her wee boy, and she was so far away from him. She wanted to hold him tight and smell his baby skin and kiss and cuddle him. What a mess it all was. When she glanced up from her thoughts, Evie was licking her plate and Violet's mother was looking round the room as if she'd lost something.

'We can't get the help,' Camilla said.

Luckily Violet reappeared. 'It's a lovely afternoon. Shall we walk in the garden? We've got wellington boots that should fit you.'

It was a relief to leave the drawing room, where Camilla was fussing over her tablets and accusing Felicity of deliberately hiding them. Felicity walked about the fancy room in her rubber gumboots, treading soil into the carpet, but no one seemed to care. If any of them had done that at home in Kiltie Street, Mammy would have skelped the hide off them.

The garden turned out to be massive, with an adjoining field at the back where there were two horses. Violet explained they rented the field to a farmer who usually had horses there or sometimes a small herd of highland cattle. Felicity didn't speak much but smoked slender cigarettes and picked early flower heads to thread in Evie's hair.

'I'm a fairy princess,' Evie cried in glee.

'Talking of princesses, any Prince Charmings on the horizon?' Felicity asked Violet.

'I'm far too busy to fall in love.'

'Falling in love is the only worthwhile game, darling. Tell her, Kathy. We don't want Violet turning into an old maid.'

But Kathy was too wise to join in what was clearly an old, much-rehearsed argument between the sisters. They wandered among the grass and the shrubs until Violet announced it was time to go. Evie scampered off to feed the horses on buttercups she'd gathered but Felicity came with them to the gate to say goodbye. They watched her go back up the driveway slowly, the gumboots mismatched with her blue silk dress. Like everything in the house, Kathy thought.

'Oh, she's dropped her hanky,' Violet murmured, crouching to pick it up.

She stuffed it in her pocket. 'I'll launder it and give it back next time I'm down. Let's hurry and get that train. Fingers crossed its running or we'll both be on a charge.'

Chapter Twelve

There were flecks of blood on the handkerchief. Violet noticed them immediately when she picked it up. She hid them by crumpling the material and putting it in her pocket before Kathy could notice. Not that she need have bothered. Kathy was back in her own thoughts. Violet's heart pounded with fear. She was angry too. Felicity had hidden how ill she was. She felt like turning round and running back to the house and demanding that Felicity admit her deceit. She knew her sister though. Felicity would deny all. Probably claim she'd cut her finger.

Instead, Violet spent the train journey back staring out at the sea and the fields without seeing them. Her thoughts were all of Felicity, who had TB and whose cough was not the remnant of a simple cold that had lingered. How had Violet been such a fool? She'd allowed Felicity to dupe her. She hadn't wanted to consider such a horrific alternative. The question was, what to do now? If Felicity refused to acknowledge her illness and didn't allow Violet to get a doctor, what could she do? Oh, and Evie! Violet gasped and covered her mouth. Was Evie infected too?

'Are you feeling sick?' Kathy asked with concern.

Violet shook her head. 'I'm right as rain. Silly me… I forgot something I had to do.'

She couldn't share this with Kathy, or anyone. Not yet. Not before she'd confronted Felicity herself. She had tried before to get Felicity to see a doctor but now she had to try harder, or beg. Whatever it took.

'Are you going to tell me or not?'

'Whatever do you mean?' Violet asked.

'I'm no daft, Violet. I saw your sister's hanky. I've been waiting for you to tell me about it. Has she seen a doctor? I'm guessing not, or else she'd be in the hospital.'

Violet groaned. 'Was it that obvious? I didn't know Felicity was so ill. She's had a cough for months but she told me it was the remains of a winter cold. She brushes me off when I try to talk to her about it.'

'She's scared.'

Felicity, scared? It hadn't occurred to Violet. Felicity was never scared. She was calm, indifferent, sarcastic and could be beastly, but she was never afraid. Not like Violet.

'What are you going to do?' Kathy asked. 'I'm here to help you, if I can.'

'You've got enough troubles,' Violet smiled weakly.

'We've all got our troubles, as you pointed out on the way down. I've been wallowing in mine and forgot about other people. I'm your pal and I'm not letting you deal with this alone.' Kathy patted Violet's arm.

'Thank you. The problem is, I'm not sure what to do. I need to think about it.'

'Do that, but not for long, eh? Your sister needs help.'

–

Violet had to wait another week before she could get away. There was a visit from the colonel to inspect the battery and the troops. This meant marching and a small parade along the lane, never mind the cleaning and inspections on camp before the colonel and his entourage arrived. One of the soldiers was put to task whitewashing the boulders at the entrance to the camp. The Campbells' herd of dairy cattle chose that week to escape from their field and invade the battery. They had to be shooed out and the reminders of their visit scooped up and delivered back to the farm for fertiliser.

Violet was glad when it was all done. She was desperate to get back home although she hadn't a clue how she was going to approach Felicity on the subject of her health.

She met the delivery man in his truck at the gate as she slung her bag and steel helmet onto her shoulder along with the hated gas-mask box.

'There's no trains today, hen, if that's where you're headed,' he shouted over to her.

Blast. What was she to do now? She thanked him and hurried back to the barracks.

'There's a bicycle at Muirhead you can borrow,' Kathy suggested. 'Gladys took it yesterday evening for a wee wander.'

'Wonderful. Just what I need. I haven't been on a bike in years. They do say one never forgets how to ride. I'll let you know if that's true.'

The farm was on the other side of the hill from the camp huts. It consisted of a cluster of whitewashed ancient buildings sheltered by a copse of pine and birch. The farmhouse itself was sturdy and well maintained and Auld Wullie's wife, Bess, was always welcoming to any of the gunner girls who came to visit. Rumours of hot freshly baked scones with pats of home-made butter and jam meant that there were plenty of visits to the Campbells' welcoming home.

'Och, you don't have to ask. You can borrow the old rattler any time. There she is, over by the barn. Put her back when you're finished,' Bess said cheerily when Violet enquired about the bicycle.

Violet eyed the beast with a certain amount of trepidation. It was painted black with a tatty leather seat and a basket on the front. The front wheel had a dent. She lifted it from the wall. Gosh, it was heavy. She slung her leg over and wobbled as she pressed down on the worn pedals. She swerved from side to side as she began to move forward but within a few minutes she had the knack of it and began to cycle more quickly down the rutted lane from the farm towards the dam. There were pot holes and dusty bumps and scattered stones as hazards on the lanes heading in the direction of the station. The nearby main road, when she reached it, would go either west to Dumbarton and Helensburgh or east towards the city of Glasgow. Violet reckoned it was a good two-hour cycle to get home from the junction but she was young and fit and thought nothing of that.

She even had enough puff to whistle 'Don't Sit Under the Apple Tree' as the 'rattler' sped along past the dam and down the side of the big house, Muirhead Hall, set in a lovely landscaped garden with the burn flowing through it. Soon she was speeding along an open lane with green fields on either side. A flock of linnets flew up with sweet trills.

'Sorry,' she shouted to them and then laughed with the sheer thrill of feeling the warm breeze in her hair and her legs pumping like mad, her muscles warm from the unexpected exercise. It felt so good. She was terribly worried about Felicity, but in the moment it was good to forget everything but the tenderness of her behind on the saddle, the sticky rubber of the handles under her fingers and the exhilaration of the sunny spring air as it rushed into her lungs.

Suddenly a rabbit flew out of the hedgerow and scampered across her path before disappearing into the hedge on the other side. Violet shrieked and lost control of the bicycle. It jerked to the side and she fell off, landing on the hard dusty lane. The bicycle came to a stop on its side, wheels spinning. Violet sat up. Her knees and palms stung madly. She assessed the damage. She'd skinned them and the blood welled up from all the scrapes. And her stockings were ruined. When she crawled over to the bicycle, she saw she had a puncture in the front tyre.

'Lovely. That's just what I need.' She rocked on her knees and licked her palms with a whimper. Golly, how they hurt!

She forced herself to pick the rattler up, and limping, she continued down the lane. Luckily she wasn't far from the main road.

'I'll keep going, and maybe I can get back on the darn thing despite the puncture,' she thought.

She limped out onto the path beside the main road and kept walking. She had only walked for ten minutes when a car drew up beside her. The occupant wound down the window.

'Hello. You look like you could use a lift. Can I drop you somewhere?'

Violet looked at him. He was rather handsome. She reckoned he was in his thirties, with dark hair and a firm jaw and brown eyes that were looking at her with some concern. He might do for Felicity, she thought hazily. Although perhaps he was too old for her.

While she was thinking that, he had leapt out of the car and taken the rattler from her. It fitted, just about, into the boot. He then guided her, in a gentlemanly fashion, into the front passenger seat.

'Joseph Gillingham, pleased to meet you.' He offered a firm, warm, large hand to her. 'Call me Joe.'

'Violet Stewart. Thanks awfully for the lift. I'm going to Helensburgh. I say, is that terribly out of your way?' Violet was appalled to hear how breathy she sounded. Gosh, he might think she fancied him the way that had come out. Of course she didn't. She didn't have time for romance these days. The little electric shock she felt when his hand had touched hers meant nothing and was more to do with how her skin stung with grazes.

She glanced at his uniform. It was officer rank, Royal Army Medical Corps.

'Actually, I'm going to the Camis Eskan Hospital on the outskirts of Helensburgh, as it happens,' he said. 'I can drop you at your destination if you tell me where. I have some time to spare.'

'Are you a doctor?' Violet asked, the cogs turning in her mind.

'I am indeed. Major Gillingham at your service.' He gave a small, self-mocking bow but kept his eyes to the road as the car sped up. 'And where have you appeared from? You look somewhat battered, if that isn't too rude to say.'

Violet did feel affronted but decided to let it pass. Clearly, he didn't find her attractive. Not that she found him attractive either. She was firm on that.

'I'm Royal Artillery,' she said proudly, pointing at her white lanyard. 'Based at the mixed battery at Muirhead.' Then she remembered the posters, 'Loose lips sink ships'.

Should she have told him that? But Joe seemed quite relaxed as he nodded.

'You should have those abrasions seen to. You'll need to keep them clean.'

'Really, it's nothing. Where are you based?'

Joe glanced at her briefly before studying the road again and Violet wondered if he'd answer.

'I'm a surgeon. I specialise in reconstructive surgery for burns injuries. I'm based in Glasgow, but I also have duties at Camis Eskan with the Polish soldiers based there.'

Gosh but his eyes were like melted dark chocolate. They were so dark, one couldn't see the pupils. And his eyelashes were black and long. Any woman would be envious of them. He must surely have a wife. Violet gathered her wayward thoughts. Goodness, what must he think of her, wool gathering like that. When she looked at him, Joe was smiling.

'What takes you to Helensburgh?' he asked.

'I'm going home for the afternoon actually. I was born and brought up there.'

'It's a pretty place.'

'Yes, it is. It's a nice area to grow up in. I hope my little niece thinks so.'

'How old is she?' Joe asked.

Violet found herself telling him about Felicity and Evie and Mrs Lafferty and her son William. Also about Mummy, but not too many details on that. He was so easy to talk to, with a pleasant way of telling her about his work and his background, but with questions about her too. So many men monopolised conversations, in Violet's opinion, so it was refreshing to find a man who didn't.

She was so engaged with their chat that she was surprised to find they were driving into the town.

'Golly, that was quick,' she exclaimed, feeling almost disappointed to be there. Soon, she and Joe would part ways.

'I can drop you at your house, if you like?' Joe said.

Violet didn't hesitate. 'That would be wonderful.'

She was very conscious of his presence in the car as they drove along and then turned right up Sinclair Street, the car powering easily up the steep hill. As they drew up outside the Stewart home, she had a bold idea. Felicity might hate her for it, but surely it was the right thing to do?

'You said you weren't in a hurry?' Violet said.

Joe brought the car to a stop outside the Stewart residence and looked at her. 'That's right.'

'This is going to sound like an awful imposition but would you… could you…' Violet faltered.

'Whatever it is, Miss Stewart, I'd be delighted.'

'Oh. You can call me Violet,' she replied, flustered. 'And you haven't heard me out yet.'

'I can wait,' Joe grinned. It caused creases in his cheeks and he looked suddenly younger. Some women would find him quite the heartthrob, she thought… She picked at the hem of her cuff until his polite cough reminded her where she was and what she needed to ask.

'It's my sister, Felicity, whom I was telling you about. She's not well, hasn't been since last summer really. She has a cough, quite persistent, and last week there was blood on her handkerchief. I'm so very worried about her but she won't seek help.'

Joe got out of the car and before Violet could move, he had her door open and was extending his hand to help her out. His fingers were just as firm and warm and steady as before.

'Let's go and see your sister.'

Mrs Lafferty was delighted to see Violet back so soon and ushered them in to the formal drawing room at the front of the house before leaving to find Felicity. The room was never used and felt chilly despite the warm spring weather. Violet was embarrassed to see that parts of the plaster had fallen from the ceiling onto the Aubusson carpet. There was soot in the fireplace and a bundle of twigs where a bird's nest had clearly fallen down the chimney. Without the maids to help, Mrs Lafferty wasn't coping with such a large house.

'Let's go and find Felicity,' Violet said hastily. 'Follow me, please.' Felicity was in the kitchen, stirring soup and shaking her head at the housekeeper. She smiled when she saw Violet and her eyes widened at the sight of Joe coming in after her.

'Ah, darling. I was just telling Mrs Lafferty that there couldn't possibly be visitors for me that required the front room. How wrong I was.'

She glided round Violet and extended her hand to Joe with a charming smile. 'Hello, I'm Felicity. And you are?'

'Major Gillingham at your service, ma'am.'

Violet had a tiny flash of satisfaction that he hadn't asked Felicity to call him Joe. Then she felt small and mean for feeling it.

'Mrs Lafferty, would you mind awfully if we spoke to Felicity on her own for a second?' Violet asked nicely.

'Not at all,' the housekeeper said. 'And I'll keep young Evie out of here too. She and her grandmother are playing cards but if she hears you're home, she'll be scampering in here nineteen to the dozen.'

'What's all the excitement about?' Felicity leaned her slim form against the solid wooden table casually.

'Let's not beat about the bush any more,' Violet said. 'I saw your hanky and the blood. Your cough isn't going away. Major Gillingham is a doctor. I want you to let him examine you.'

'Darling...' Felicity began.

'No!' Violet cut across her sharply. 'No more dissembling, no more excuses and fobbing me off. I won't have it. You have Evie to consider. If there's something wrong...'

Felicity's face was white with its usual high colour over the cheekbones but she seemed to pale further at Violet's words. Meekly, she bowed her head. In a way it made things worse, because it was not like Felicity to give in. There was a terrible gnawing fear in Violet's belly as she watched her sister lead the doctor out of the kitchen to find a small room to speak in. Joe took his black bag with him that he'd carried from the car. Violet stirred the soup for want of anything else to speed the time up. Even so, she felt as if a lifetime had passed before they came back, both looking subdued and serious.

'Well?' she said, setting the dripping spoon down on the table, never minding the stains it would make.

'You tell her,' Felicity said.

'I've done a cursory examination and we've talked about your sister's symptoms,' Joe Gillingham said. 'I'd like a second opinion, but I'm fairly sure that Felicity has tuberculosis. I want to take her in to a chap I know who deals with the disease. He's a consultant, excellent at his job.'

Violet only heard the word 'tuberculosis'. It was her fear, and now he'd said it. Made it real.

'Will she...?' No, she couldn't voice her greatest terror. That Felicity could die. Violet couldn't imagine life without her sarcastic, witty, big sister and her sometimes biting tongue. She loved her. Oh, and Evie. What would they do?

Joe put up a hand. 'Let's not get ahead of ourselves. Let's get Felicity into hospital for some tests. There are treatments, and people do get cured. Will you let me arrange all this for you?'

'Would you do that for us? Even though we don't know you?' Violet said.

Felicity raised an eyebrow. 'How intriguing. Don't you know each other?'

'Long story involving a bicycle and a rabbit. Anyway, we need to talk about you.'

'What will I do with Evie if I'm away in hospital?' Felicity frowned. 'I can hardly leave her with Mummy.'

'Of course you can leave her with me.' Camilla appeared in the kitchen doorway. 'Don't bother to explain. I overheard everything. I don't suppose you would have told me the truth otherwise. It will be your fault if my knees ache this evening. I shouldn't be standing up, I should be resting.'

'You don't like children.'

'Mavis will take care of her. Evie and I play cards.'

'That's sorted then,' Felicity said drily.

Camilla tottered away back to her drawing room. There had been no concern or sympathy expressed for Felicity, but in her own way, Mummy was doing her bit, Violet supposed. Of course it helped that somehow she had bonded with Evie.

'I have to get going,' Joe said to Violet. 'I'll arrange a car to come and collect you and the bicycle and take you back to your camp.' He turned to Felicity. 'You'll get a letter with an appointment. Please don't disappoint your sister by turning it down.'

Violet saw him to the door. 'Thank you for all your help today. Goodness, you rescued me and you may have saved Felicity's life.'

Joe grinned. 'I can't resist a damsel in distress, and I'm a doctor. All in a day's work.'

'You don't need to organise a car for me.'

'Of course I do. How else are you going to get back when the trains aren't running? Let me do this for you.'

'Thank you again.' Violet smiled, and Joe's returning smile did something very odd to her insides.

She watched his upright back as he walked down the driveway. His black bag swung from his hand and his gait was steady but fast. She lingered until he vanished round the curve behind the azaleas before returning to the kitchen, where Felicity had taken the long-simmered soup off the range.

Violet rushed to her and clasped her arms around her. Felicity tolerated her embrace for a moment before pushing her off.

'I'm not dead yet,' she said.

'Oh, don't say such a thing,' Violet gasped. 'You're not going to die. You heard Joe. I mean Major Gillingham. There are cures. When that letter arrives, you must reply immediately and for God's sake, for once in your life, do what you're told.'

Felicity cleared her throat and glanced at Violet. All her affectations had been wiped away. 'I'm scared,' she said.

'Oh, darling.' Violet hugged her, ignoring her sister's slight wince. 'I'm scared too, but we're in this together. I'm going to be with you all the way. You're going to get better. For Evie's sake and for my sake. I can't lose you.'

'You're not going to lose me, silly. I'll be a good girl and do what your Major Gillingham tells me to. Besides, I won't give Mummy the satisfaction.'

'Whatever do you mean?'

Felicity sighed and sat on one of the kitchen stools. 'When Ian and I moved into the fishermen's cottage, I sent a sketch of it to Mummy and Daddy and described where it was and the village and how poor the inhabitants were. I meant it all sympathetically, but Mummy wrote back to say there would be no more money until I came to my senses and left Ian and that she wouldn't be at all surprised if I caught tuberculosis or some other dreadful disease of the poor and it would serve me right.'

'How like Mummy.'

'Yes. So I'm not going to succumb to this and let her be proved right. I'll do whatever it takes to come back to you and Evie.'

'I love you,' Violet cried.

'Let's not get all soppy, darling. Stiff upper lip and all that. Where are my cigarettes? I'm dying for one.'

'I've taken them. You can't smoke any more. Promise me?'

Felicity shrugged. 'Unless I can persuade Mrs Lafferty to buy some, I haven't the energy to walk downtown to buy more. So, yes, I promise.'

'I've got to go,' Violet said reluctantly. 'I do hope Joe, I mean Major Gillingham, sends that car soon.'

'Honestly, Violet, you are hopeless. I can see that he's "Joe" to you so do stop pretending otherwise.'

'I wondered if you might like him? He's rather dashing. He's probably married though.'

'He's not married, he's a widower. I asked him. His wife died five years ago. Cancer, poor girl.'

'You did not. How terribly rude of you. We don't know him at all. Oh, what must he think of us!' Violet cried.

'He thinks I'm a medical case, but he thinks you are quite delicious,' Felicity told her with a glint of her old spirit in her eyes.

'Now you're being ridiculous.'

'He's far too old for me, but he's just about perfect for you,' Felicity added.

'That makes no sense at all.'

Chapter Thirteen

In the six weeks since the awful news about Don, Kathy had gradually come to terms with it. The dreadful numbness had passed and when she thought about him it was with sadness and regret, although she knew she hadn't loved him and would not have married him if he had lived.

She missed Bridie and Jennifer's good-natured company. It was lovely to get their letters and to write her own letters back but it wasn't the same as having them there. Luckily Violet had turned out to be a good friend too.

'Ouch!' Kathy cried.

'Sorry. Do hold still. It's almost impossible to wind your hair round the curler without tugging on it otherwise,' Violet replied, not sounding sorry at all.

'I managed yours all right.'

'Mine is silkier. You're very lucky to have such luscious locks.' Violet pulled the last section of Kathy's red hair expertly onto the metal curler between its two prongs, closed them and wound it round and round. 'There you go. Tomorrow you will have the most wonderful waves.'

'It's worth a painful night.' Kathy glanced around the barrack room where the others were also putting their hair in curlers. 'I hope it's appreciated when we go to that school hall tomorrow.'

'I could do with a dance and a jolly time,' Violet agreed.

'How is Felicity?' Kathy asked, knowing that Violet was worried about her sister, who was now in hospital.

Violet shook her head but mustered a smile. 'As far as I know, she hasn't got any worse. I haven't been allowed to visit yet. Thank goodness Evie and the rest of us don't appear to have contracted the dreaded disease. I couldn't have borne it if Evie was sick with it.'

Kathy opened her mouth to answer when the sound of a whistle pierced the air, closely followed by the shrill clang of an alarm that went on and on.

'Steel helmets on, girls,' Violet shouted. 'Must be an enemy plane spotted. Quickly now, we know what we have to do.'

Steel helmets were rammed on top of curlers as the gunner girls ran to their stations in an orderly fashion. All that drill was finally worth it, Kathy thought as she went, her skin tight with anticipation. None of them were panicking. Kathy knew, as they all did from their regular practice, that there was enough time to get into position. Battery Headquarters would have rung the telephone operator in the anti-aircraft central command post at the camp where any planes seen were plotted on a map. If it was an enemy plane heading in their direction then the alarms were set off.

Outside the barracks hut, dusk was falling and powerful searchlights were scanning the sky in long, white columns. They reached the predictor and height and range finder as the male soldiers loaded the shells into the guns. The air was suddenly full of the women's shouts of their calculations, the noise of the generator muffled by the powerful crump of the guns. Above them the sky, now darkening rapidly, blossomed with flashes of light illuminating the camp. It was an eerie sight to see the emplacements silhouetted against the fields, the woodlands black shapes beyond. Kathy wondered briefly how Auld Wullie and Bess felt, being so close to the action in the Muirhead Farm. She felt excited and scared all at once but also proud to be part of her team. They were Royal Artillery and they were in the thick of it!

As the shells were fired, the noise and heat seemed to suck the air away and Kathy gasped, her mouth dry. She wanted to squeeze her hands over her ears but couldn't. The calculations changed constantly, tracking the lone aeroplane. Bloody hell, why wasn't it shot down by now? A direct hit was unlikely but the gunners were aiming to force the plane off course so that any bombs missed their targets. The most likely target was the shipyards at nearby Clydebank and the Clyde. In response to ack-ack fire, the aeroplanes tried to zigzag to avoid being hit, but in order to drop their bombs accurately, they needed a long, straight flight in the run-up to their target.

Had they done enough? Kathy thought desperately. She tried not to imagine the damage wrought by enemy bombs. She had experienced the Glasgow blitz back in March 1941, huddled in the family's Anderson shelter praying there wouldn't be a direct hit and waiting for the all clear. When they had finally emerged, rows of nearby tenements had been devastated, killing families and leaving buildings ripped open to the elements or completely vanished, leaving only gaping craters.

The Nazis mustn't be allowed to do that again, she vowed. Her throat was sore from yelling the numbers over the roar of the guns. Something thudded onto her helmet and there was a shriek from someone nearby. Shrapnel was raining down on them. Hot pieces of metal scattered on the ground and still the women held their positions, knowing that it was vital that the soldiers loading the guns knew where to fire.

Suddenly there was a shout as the guns stopped. 'It's a goner! Bloody thing's hit.'

A cheer went up and Kathy clapped her hands and grinned like a fool. All around her, the other girls were clapping too as if they were at a show. Oh, it felt marvellous and odd to have survived together and fought the enemy and won. Faces were sweating and streaked with dirt. Helmets were dented by shrapnel. Gladys was shivering and another girl burst into tears.

The distant sound of an aeroplane's engine, spluttering and clearly in trouble, reached them.

'It's ditching in the sea,' Kathy said. 'It hasn't bombed the shipyards. Thank God.'

The girls crowded together as the shock wore off and they realised the action was over.

'Me curlers 'ave come out,' one of them complained. Gladys giggled and suddenly they were all snorting with laughter, holding their sides and feeling the belly laughs ease away the tension of the night.

Kathy and Violet were first back to the barracks. Kathy's back ached and Violet had sustained a cut from falling shrapnel, which she brushed off as minor but Kathy insisted she must clean and dress.

'I'll wash it for you. There's Germolene ointment in the first aid kit and I'll put a bandage on the cut so no more arguing,' Kathy said firmly.

It didn't take long for Kathy to tend to Violet's arm and soon it was wrapped in clean crepe bandage.

There was a whimper from the back of the room. Kathy grasped Violet's uninjured arm and raised her eyebrows. Violet shook her head and shrugged helplessly. No one was visible. The whimper came again.

'Who's there?' Kathy called, leaving Violet and walking up towards the end bed.

In the far corner, Judith was curled up on the floor, her head on her bent knees and her arms placed protectively over them.

'It's all right. It's over now, you don't need to be scared. Let's get you up,' Kathy said gently.

In that moment, she felt nothing but pity for Judith. She wasn't a gunner girl, she was simply a cook, and the whole evening must have been terrifying for her. She wasn't even in barracks with the other general staff, having never received an order to move across to the other huts. She was all by herself in the Royal Artillery girls' room with no one to turn to for comfort. She hadn't made any friends. How sad that was. Kathy realised she wasn't afraid of Judith any more. She had her own set of friends who had stuck up for her and refused to listen to Judith's nasty gossip about Dennis. Judith was powerless to hurt her any longer.

It took a German raider to make me realise that, Kathy thought, her lip turned up in silent, wry humour.

'Come along, listen to Kathy,' Violet was saying as she bent over Judith's curled body.

Between them, they were able to haul her up. She was heavy and they staggered with the weight but managed to get her sitting on her bed. Judith's face was streaked with tears and mucus.

'I'll get my towel to wipe your face,' Violet said.

She was as good as her word, passing the towel to Kathy and then quietly going, leaving the two girls alone.

Kathy sat beside Judith and took her damp hand. 'It's done. The aeroplane is gone for good and listen – camp's quiet again. Just the cleaning up to do. That'll be tomorrow's job. The others will be in soon, so let's get you sorted.'

Judith took a great sobbing gulp and wiped the back of her wrist across her nose. Her eyes focussed as if she was back in the world and seeing Kathy for the first time.

'Get away from me,' she hissed.

She pushed Kathy hard in the chest. Kathy reeled from the unexpected blow and nearly fell off the bed. She stood up, annoyed.

'I'm trying to help you.'

'I don't need your help. I can look after ma self so I can. I'm no taking direction from the likes of you,' Judith growled.

'Why do you dislike me so much?'

'You've no idea. Really?' Judith sneered.

Kathy rubbed her chest. It felt bruised. 'No, I don't. You were happy enough to come out to the cinema with me that time after… after I came home. I wanted to thank you for covering for me, to make it up to you. Mammy told me that Mrs Lennox kept you in, wouldn't let you out of an evening for a wee while.'

'A wee while? You're unbelievable. It wasnae a *wee while*, it was months wi' no cash. I had to gie her all ma pay. And she battered me. Ma rib's still no healed. All because of you.'

Kathy stepped back at Judith's venomous tone.

'I'm sorry…' she spluttered. 'I didn't know.'

'That's because you're that wrapped up in yourself. Butter wouldnae melt in yer mouth. Yer Mammy being all concerned. She shoulda thrown you out after what you did. Ma Auntie Irene would've, had it been me wi' a wean on the way, I tell ye.'

'Is that why you're here? Are you following me to get revenge?'

Judith looked so surprised at that, Kathy felt a ripple of hysterical laughter come up. But none of this was funny. It wasn't just that Judith didn't like her and enjoyed bullying. She actually hated her.

'I'm no following ye. I got posted here just like you did.'

'Look, I really am sorry that your aunt was so awful to you. But you have to remember, you made me pay you money to cover for me. You didn't do it out of the goodness of your heart. And I... I never meant to get pregnant. It was all a terrible mistake. I was young and daft.'

Judith's mouth twisted. Her eyes were fierce as she stared at Kathy.

'Aye, yer daft, that's for sure.'

Kathy was stung. 'Aye, and you're awful mouthy for a girl with no friends. No one likes you. You've got a reputation for chasing the men, who also don't like you.'

She stomped away, furious. Where were the others? She opened the door and saw Violet and the rest of the squad politely waiting in the fresh night air.

'We've been in the canteen,' Violet smiled with a question in her gaze. 'Cook's got bacon sandwiches on the go. I brought you and Judith some. We were about to come in.'

'Aye, in youse come,' Kathy said, grateful for Violet's thoughtfulness. For keeping the others out of the room so that she and Judith could sort themselves out. Only they hadn't. Not really. She was shaking from rage and shock.

She forced herself to calm down. She'd tell Violet later but there was no need for the others to know what had happened.

Soon the buzz of the evening deflated and they all declared they were exhausted. Lights went off and Kathy lay in her bed, the scratchy blanket tickling her chin. She was conscious of Judith not far away, lying in her bunk and probably cursing Kathy. Well, she wouldn't think about that. Instead, she thought of Don and how proud he'd have been of her tonight. And Alisdair? She wished he could have seen her working the instruments which had helped defeat that lone raider over the coast. Did he ever spare a thought for her? Or had he completely forgotten the girl he bumped into all those months ago?

–

The next morning, under Cook's beady gaze, Judith cleared away the breakfast trays and scrubbed the tables. The vegetables for the midday meal had been peeled and the pastry was covered by fresh cloths.

'Go and check if the dairy van's coming today,' Cook ordered the girl mopping the floor.

'I'll go,' Judith said, glad to have an excuse to leave the stuffy room because no doubt the cook would find more chores for her to do very soon.

She had no intention of finding the dairy van. As soon as she escaped the canteen, she walked through the busy camp and out past the sentry, who was smoking a cigarette and didn't even acknowledge her. A truck passed her going the other way into the camp, its engine rumbling, sending a blast of grit and warm air against her legs. She caught the sign 'Buttercup Dairy' on its side. Cook would be pleased, stupid woman. All she thought about was food and drink. It was tedious. All of it. She felt her weariness lift as she walked the country track, not caring where she went. She just had to get away for a wee while. Last night was awful. She'd been terrified. But worse, she'd been humiliated by that Kathy Dougal finding her hiding from the noise.

The birdsong was sweet in the willows and there were daffodils and bluebells stuffed with fat bees in the grassy edges of the track. The farmhouse came into view and Judith stopped. Bess, the farmer's wife, was chopping logs in the front yard. Every few minutes, she stopped to wipe her brow before continuing. A tractor was ploughing the nearby field, flocks of grey gulls and black crows in its wake. A young woman with an iron bucket and spade was walking up the side of the field hedgerow. In the adjacent field, lambs scampered around their mothers.

'Are you going to watch me all day or do you want to help?' Bess said.

Judith blinked. Her feet had taken her closer into the farm's yard as she'd watched all the goings on. Bess pointed to the axe.

'Chop a few logs before you go, there's a love.'

Before Judith had a chance to refuse, Bess's plump shape had disappeared into the farmhouse. Almost against her will, Judith picked up the haft of the axe. The wood was warm from Bess's hands and felt smooth to her touch. She lifted it, felt its weight and shifted until the balance felt right in her grip. There was a log in place on the large stone in front of her. Judith took the axe and swung it down hard. There was a satisfying cracking sound. She swung again and again. The log split in half and bounced away. She put the axe down and collected the log pieces.

There was a stack which Bess had made so she added them to it. Then she picked up another log. It was heavy but she managed to get it onto the stone. Lifting the axe, she went to work on it.

There was a rhythmic quality to chopping logs. Judith's arms ached as they stretched to the task. Her breath came quickly, full of sweet spring air. She slammed the axe hard into the wood. She thought about her aunt and the cook and the endless preparation of food and how bored and lonely she was and the axe hit and hit and hit with her fury.

She felt Bess come out to watch her but she didn't stop. Sweat trickled into her eyes, making them sting. A stitch in her side made her gasp and put the axe down. She was aware of a figure near her. Thinking it was Bess, she turned to say she'd done enough for free. But it wasn't Bess. It was Young Wullie. He looked at her and gave a nod as if to say she'd done well.

Judith had overhead the other girls saying how attractive he might be if it wasn't for his dourness. He was nice looking, she had to agree. He had a square jaw, strong features and very blue eyes. His hair was thick and corn-coloured. He wasn't tall but he was broadly built and taller than her. Judith didn't like a lot of gab anyway. If Wullie wasn't one for chatting, that suited her. She'd only come here to get away from camp in any case.

'There's food in the kitchen. Ma said to tell you to go in. The others are there.'

Wullie turned on his heel and left. She watched him stride across to the farmhouse and shortly afterwards come out again to the gate and into the field with the tractor. Moments later, the machine was revving up and began to finish the plough. The turned earth was a rich, dark brown and the gulls shrieked and followed the tractor.

Judith found herself going into the big farmhouse almost against her will. She wasn't meant to be here. Inside, the kitchen was a large, cosy room with thick rugs covering most of the stone floor. Heavy curtains hung at the sides of the windows. The range was beautifully tiled with shining brass fittings. It smelled of baking. Bess was at the range, stirring a black pot, and two young women, dressed in land girl uniforms, sat at the table.

'Ah, there you are. Sit yourself down, my love, and have some griddle scones while they're hot.'

One of the land girls smiled and patted the seat beside her. Judith sat and listened to them chatter and giggle. Bess put a plate of scones with a generous pat of butter and a jar of blackcurrant jam with a spoon in front of her.

'You deserve that. Wullie says you did a fine job with the wood.' Bessie smiled and patted Judith's shoulder.

Judith sat up straighter with the praise. It was nice in the farmhouse. No one expected her to join in the conversation and no one seemed to be judging her either. Young Wullie came in. He glanced at Judith. She kept her eyes on her plate but she heard Bess teasing him and his low reply and a deep chuckle. So the man could laugh. Who'd have thought it. Aye, well, she was one to talk. Judith couldn't remember the last time she'd been happy enough to giggle like the daft lassies beside her.

All too soon, Bess was clapping her hands and shooing the land girls fondly from the warmth of the kitchen. Wullie had already gone. Reluctantly, Judith got up too.

'I can chop more wood,' she offered.

'That's a kind thought, love, but I guess they'll be expecting you back at camp. Am I right? Here, Wullie's taking the tractor over there now to plough the potato field. You can drive over with him.'

Before Judith could protest, Bess was shouting out of the door for Wullie and pushing her in the back, steering her to the tractor that was now out of the field and at the edge of the yard.

'Come back and see me. I have plenty of wee tasks for a strong girl like you,' Bess grinned.

'I will,' Judith said, surprising herself.

Young Wullie waved at her impatiently and she clambered up to sit beside him in the tractor. It smelled of soil and sheep's wool and fresh sweat. She realised it was Wullie's sweat and that she didn't mind it at all.

'Ma likes you,' Wullie said as he started up the engine.

A warmth spread through Judith's chest. She liked Bess too. That good feeling ebbed quickly. No one else liked her. And no wonder. She hadn't exactly made the best of things or been nice to anyone. She was so... *angry...* at the world.

Wullie didn't say any more and Judith was content to see the fields from the high seat in the tractor without attempting to converse. It was a bumpy ride to the camp. How different it was from Kiltie Street and living in the city. But she liked it, could learn to love it. She didn't miss Glasgow's smog and being cheek to jowl with other people and the smell of the chemical and dye works up along the canal. Aye, there were smells here too, but these didn't bother her.

'I should've been a land girl,' she said out loud.

Wullie brought the tractor to a stop outside the camp gates. 'Hop down now. Unless you want to plough this tattie field.'

He was joking, she knew that, but she wouldn't have minded ploughing the field. Not one whit. There was a new energy to her steps as she went back to face Cook's wrath.

Chapter Fourteen

Mavis Lafferty's letter was brief.

Dear Violet, she wrote.

> *You must come home as soon as you can. Your mother is exhausted and Evie needs a firm hand. The situation cannot continue.*
> > *Yours sincerely*
> > *Mavis Lafferty.*

It was the first Sunday in May and Violet was able to leave the camp and take the familiar journey along the west coast to home. If anything, the trains were even more unreliable on Sundays and she held her breath, waiting for the carriages to be shunted into a siding and left for hours, but in the end she reached Helensburgh with no disruptions. The contents of Mrs Lafferty's letter ran through her mind in a loop. What was waiting for her in the house at the top of the hill? It was unlike the housekeeper to write to her so whatever it was, it must be serious. Violet walked up Sinclair Street barely feeling the pull of muscles in her legs, the lovely views of cherry trees in blossom along the side streets going unnoticed.

'Violet, thank goodness you're here,' Mrs Lafferty said when she opened the door.

'I got your letter, but this is the first day I could come. Is everyone all right?'

'In a manner of speaking. Shall we sit in the front room?' Mrs Lafferty asked.

Violet shook her head. 'The kitchen will be warmer. Besides, I'd rather talk to you without Mummy.'

'You should let your mother know you are here,' Mavis said. She glanced at Violet and paused. 'Perhaps you're right. We should speak first, and then you can decide what to do.'

'Where's Evie?' Violet was disappointed that her niece hadn't rushed to greet her.

'That's just it,' Mavis said, collapsing into a kitchen chair. 'We can't keep her any longer, Violet. You'll have to do something.'

'What on earth's happened? Here, let me make us a pot of tea. You look like you need a cup.' Violet filled the kettle and put it on the range to heat. She was worried about the housekeeper, who was pale and agitated. Poor Mrs Lafferty. She was still getting over William's loss at sea, but clearly something more was bothering her too.

'Tell me what's happened,' Violet said, sitting opposite the housekeeper.

'I'm not as young as I used to be. That's the problem. Evie *is* young and full of mischief, and I haven't the energy to chase after her. Camilla, I'm sorry to say, is no help at all. In fact, I'm thinking of retiring altogether. With William gone, I've no need to keep earning to put a nest egg by for him. And this house is so large, without the two maids it's impossible for me to keep it clean and tidy. I can remember this place in its heyday, Violet. Oh, the parties your parents used to host, and the visitors that came. It was a wonderful atmosphere. We even had a butler before your father... before the money troubles began.'

'I can remember it a little. Felicity and I used to sit on the stairs and peek at the ladies in their beautiful dresses. The maids had black dresses and white lace aprons and gave us winks and grins because they knew we were there. They used to sneak us pastries too.'

Mavis laughed. 'I sent those up for you. Did you think I didn't know you were there? Camilla would have had a fit if she'd seen you.'

'I never realised you knew. We hid when we saw you. It was all part of the excitement. Of course it was Felicity who made us watch or hide. She was always the naughty one.'

'How is Felicity? Dear me, where are my manners, I should have asked that first of all.'

Mavis looked genuinely distressed and Violet realised how overwrought the older woman was.

'Felicity is comfortable, that's all I know. Major Gillingham sent me a couple of short letters to tell me, as his friend is in charge of the hospital where she was sent. I'm hoping to be allowed to visit very soon.'

'Please take her my best wishes. Poor Felicity. You're right, she was always the naughty one as a child. Her daughter has taken after her. Don't get me wrong, I love Evie dearly, as much as I love you and Felicity. You're like my own daughters. But I'm exhausted chasing after Evie and that's the truth of the matter.'

Violet made tea and poured two cups. She waited until Mavis had taken a good, long restorative sip from hers.

'Where would you retire to?' Violet asked.

'I have a brother up in Inverness who's been pestering me for an age to come and keep house for him. This time I've decided to say yes.'

It was a very firm answer and Violet realised, with a sinking heart, that Mrs Lafferty had already made up her mind.

'What will Mummy do?' she said out loud, her thoughts buzzing at this new problem.

'She will do what everyone else does. Make do and carry on,' Mavis said stoutly. 'I am very sorry, but I can no longer put her first. I won't change my mind.'

'Oh, no, you must do what is right for you,' Violet agreed. 'Goodness knows, you've given years to our family. I'll go and see where Evie is now and I must work out what to do for the best.'

She left the housekeeper drinking tea and went through to the sitting room, wondering why it was so quiet. Camilla was asleep in the armchair beside the fire, her head thrown back against the antimacassar, and she was gently snoring. It sounded like a cat's purr. Evie was at the wall, in a blue dress with black gum boots, reminding Violet ever so much of Felicity. She had a paintbrush in her right hand and a tube of oil colour in her left and was happily daubing yellow blobs onto the Chinese silk wallpaper. She was so absorbed in her task that she hadn't heard Violet.

'Evie Stewart, what are you doing?' Violet injected a stern note into her voice.

'Auntie Violet!' Evie squealed and dropped the brush and the tube of paint.

Violet winced at the thought of it landing on the carpet but Evie flung herself into her arms and she felt the hot little body squirm against her. She hugged Evie tightly.

'Is Mama home?' Evie asked, pulling back to look into Violet's face.

A scent of oil paint, biscuits and dirty hair wafted off her. Violet hugged her again.

'Mama is still in hospital, darling. You know she's not very well, don't you? But she's going to improve. You aren't allowed to see her in case you catch her illness but soon she'll be able to write you a letter. She loves you very much.'

Evie burst into tears. Violet's army jacket dampened.

'I miss Mama,' Evie sobbed.

'I miss your Mama too,' Violet said, her own eyes welling up. 'But we have to be brave, darling.'

'I want to live with you, Auntie Violet,' Evie wailed. 'I don't like it here.'

'I thought you loved being with Mrs Lafferty and Granny?'

'I do… but there's no one to play with.'

'What's all the racket?' Camilla's testy voice broke in. 'You've woken me up.'

'Hello, Mummy. How are you? Evie's upset. She's missing Felicity.'

'Where is Mavis? My throat's parched and I'm sure it must be time for luncheon.'

'I'll bring you a cup of tea, and then we have to have a serious chat about Evie,' Violet said.

Evie followed her through to the kitchen and helpfully carried the tin of shortbread while Violet took two cups of tea back through to where Camilla shifted irritably in her armchair.

'There you are, Mummy, a lovely cup of tea. Evie, darling, give Granny a slice of shortbread. Good girl. Why don't you take the tin back to the kitchen and then find Mrs Lafferty? I heard her upstairs.'

Good, that got rid of Evie for at least a few minutes while she spoke to Camilla. Violet waited until half the cup of tea and the whole slice of shortbread had been consumed before she spoke.

'You said you'd look after Evie. She smells as if she hasn't had a bath in days.'

'I said we would play cards. The girl doesn't want to play.'

'She's a small child and she's missing her mother. Mrs Lafferty isn't coping and it looks as if you aren't either.' When Violet looked closely at Camilla she thought her mother did look tired. 'I'm taking Evie with me. This can't go on.'

The decision had been made in a split second, but Violet had no idea what she was going to do with her niece. Oh dear. She missed Felicity terribly with an almost physical pull of her heart. For a brief moment she felt the old sensation of being alone, but then she remembered Kathy and the other girls waiting for her at the camp and it perked her up and made her feel stronger.

'You must do what you see fit. It's not as if I am ever consulted on what goes on in my own house.' Camilla sniffed.

'Very soon you will be making all the decisions,' Violet warned. 'Mrs Lafferty is going to live with her brother and will finally be able to put her feet up after all the years of service she's given you.'

'She wouldn't dare!' Camilla huffed, her face reddening as she struggled upright in the soft cushioned chair.

'I'm afraid she would and she has,' Violet replied calmly. 'Which means you'll have to make your own meals.'

'I can't do that,' Camilla said, sounding aggrieved. 'You'll have to come and live with me if Mavis leaves.'

'I'm sorry, Mummy, but that's quite impossible. The army won't let me. You haven't even asked after Felicity.'

'How is Felicity?'

Violet shook her head in exasperation and went to find Evie. She said goodbye to Mavis Lafferty, extracting a promise of her brother's address so that they wouldn't lose touch. With Mavis's help, she filled Evie's suitcase and helped the little girl on with her coat and shoes.

'Come along, Evie. Say goodbye to Mrs Lafferty and then run along and say goodbye to Granny too. I'll wait for you at the gate with the suitcase. Don't forget teddy.'

–

What had she done? Violet had yet to come up with an answer as to where Evie could live as they walked along the country lane towards the camp. Evie skipped happily beside her, tugging at her hand and pointing to the sheep and the bluebells and the skylarks trilling in the skies above.

'Ooh, lovely music. I like that, Auntie Violet,' Evie cried.

The loudspeakers in the camp were blasting out Glenn Miller big band jazz melodies as they did every Sunday afternoon. Violet walked past the guard without challenge and into the camp, holding Evie's hand in a firm grasp. There were trucks and soldiers busy at tasks and she didn't want to lose her or risk an accident. She wasn't quite sure where to go when she heard her name shouted across the yard. Turning, she saw her commanding officer.

'Stewart. My office. Now!'

Violet's stomach dropped horribly but she managed a small smile and a salute. The officer stalked away, back ramrod straight. Evie glanced at Violet doubtfully.

'Come along. It's going to be fine,' Violet said, managing to avoid a wobble in her voice. She smiled brightly.

Soon they were standing in front of the ATS officer's desk, side by side. On the other side of the desk, Violet's superior was tapping her fingernails on the wood.

'Who is this, Corporal Stewart? There are no children allowed on the camp.'

'This is my niece, Evie. I didn't know where else to take her. I've got nowhere to go...'

'Take a seat, both of you, and tell me the situation,' the officer said in a more kindly tone.

The whole sorry tale poured out of Violet. 'And so you see, I couldn't leave her there, but now I don't know what to do...' she finished lamely.

'She can't stay here. You must know that. I suggest that you take young Evie into the barrack room and have a good think. There must be someone who will take her. If not, then there are orphanages in Glasgow who must be able to place her.'

Evie was not going to an orphanage. Felicity would hate that. There must be another answer but Violet, for the life of her, couldn't think of it. She took Evie's hand again and walked over to the barrack, ignoring the curious glances and occasional calls from the soldiers.

On Sunday afternoons, many of the women left camp for walks in the fields or the nearby bluebell woods or to visit Bess at the farmhouse where it was well known there would be good food and a generous welcome. Most of them were too far from home to visit family and Wullie and Bess's lovely home had become a substitute. As a result, only Kathy and a couple of others were there when Violet and Evie walked in.

'Hello Evie. Have you come for a visit?' Kathy grinned, raising her eyebrows to Violet in a silent question.

'I've come to live with Auntie Violet,' Evie said, jumping up onto Kathy's bunk and swinging her legs.

'Is that so? Here, do you want to try on my cap? See that lady over there, she's called Gladys, and if you ask her nicely she'll let you see in her mirror. I need to talk to your auntie.'

While Evie was focussed on preening in the mirror, Kathy whispered to Violet.

'What is going on?'

Violet groaned. 'I have to find a place for Evie to live or I'm going to have to leave the army to care for her. I owe it to Felicity. I can't let Evie go to an orphanage, but how will I manage when I won't have any wages? I can't imagine Mummy giving me any money. I suppose I could go and live with Mummy, but with Mrs Lafferty leaving, I'll be general dogsbody and I'll never escape. Mummy will have me at her beck and call. But at least Evie will have a home.'

'Slow up a bit, will you,' Kathy said. 'Tell me the whole story.'

Violet repeated her tale and Kathy listened without interrupting. When Violet had finished there was a moment of silence before Kathy frowned.

'It's hopeless, isn't it?' Violet said sadly, seeing her friend's solemn face.

Kathy clapped her hands suddenly, making Violet jump.

'I've got it. Evie can stay at Kiltie Street with Mammy and Harry. Mammy's always saying how having Dennis keeps her young. One more wean won't make a difference.' This wasn't strictly true and Kathy sent up a silent prayer that Mammy wouldn't mind taking on another child, remembering how tired she'd been. It was something of an emergency, after all. She tried to quell her doubts.

'Oh, but I couldn't possibly impose...' Violet said, unable to extinguish a tiny flicker of hope. 'I've never met your mother and step-father. Why would they take in a child they've never met before?'

Kathy shrugged. 'Because they're good people, and you're my friend and you need help.'

Violet reached over and squeezed Kathy in a wrap-around hug. 'You really are my friend. Thank you so much. Can you keep an eye on Evie? I have to go back to my officer and tell her I've got a solution. If you really are sure?'

'I am sure. I'll write to Mammy this instant but I know she'll say yes.'

-

Violet, Kathy and Evie reached Kiltie Street before the letter could be sent. Passes had been quickly provided with strict instructions to place the child and return empty-handed for duty the next day.

'Will your mother be all right putting me up for the night?' Violet asked, as the bus swerved a corner making them slide across the seat into each other.

'Of course she will. There's not much space but if you don't mind sharing a bed with Evie we'll be fine.'

'I don't mind, Auntie Violet,' Evie piped up, her face pressed against the bus window, staring out with eager interest at the passers-by and the tall buildings.

'Well, if you don't mind, then I don't either,' Violet smiled.

'My sister Jeannie's baby is due any day,' Kathy said. 'I'm excited to be an auntie.'

'Golly, you never mentioned that! Surely your mother can't take on Evie when there will be a new baby in the flat?'

'You haven't met Mammy. She loves babies and children. Don't worry.'

Violet couldn't help worrying as the bus drew up at the bus stop near Kiltie Street. She felt quite strongly that she was imposing on the Dougal family but couldn't see an alternative which didn't involve her giving up the Royal Artillery and having no income to live on. She decided to observe carefully, and if there was any sign that Evie was not welcome, she would take her niece away again and resign herself to a life as a drudge to her own mother.

Despite her worry, she smiled as they walked around the corner and into Kiltie Street. She had once dated a man who lived here while she was stationed in Glasgow. Roy Allen, the man who had been in love with someone else. Violet had been relocated to Shopshire in any case so it would have been difficult to maintain their relationship even without that.

She had fond memories of Kiltie Street and its black-stoned tenement buildings and friendly inhabitants. Even the aroma of the nearby canal and the factories, chemical and rubber works that lingered in the air smelled good to her, mixed in with her memories as they were. She remembered attending a bring-and-buy sale with Roy in the street once and the happy bustle as the local women bagged bargains.

Roy had been good company and they had had fun going to dances and meals. Actually, Violet thought, I miss having a boyfriend. The thought surprised her. She was happy with her friends and the gunner girls she commanded and she liked living at Muirhead Farm in the Royal Artillery camp. Goodness, she hardly had time for a boyfriend, she was so busy.

'Here we are,' Kathy said, bringing Violet abruptly back to the present moment. 'Number four. Up the steps, Evie, and chap on the door to your left.'

'Who lives in there?' Evie said, rubbing her nose.

'Chap it and find out,' Kathy laughed.

'She means knock on it,' Violet said, when Evie looked puzzled.

'Aye, that's what I mean. I forgot youse two aren't from here. You'll soon learn from the weans in the street what to say.'

Violet hid a smile. She would love to see Felicity's expression when Evie came back speaking Glaswegian. The door opened and a young woman with dark hair and grey eyes and a tiny strawberry mark on her cheek stood there. Her hands were pressed to her back and her belly was so swollen that she filled the narrow doorway.

'I haven't missed the big news then,' Kathy said cheekily, touching the woman's stomach.

'I can't wait for him or her to meet the world,' Jeannie groaned. 'My back's aching and I've not been able to see ma feet for weeks.'

'Violet, this is my big sister, Jeannie, as you might have guessed.'

'Hello, come away in.' Jeannie smiled politely. 'You should've written, Kathy, to say you were coming. Mammy'll kill you for not giving her notice of guests.'

'I'm terribly sorry,' Violet chipped in. 'It was a bit of an emergency, actually.'

'Let us in the door and we'll explain,' Kathy said, stepping across the threshold as Jeannie moved her bulky body to let them enter the flat.

Kathy's home was small but very neat and clean, Violet noted. In layout it reminded her a little of Roy's home, but whereas Roy's family all lived in a single room, or 'single end' as he'd told her it was called, the Woodleys seemed to have more space. They were ushered into what Jeannie called the parlour. A moment later a woman rushed in to greet them. She had Jeannie's dark hair, although hers was laced with grey, but her face was very like Kathy's.

'Kathy love, it's good to see you.' She swept Kathy into a bear hug and kissed her cheek before looking kindly at Violet and Evie.

'Mammy, this here's my good friend Violet Stewart and her wee niece, Evie. They need our help, so they do.'

'Of course. What can we do?'

Mary Woodley sat in the nearest armchair and indicated for them all to take a seat. Jeannie said she'd make tea and staggered out. Violet was concerned in case she toppled over but no one else appeared to be.

'She's overdue,' Mary said. 'It does her good to walk about. Maybe it'll jiggle the babbie into moving. Monica Wiley, the midwife, she's been round yesterday and today to keep a wee check on things. Can't be long now, fingers crossed.'

'Gosh, we really haven't come at a good moment at all,' Violet said awkwardly. 'I'm in a bit of a pickle, but I really can't expect you to help. Evie, we must go.'

'Hang on a wee minute.' Mary waved her hands when Violet made to get up from the sofa. 'You haven't said why you're here yet. If you tell me, we can sort it all out one way or another.'

'I'll help Jeannie with the tea,' Kathy leapt up and disappeared.

'That's got to be a first,' Mary winked at Violet and laughed. 'She's not one for helping out much, our Kathy.'

'Really? She's awfully good at her job, Mrs Woodley. She was splendid when the guns were firing recently. Kept the others' spirits up and helped a girl who was frightened.'

'My Kathy did that?' There was a pride in Mary's voice and Violet was glad she'd told her.

'Yes, she truly did. She's a pleasure to work alongside.'

'So, what can we do for you, hen?'

'I hardly feel I should ask...'

But Violet found herself telling Mary the tale, beginning with Felicity's illness and Camilla's inability to cope and ending with their reception on camp by her commanding officer.

'Evie must stay here with us,' Mary said firmly. 'Unless your sister wants her to be evacuated? I've got my wee boy, Dennis, still at home and there's no been any bombing since last year so most of the local children are back, although my two, Isa and Bob, are still living on my cousin's farm. They could come home but they love it so much they asked to stay.'

Violet thought of the lone raider and the boom and crack of the ack-ack guns at Muirhead as they shot it out of the sky. It was true there hadn't been bombing in Glasgow since 1943 but that didn't mean that Hitler couldn't decide to give them another doing at any moment. Not just a single raider who may have been lost but a whole squadron of bombers. She shivered inwardly.

'Felicity was adamant that she wanted Evie to stay near to me,' Violet said. 'This is as close as can be, given the circumstances. Thank you so much, Mrs Woodley.'

'It's no bother at all. We'll love having Evie to stay. She'll be company for Dennis and a help with Jeannie's wee one once it's born.'

'I love babies.' Evie clapped her hands with glee.

Violet opened then shut her mouth. Evie didn't know any babies. Still, she looked excited at the prospect of living here, which was a relief.

'It won't be forever,' Violet said. 'Only until Felicity is better.'

Mary patted her knee sympathetically. Jeannie and Kathy came back with the tea tray and they sat and drank tea and ate scones together. Mary and Jeannie then excused themselves to go and wash up the crockery and wouldn't hear of their guests helping.

Kathy vanished and reappeared with a sleepy toddler on her hip. He had the same flaming red hair as she did and the same grey eyes and freckles. They were so startlingly similar that Violet had to look twice.

'My step-dad Harry is out at his allotment, but look who I found in my bed. This here's Dennis. Say hello to Violet and Evie, who's going to be your new pal.'

Dennis curled shyly into Kathy's neck and sucked his thumb. She put him down on the ground on his two sturdy legs and kissed the top of his head.

'Go and play nice,' she instructed, turning him in Evie's direction.

Watching them together, something clicked in Violet's head. She looked at Kathy with new eyes. She waited until the two children had held hands and wandered out of the room before she spoke.

'He's yours, isn't he?' Violet said quietly.

Kathy looked as if she would deny it before her shoulders slumped and she nodded.

'How did you know?'

'I didn't... there was something about the way you are together, it's obvious that you're not his sister. That you're his mother. Oh, blooming heck, Judith was telling the truth. That day... in the barracks... we assumed she was being nasty, stirring us up for some reason, when she said you'd had a baby with a soldier, but she wasn't, was she?'

Kathy flushed a dull red and she sat heavily on the sofa next to Violet, half-turned so they could talk.

'I lied to you all. I'm sorry, but I had to. If the other girls knew the truth, they would be shocked and disgusted. It's shameful.'

'Did Bridie know?'

'Aye. I had to tell her once she got pregnant. I wanted her to know it wasn't the end of the world, that things could work out somehow. I've made a mess of it all now though, haven't I? You probably hate me for it.' Kathy sniffled.

'I don't hate you at all,' Violet said gently, taking Kathy's hand in her own. 'I think you must have been incredibly brave to go through what you did and to give up your baby to be brought up as your brother.'

'But I've done wrong by Judith.'

'Judith was wrong to tell them about Dennis, but she wasn't lying. She's being shunned as a liar. At some point, when you're ready, it's only fair to right that. None of them will judge you badly for a mistake you made when you were younger.'

Kathy knew that Violet was right. Only she wasn't ready to share her secret. Not yet. She couldn't bear to see the others' expressions if she told them about her wee son. She didn't want her secret to spread either. She thought of Alisdair Meikle and imagined the revulsion in those green eyes and shivered. He hadn't wanted to know her after their first meeting, and she could guess why if Judith had carried out her threat. And if Alisdair didn't want to be around her, others might react the same way. Violet might know her secret but no one else must, Kathy resolved.

Chapter Fifteen

Robroyston Hospital and sanatorium lay on the far side of Glasgow in an area dotted with farms. On the right-hand side of the road, there was a huge area of marshes with tall swaying reeds and plenty of swans and ducks on its shore. On the left of the road, there were vast rhubarb fields.

'It was very kind of you to take me in your car,' Violet said.

'It's no bother at all.' Joe smiled, his hands relaxed on the steering wheel as the car drove smoothly along. 'I knew you would want to see Felicity as soon as she was allowed visitors.'

'How is she?'

'The X-ray showed tuberculosis in her right lung, so she will have to stay in the sanatorium for a good six to nine months, but she has a very good chance of a complete cure within the year if all goes well.'

'Thank goodness. I was afraid… well, that it would be bad news all round,' Violet said.

'They collapsed her lung to allow it to rest and heal. You must prepare yourself, Felicity has lost some weight but the fresh air and good food will help in her recovery. There are no guarantees but we must pray and have faith in the medical profession.'

The impressive hospital entrance came into view as Joe swung the car round the curve in the road and along the wide street towards the two main buildings. There were other brick houses which Violet decided must be further wards. There were also formal gardens with pine trees and Violet saw tennis courts, a putting green and a bowling green, all of which were in use by patients.

'There are four hundred and fifty TB beds here,' Joe told her. 'That's almost half of all beds for treating tuberculosis in Glasgow. It's a big place. It treats other diseases too.'

Violet felt quite small standing in the shadow of the hospital, waiting while Joe greeted one of the doctors. He hurried over to her.

'Sorry about that. Doctor Morris is a friend of mine. He works at Camis Eskan too on occasion. Let's find Felicity, shall we?'

He offered his crooked arm and Violet slid hers into his, wondering if he was simply being friendly. He did seem awfully keen to see Felicity. Had he succumbed to her sister's charms? It was possible. Felicity could be very charming when she felt like it. Violet was all too conscious of his nearness. He smelled of citrus and Sobranie and something indefinable but delicious.

They entered the high-ceilinged main building. Joe knew where he was going and all Violet had to do was keep up with his long legs. He adjusted his stride to match hers and she smiled up at him. Soon they had reached the ward. Violet was surprised to see that all the patients were outside rather than in the room. There were French doors all along the far wall and they were all open to the elements. She slipped her arm out of Joe's, and followed him out onto the veranda. The beds were lined up under an awning. At least they wouldn't get rained on, she thought.

'Fresh air is essential for healing TB,' Joe said. 'I know it looks odd but it works. We can't stay long, Violet. We mustn't wear Felicity out. There she is, along at the end. You go and visit while I have a chat with Matron.'

Violet glanced along the beds, seeing pale, weary faces, many of them quite gaunt. Some patients smiled or met her gaze hopefully but others closed their eyes or looked away. Perhaps they never had visitors and had given up hoping. Felicity was grinning. Golly, but Joe was right. She was terribly thin and her cheekbones had gone from elegant to skull-like. Violet smiled brightly. Felicity mustn't know how shocked she was.

'Hello, darling girl. It's me,' she whispered as she dodged the beds and finally reached her sister.

'Dearest, I may have the dreaded consumption but I still have my eyesight, so I can see that it's you indeed. There's no need to look so appalled, darling. I know I've lost weight but nurse is force feeding me and I'm getting plenty of lovely fresh air as you can see. Whether I like it or not.'

'Is it too awful?' Violet whispered.

'It isn't. Not really. Even the artificial pneumothorax. They gave me an anaesthetic and I didn't feel a thing. My chest was pretty sore the next day and of course I've had the blasted procedure again but that's par for the course apparently.'

'Oh, Felicity. I'm so sorry,' Violet said.

'You needn't be,' Felicity snapped.

Her head fell back and Violet saw that her skin was almost the same colour as the ivory pillow case.

Felicity sighed. 'I'm sorry, dearest. I mustn't take it out on you. The thing is, I have to rest all the while. I'm not allowed to sit up or read or knit. Have you tried eating and drinking while lying prostrate? I can't recommend it.'

'I'm very glad you're...'

'Not dead?'

'Must you tease about everything?' Violet cried. Honestly, she'd forgotten how annoying Felicity could be.

'That's better, dear. I'd rather tease and act normally and I'd rather you did too. Some of the rare visitors whisper and tiptoe about the other patients as if they are already in the grave. I don't like it. Not one bit. Promise me, Violet, to treat me as you always have? I am more than this horrid disease. I'm still me.'

'I promise. I hadn't thought of it like that. Would you like to hear about Evie? She wasn't allowed to visit but she sends her love.'

Tears welled up in Felicity's eyes and trickled down the sides of her face onto the pillow. As her arms were tucked under the blanket she couldn't wipe them away. Violet did it for her with her clean handkerchief and neither of them mentioned it.

'She's very happy living with Kathy's family in Glasgow. We get regular updates in Kathy's letters from home. If you want her to be evacuated, let me know. Kathy's brother and sister are on a farm apparently although there are plenty of children back in the city.'

'I know it's selfish, but I want to know that Evie isn't far away from either of us,' Felicity said. 'I couldn't bear it if we were separated further. I wasn't surprised to get your letter about Mummy not coping and poor Mrs Lafferty. Although I expect Mrs Lafferty will be enjoying a retirement that puts hundreds of miles between her and Camilla.'

There was a small silence between them. It wasn't the easiest place for a reunion. There was no chair for Violet so that she had to stand beside the bed, looming over Felicity's frail figure.

'Did you bring the dashing Doctor Joe?' Felicity asked, turning away to cough.

'He kindly brought me. Would you like to speak to him?'

'No need. I suspect he'd rather speak to you,' Felicity smiled. 'You like him, don't you?'

'He's been very kind, writing and letting me know how you are.'

'You're not fooling anyone, Violet Stewart. You're besotted with the man. Don't let him slip through your fingers. Life is far too short.'

'Do be quiet. He'll hear you,' Violet hissed.

That only set Felicity to giggling, which quickly turned to more coughs.

'I see a nurse hurrying in our direction,' Violet said. 'I think I'll be told to go as I'm wearing you out. I'll come again if I'm allowed. Take care, darling, and do get better soon.'

'Wait a moment – how are we paying for all this?'

'Mummy's paying. Apparently she had some money stashed away in a stocking under her bed for a rainy day. She appeared with it and told me to use it for your treatment. When I get annoyed that she never asks if you are all right, I remember the stocking full of cash. She does care after all. She just finds it impossible to show it.'

'Blow me down with a feather,' Felicity breathed.

Violet reckoned she could blow her down with a feather she was so fragile, but she knew what Felicity meant. It had been a surprise to her too that Mummy

218

had made the gesture. Neither the money nor Felicity had been mentioned since in the infrequent letters that arrived at camp from Camilla but it didn't matter. Felicity's treatment could be paid for and that was what mattered most.

The nurse arrived at Felicity's bed, looking stern.

'Goodbye, dearest. Chin up and all that. I'll be back soon, if I'm allowed,' Violet said. 'Thank you, nurse. I can make my own way out.'

She didn't look back at Felicity, afraid that if she did, she would break down and sob and embarrass them both. Her sister looked so small and vulnerable and so terribly sick. She prayed that Joe was right and that Felicity really would make a full recovery in the next year.

Joe was waiting for her in the corridor at the far end of the ward. His smile did something to Violet's insides. Should any man be allowed to have such a firm jaw and just the hint of a dimple in his right cheek? *You're besotted with the man.* Felicity's words came back to her. Perhaps she was. She certainly found him very attractive, despite what she reckoned was a ten-year age gap. She had never much cared for men her own age, finding them rather shallow and with few interests that matched hers. Roy Allen had been different, with his strong political views and desire to make the world better for working-class people. Roy had been very knowledgeable about the war and geography and had taught himself all sorts of subjects. But he had been the exception that proved the rule. Most men his age did not intrigue Violet at all.

'How did you find her?' Joe asked, taking Violet's arm again as casually as if they were a couple.

'Oh, Joe, she's awfully ill, isn't she?' Violet burst out, a little sob escaping before she could stop it.

Joe stopped right there in the corridor, never minding the nurses trotting past importantly and a doctor flying up and past them, his white coat flapping.

'You mustn't get upset. You've had a shock, seeing her like that, but I spoke with the matron and Felicity is making good progress.'

'Is she really? Only... it doesn't seem like it.'

'I wouldn't tell you that if it wasn't true,' Joe chided her gently. 'I promise only ever to tell you the truth. Even if it's unpalatable. It won't come to that though, I hope. We must have every confidence that your sister will be with us for many years to come. And young Evie will get her mother back.'

'Thank you,' Violet said simply.

They carried on through the corridors and past the wards and out into the car park. Joe opened the car door for Violet to slide into the passenger seat before going round and getting behind the wheel himself. He paused.

'Look, you're upset. I'm not expected back at the hospital until later. Do you fancy a small detour to take your mind off all this?'

'Where to?' Violet's spirits lifted at the thought of a little more time with him.

'Ah, that would be telling. I'll show you instead.'

They drove out of the hospital and along and through a narrow road flanked with yet more rhubarb until they reached a junction. Ahead of them the road in both directions was fringed with hawthorn hedges bursting with white blossom and from the open window of the car, Violet heard the sweet sound of yellowhammers in full song. Joe turned left along the country road, the hedge on one side and a dry stone wall covered in soft green mosses on the other. Beyond them were fields of cows and sheep, and some with crops. How could there be a war on when it was all so idyllic?

Joe soon brought the car to a halt, parking it in a dusty space near a field gate.

'We'll have to walk from here. It's not far.'

As Violet had her stout army shoes on, she didn't mind. In fact, it was pleasant to be in the warm, fresh air after breathing in the carbolic smell of the hospital, and she was with Joe. She couldn't imagine being happier anywhere else at that precise moment and knew that Felicity would be glad for her.

A few minutes' walk alongside the hedgerow brought them to a gap in its length and an area of tangled bramble and long grass with pretty pink cuckoo flowers scattered through it. In the middle of the vegetation stood a tall red granite Celtic cross. Carved on its surface was a sword, a lion rampant and the words 'in defence'. There was also a plaque at the bottom. Curious, Violet pulled away at the overgrown grasses and waded forward, trying to avoid the snaking bramble which snagged at her cuffs and her skirt. She bent down and cleared the plaque to see the engraved writing.

> We are not here to sue for peace but to fight
> for the freedom of our country

'What is this place?' Violet turned to Joe, her eyebrows raised.

He had been standing back as if enjoying her discovery.

'It's a monument to William Wallace. It's rather neglected, as you can see, and I doubt many people except locals know that it's still here. But it's a wonderful piece of history. Imagine, Wallace slept in a farm cottage on this exact spot over six hundred years ago for what turned out to be his last night as a free man before he was betrayed and captured.'

'I'm afraid my grasp of history is rather poor,' Violet said. 'Schoolgirl level. I know Wallace is a Scottish hero but I had no idea he was here near Glasgow. I thought he roamed the Highlands.'

Joe laughed. It was such a rich, hearty sound that Violet wanted to laugh too.

'Don't tease me,' she protested, half meaning it.

'I'm not teasing, honestly. It was just that you looked so guilty for not knowing your history. I'm not sure many people know this stuff, to be honest.'

'I do feel a bit that way,' Violet agreed with a sheepish grin. 'Tell me more.'

'Actually, I can do better than that. Come with me. A little further on, there's another interesting item.'

Violet followed him further into the fields until he veered back to an ancient stone wall. Set into the stonework was a well with a small pool of clear water.

'This is Wallace's Well,' Joe explained. 'It is said that here he took his last drink as a free man.'

'Poor old Wallace. Imagine having a lovely drink of cold water and looking up to find your enemies upon you. Actually, that inscription on the cross about fighting for your country's freedom feels very relevant today. Almost as if Wallace was speaking about our own war. I wonder if it ever ends, all the fighting over the ages. They said the last one was the war to end all wars and yet here we are again. If you and I came back here in fifty years, would we be at war yet again?'

'I very much hope this war will end soon,' Joe said. 'Things are looking much more hopeful for us and our allies, but I suspect the end game has yet to play out.'

He crouched down by the well, examining the ancient stones. Violet watched him.

'I had no idea you were so keen on history,' she said. 'You should come and use my father's library. It's full of history books. Felicity and I were never that interested and so they simply gather dust.'

She blushed. Did he think she was inviting him because she... *liked*... him? Was it that blooming obvious?

Joe stood up. 'I'd like that very much, thanks. I have a good library of my own at home in Edinburgh but I'm always glad to find new books to explore.'

They both stared at the well. Violet was thinking about how tall he was and how well his jacket fitted across his shoulders and about how the air between them seemed to crackle. But what was Joe thinking?

'How old are you, Violet?' Joe asked suddenly. 'Nineteen, twenty? Not any older, I'm sure.'

'I'm twenty-four.'

'And I'm thirty-four. Do you think it matters? Anyway, I'm sure you have lots of boyfriends, don't you? A beautiful young woman like you. Of course you do,' Joe murmured.

'You seem to have answered your own question without waiting for my answer,' Violet replied. 'Actually, I don't have a boyfriend, and for a long while I haven't been at all bothered about having one.'

Joe looked disappointed. 'You don't want one. I see. I suppose this war does put things into perspective, doesn't it. You're very sensible. There's no point getting involved with someone when people get moved around at a moment's notice or worse.'

'What I meant was, I haven't met anyone interesting, or hadn't until recently, and I'd rather convinced myself that I hadn't time for that sort of thing,' Violet said hastily. She turned to him carefully. 'Felicity said you were married and that you lost your wife. I'm so sorry.'

'No need to be sorry. It's been five years since Eloise passed. She was very sick and in pain. At the end it was a blessing.'

'You still miss her.'

'When you lose someone, I'm not sure you ever stop missing them,' Joe said. 'But it becomes easier to live with in time. Look, Violet... I'm a widower and I'm ten years older than you and no great catch but... would you do me the honour of having dinner with me? It doesn't have to mean anything...'

'Yes, Doctor Joe, I would love to have dinner with you,' Violet beamed. 'I don't know when until I see my rota but we usually have Sunday off and an evening mid-week.'

'Wonderful.'

Joe began to whistle as they wandered slowly back from Wallace's Well towards the monument and then the car.

'Oh, and Joe...' Violet said, as they walked along together.

He raised an eyebrow and waited for her to speak.

Violet smiled shyly at him. 'I wanted to tell you that it does. It does mean something to me.'

-

Violet was humming under her breath as she trudged in through the camp gates and past the guard, having assured him she was friend and not foe. She couldn't help the delight that rippled through her. Joe was taking her to dinner. He liked her, maybe even as much as she liked him. She couldn't wait.

The alarms sounded, long and piercing and loud, and Violet cursed. Not now. She'd been looking forward to lying on her bunk thinking of Joe Gillingham. She ran into the barrack and saw the others jumping up, ramming steel helmets onto their heads and preparing for action.

She grabbed her own helmet and gave orders, making sure each gunner girl knew where to go and what to do. She hardly needed to. She was proud to see each of her squad calmly head up the hill to the anti-aircraft guns and take their stations at the predictor and height finder. She also glimpsed Judith among the canteen staff hurrying towards the concrete shelters and was glad to see that there were no hysterics or panic among the staff this time. Ahead of her, the gunner girls were working together like a well-oiled machine, all their practice and the previous attack having primed them perfectly.

She looked up into the bright sky and saw two aeroplanes and heard the sound of their engines. The German planes hadn't waited until dark to fly across the west coast. They were going to pay a mighty price for their impudence. Soon, the air was full of shouts as the girls communicated the aeroplanes' co-ordinates and the guns were loaded with shells and the familiar crump and whoosh of them firing began. In the daylight, the shells exploded to create black puffs scattered across the sky.

Shrapnel thudded down, hitting Violet's steel helmet as she ducked behind the concrete wall. When she stood up again, she heard the long whine of a stricken aeroplane engine and the rippling cheer that went up from the Royal

Artillery soldiers. More shells were loaded and fired but the remaining plane veered away. Hopefully all the way back to Germany, Violet thought grimly.

'Reckon that first one went into the briny,' someone shouted.

'Let's hope 'is pal follows toot sweet,' another soldier replied with a grin.

There was a raw headiness that followed such intense action. Violet felt it and she saw it in the faces of her unit as Kathy came towards her, followed by Gladys and the others. It was a mixture of relief at surviving danger and exhilaration at beating the enemy and pride at protecting the Clydeside shipyards and all the people that lived in the district.

Flinging off their heavy helmets and jackets, the women sank onto bunks and into chairs in their barracks. They could afford a small rest before the clear-up began, Violet had agreed.

'I don't know about you lot but I need a bath,' Gladys complained.

No one could disagree with that. Gladys's face was streaked with dirt and perspiration and they knew they all looked just like her.

'We all need a wash, but do youse know what we need more?' Kathy asked.

Violet looked at her friend. Kathy's grey eyes were sparkling and her dirty face was flushed pink with exertion but she looked marvellously alive and gave off waves of nervous energy. When she glanced about, no one was sitting still. Toes were tapping, fingers rubbing together and a couple of the girls were pacing up and down the room. It was all part of the reaction to the unexpected end of a peaceful Sunday afternoon.

'What do we need?' Gladys said, wiping her face with her jacket sleeve.

'We need to put on a show,' Kathy said triumphantly. 'Something to cheer us all up and entertain the rest of the camp.'

'You wanted a show at Christmas and never got it. You've had a hankering for this since then, haven't you?' one of the other girls laughed.

'Aye, so I have,' Kathy grinned. 'But it's no just for me. We'll all muck in and enjoy it. What do you say? Besides, I've got something to celebrate. As you all know I became an auntie this week to my wee niece Flora.'

They turned as a unit to Violet. She was in two minds. They had an awful lot of work to do. Not just the clear-up from this evening's onslaught and the possibility of more airborne attacks but the everyday marching and training and camp chores. Then there was sentry duty and spotting duty and… oh, she could go on. But the ring of expectant faces made her stop. Perhaps Kathy was right. They could all do with an event that would be cheerful, good fun and would raise spirits and keep morale high.

'I think it's a jolly good idea,' Violet said with a smile. 'As long as the show doesn't get in the way of your duties as Royal Artillery soldiers, my gunner girls, then please do carry on. Only, I'm warning you, don't put me down for a singing slot or the audience will run for the hills.'

Chapter Sixteen

The mood in the camp was buoyant with news of the D-Day Normandy landings. On Tuesday the sixth of June, while they had slept, Allied forces had launched a combined naval, air and land assault on Nazi-occupied France. Airborne forces had parachuted into drop zones across northern France with ground troops then landed across the beaches. By the end of the day, the Allies had established a foothold along the coast and now there was optimism that they could begin their advance into France, although no one expected that to happen without serious defence by the German army. Although they knew there would be further tough battles ahead, the feeling throughout the country was that this could be the beginning of the end of the long years of the war.

It was the perfect time to put on a show, Kathy thought, sharing the excitement and fervour of the soldiers and gunner girls at the news on the camp wireless and in the newspapers that circulated, getting grubbier with each pair of hands that eagerly grabbed them.

Permissions to hold an evening of entertainment were sought and received from the major, the captain and the junior commander in charge of the ATS. A group of soldiers offered to construct a makeshift stage and so hunting parties were sent to the bluebell woods to seek out the best logs. In between camp duties, the sounds of saws and swearing were to be heard as the stage began to take shape.

One of the gunner girls had a small talent as an artist and she was put to work making leaflets to put up round the camp. As paper was in short supply, all the girls contributed whatever they could in the way of writing paper to make this work.

'They don't have to be large, but if we can't have proper leaflet sizes, let's make them colourful,' Kathy suggested. 'There's paint in the storeroom in the cottage. Ask the captain if we can borrow some of that.'

The girl nodded and scurried away with another couple of girls in the unit.

'What else do we need?' Violet asked.

Kathy frowned. 'The stage is getting built as we speak, Lily is doing the leaflets and Cook has volunteered to make refreshments. What we need are more acts. So far all we've got is a soldier who was an opera singer before the war who's offered to sing an aria from *Carmen*.'

'Gosh, how lovely.'

'Aye, well, I've no idea what an aria is but I'm guessing it's a song.'

'That's right. Before the war, I went to see *Carmen* with Mummy and Daddy in London. It was quite magical,' Violet sighed.

Kathy considered Violet to be her best friend now that Bridie and Jennifer had gone but at certain moments, like now, it was brought home very sharply to her that they came from different classes. The Dougals had never been to London. Even if they had gone, they'd never have wished to see an opera. Mammy and Jeannie liked musicals while Kathy loved the new big band tunes of Glenn Miller and before the war she'd liked any tune on the wireless with a bit of zip to it.

'I'm sure Private Graham will be just as magical. In the meantime, who else can we rope in?' she said.

'I heard Gladys and the others are considering a chorus girls line-up of some sort. I'm not sure what I can offer. I can't sing for toffee and I'm not funny so no comedy turns either,' Violet said.

'I'm not talented at all, but since it was my idea, I feel I have to do something on that handmade stage. I cannae sing or dance except a highland jig that Mammy taught me and Jeannie when we were wee. She learned it from her mammy who came from the Western Isles.'

'That's it! We can do a double act, because I can do a highland dance too,' Violet said eagerly. 'Felicity and I had dance classes as children and our dance teacher was very keen that we learn traditional dancing as well as foxtrot and waltzing, and so on.'

'I suppose we don't have to be top notch,' Kathy agreed. 'It's more about making an effort.'

Violet nudged her and pretended to look hurt. 'Are you saying we'll be rubbish?'

'Och no, not at all. With a wee bit of practice we'll only be half-rubbish,' Kathy joked.

The other girls trooped in to the barrack room, all talking about the show. Judith slunk in behind them and went to her bunk at the back of the room without joining in. Gladys came over to Kathy and Violet.

'A couple of the lads are going to do an Arthur Askey comedy turn with "Kiss Me Goodnight, Sergeant Major". We've got a conjuror and a mime artist signed up too. One chap says he's a ventriloquist but we heard him practise and he's terrible.'

'At least he's willing to make a fool of himself,' Kathy said. 'For that, I'm thankful. We cannae have an empty stage.' She thought for a moment. 'There's a good variety of acts, but the men have got a solo singer and we haven't. That's what's missing from our side. Has anyone here got a strong voice and can hold a tune?'

Everyone looked about and most were shaking their heads.

'We have one powerful singer in our midst,' Gladys said. 'We've all heard her in the showers.'

'Spill the beans, hen,' Kathy said impatiently. 'Don't be shy.'

'It's Judith,' Gladys said.

There were several intakes of breath and they all turned to the back of the room where Judith was taking off her shoes. She sat up at hearing her name and looked wary.

Kathy felt a pang of guilt. She hadn't forgotten Violet's words when they had visited Kiltie Street. She owed Judith, even if she wasn't ready to put things right by exposing her secret to the rest of the unit. Judith hadn't been horrible to Kathy for weeks. In fact, when she thought about it, she realised she'd hardly seen Judith for weeks apart from evenings in the barrack. Now, when serving up food, the other girl ignored her for the most part. During her free hours, she seemed to slip away from the camp.

'Judith, will you help us out?' she said, fully expecting it to be thrown right back in her face.

Maybe she'd deserve it if Judith said no or ignored them all. Although Judith hadn't been fair to Kathy either. They were both to blame for the history between them. It was a shame it had spilled over into the barrack where Judith had made no friends with her attitude. Was this an opportunity now to change that?

With more energy and kindness, Kathy spoke again as Judith simply stared at them all, like a cornered cat, claws sheathed for now.

'We would love you to take part in the show. If Gladys thinks your voice is strong and you can hold a melody, we can find some great songs for you. What do you say?'

For a dreadful, heart-stopping second, Kathy thought Judith was going to launch herself forward with fists at the ready. Certainly the old Judith, the one Kathy met so often in the streets around Kiltie Street, would have. This Judith, tempered by months in the ATS with its training and discipline, glanced at each face slowly before replying.

'If youse want me to. All right.' She shrugged carelessly, but a dull stain of colour spread up her neck to her chin.

'That's wonderful news,' Violet said cheerfully, going to Judith and hugging her.

The look of surprise on Judith's rather harsh features made Kathy want to giggle. She suppressed the urge. Gladys smiled widely and pulled Judith into the circle, making her sit on a chair beside the nearest bunk.

'You'll be our star of the show,' she said. 'Won't she girls?'

They all nodded and the chat turned to what Judith should wear, with girls offering dresses and skirts and blouses. Judith looked stunned. Kathy shared a smile with Violet.

'Looks like they've forgiven her all her missteps,' Violet whispered away from the group.

'She's mellowed somehow,' Kathy whispered back. 'Something's changed in her. We can all sense it. I think she'll find she's got some new friends finally today.'

'And you?' Violet asked, meaningfully.

Kathy shook her head. 'I can't. Not yet. I will tell them all my secret, but I'm not ready. Don't make me, will you?'

'Of course not. I don't believe it will make any difference now to Judith making friends. It's up to her not to spoil this opportunity. The girls are being very generous forgetting all the small ways she was spiteful to them. Don't think I didn't notice the spilt cocoa, ripped tights, items being misplaced and little acid comments she made. I did have a word with her but to no avail. I hope that is all in the past now.'

'Gladys is a softie. She'll lead the way for how the others behave. I know she's felt bad about Judith being ignored in spite of her behaviour.'

'Selfishly, I'm glad we are once again a cohesive group. It's better for morale,' Violet said.

'Morale will be very high once the show is on. I promise.' Kathy rubbed her hands together gleefully.

–

Judith's feet found their way as usual to Bess's welcoming farmhouse. She had been escaping here whenever she could for the last month or so, ever since the day she had chopped wood and taken a ride in Young Wullie's tractor. Wullie's father, Auld Wullie, turned out to be a friendly sort and didn't mind Judith trailing along, asking questions about how the farm was run. It held a fascination for her. Especially watching the crops and lambs growing.

When Auld Wullie wasn't available, she watched the land girls in their tasks and spoke to Young Wullie, if he wasn't too busy to answer her queries. In fact, if she thought about it, he was around a lot lately. Was she imagining it, or did he enjoy her company? She found herself looking forward to seeing him. Like his father, he had a wealth of knowledge about farming and life on the land. But most of all, she liked the sensation of his blue eyes flickering thoughtfully over her face.

'Someone smelled the pies coming out of the oven,' Bess chuckled when Judith went inside. 'Sit yourself down with a fork and knife, my girl, and tuck into this. Mind, you can help with the washing up after.'

The two land girls greeted her kindly. They were in for their midday meal although it was almost two o'clock in the afternoon. Judith had already served hundreds of meals in the canteen before Cook had given her a couple of hours to herself. She tried not to think of the peas needing shelling and the bread and butter puddings to make when she returned.

It was rabbit pie; the meat was tender with a thick, salty gravy and flaky pie crust. Bess served up cabbage and potatoes. Judith ate hungrily despite having had a canteen meal earlier. It was followed by a summer pudding, crammed full of blackberries, redcurrants and raspberries.

'Where's Wullie?' she asked, meaning the younger man.

Bess eyed her curiously but smiled. 'He's away with the gun after the wood pigeons. They take the seed and strip the buds, a real pest so they are. There are far too many of them but luckily for us they make a tasty pie. Wullie's a good shot, he'll bring back more than a few brace.'

The land girls ate very quickly, thanked Bess for the food and hurried back to their tasks outdoors. Judith took the dirty plates over to the Belfast sink and washed them. She didn't mind doing that for Bess. She liked spending time in the farmhouse kitchen. It was peaceful and quiet and safe. No one was going to clip her ear or give her a belt to her head like her aunt had done if she thought Judith was daydreaming and slacking off.

'Penny for them?' Bess said, taking the dishes and drying them before reaching up to the Welsh dresser to place them properly.

'Why isn't Wullie away fighting?' Judith asked. It wasn't what she'd been thinking but she had wondered about it.

Bess paused, a plate with blue-and-white pictures of farming life in her work-coarsened hand. 'You haven't asked him that, have you?'

Judith shook her head.

Bess pursed her lips. 'Aye, well. Don't, lass. We lost two sons in the first year of the war and the ministry let us keep our youngest. Besides, Wullie's eyesight was borderline in the tests. If you feel he's frowning at you, he's probably just trying to bring you into focus. He's too proud to wear glasses, that one.' She sighed. 'Wullie feels the loss of his brothers very keenly.'

Judith washed the last plate very slowly. The water was hot to her skin and she watched the flakes of pastry float on its surface. The words came out of her awkwardly, she was so unused to sympathising with others. 'You and Auld Wullie must feel their loss too. I'm sorry.'

'Aye. We don't dwell on it. Wullie doesn't like to talk about it. By the by, don't be letting him hear you call him Auld Wullie. I know that's how he's known in the camp but you'd better call him Mr Campbell with some respect.'

Bess's tone was friendly so Judith didn't mind the chiding. She nodded so that Bess knew she'd heard and rinsed the plate to hand it to the older woman.

'I hear there's a show planned. Want to tell me all about it?' Bess said, when the plates were done and two cups of tea poured.

She motioned Judith back to the table. Bess seemed to know everything that went on in the camp although she rarely ventured there herself. Auld Wullie did appear with very welcome baskets of scones or jars of preserves from time to time with messages to Cook from Bess. Perhaps, in return, news was spread to the farmhouse.

'I'm going to sing,' Judith said.

She still wondered why Gladys had suggested it. She'd been horrible to them all because she was jealous of their friendships and she had been the outsider. She could admit that now. Her unhappiness had made her lash out. And she had been angry with Aunt Irene and her life. These past weeks, on the farm, she had found a peace that soaked into her bones. She had found a love of growing things, a feel for the rich soil and a delight in the warm, spring air that brought scents of May blossom and bluebells along with the richer stink of manure and cattle and pigs. Maybe Young Wullie's presence had something to do with her mood too. She liked him fine.

'Singing, is it? Well done, you. I didn't know you had a good singing voice. You never told me.' Bess smiled approvingly.

'I didn't know either. I mean... I've got strong lungs, I can belt out a song but I never thought it... *good*.'

'So, how did you get into the show?'

'I was volunteered by the other girls,' Judith said, hearing the wonder in her own voice.

'That's nice. It's a lovely feeling having friends to buoy you up. They must like you very much.'

Judith felt her own mouth widening into a reluctant smile. Maybe they did like her. She had stopped being mean and playing little tricks on them. She didn't need to any more. She was busy at work and when she wasn't there, she was here with Bess or outside learning new facts about farming. How odd, that while she was happier in herself, now the other girls liked her better for it.

'Will you come?' she asked. 'You and Auld... Mr Campbell, and mebbe Wullie if he can make it?'

Bess's answering beam made Judith feel warm inside. 'That's a very kind invitation, lass. We'd be delighted to come to the show and we'll be watching out for your star turn.'

Judith walked back to camp round the bottom of the hill. The shapes of the four gun emplacements loomed above. She had a cotton bag of lettuce and two jars of marrow jam to give to Cook from Bess. Deep from the woods, she heard a shot ring out. Young Wullie still shooting the wood pigeons. No doubt a few would end up in the canteen dinners.

She thought about the show again and how the girls had crowded round congratulating her on her singing voice. Kathy had hung back though, muttering with that pal of hers, Violet. Judith might be friends with Gladys and her crew, but not with Kathy Dougal. They had unfinished business. Judith had told them all the truth about Kathy and she had flat out lied to their faces and denied it, making the others hate her. If Judith had a chance to show that cow up and make mischief for her, she would take it.

–

It had been originally planned that the show would be put on in the canteen but the weather was so hot and calm that they decided to hold it outside. The long dining tables and chairs were moved from the canteen and set up in rows in front of the stage.

'Did you hear the news?' Violet cried as she hurried towards Kathy.

'If it's about the piano, there's a laddie says he can fix it before this evening,' Kathy said. 'He used to be a piano tuner, luckily for us. Him and his pals have planned how to get it outside onto the stage too. Something to do with rope and pulleys. Don't ask.'

'Not that news, although that's super in itself. Otherwise we'd have no music to dance to. My news is that the colonel himself is coming to the performance. Rumour has it that it's more to do with Bess's secret fish custard recipe than our talents but nevertheless it's quite something. He'll dine at the farmhouse and then come to see the show.'

'Is that good news?' Kathy squeaked. 'I'm shaking with nerves as it is. What if it all goes wrong?'

'Court martial?' Violet joked weakly. 'Anyway, it's going to be marvellous, so I won't hear any more negative comments and that's an order.'

Kathy saluted smartly with a grin before a wail from Gladys made her rush off to solve yet another prop disaster. Someone had ripped a sheet which had been borrowed to create robes for a theatrical dialogue set in Ancient Rome. The ATS orderly in charge of store supplies was none too happy.

-

The show was introduced by the major himself as if he had personally done all the organising and the hard work. Kathy and the rest of the performers were inside the canteen going over last-minute rehearsals. She peered out, ready to call the first act once the major had finished speaking. She could see the colonel in the front row along with Auld Wullie and Bess, the captain, the ATS officers in charge and the local church minister who came every Sunday to the camp. In the rows behind were the soldiers who had been given permission to attend. It looked like most of the camp had turned up. As promised, the piano had made it onto the stage and Kathy crossed her fingers that it was now in tune.

Behind her was a thick murmur of lines being read out, songs being hummed and not a few muffled shrieks as last-minute nerves took hold. Finally, the major was stepping carefully down the planked steps.

'Private Graham,' Kathy shouted. 'You're up first.'

They might as well begin with their most talented act, she had decided. They had an actual trained opera singer in their midst. Unfortunately he'd be followed by raw amateurs, but hopefully eagerness would make up for any theatrical flaws. They all listened to the young man's powerful voice as he sang the well-known aria from *Carmen*. It made the tiny hairs on the back of Kathy's neck stand up, it was so beautiful. She hadn't known such music existed. The applause was loud and long and the front row of brass even stood to show their appreciation.

Soon, they were rattling through the acts. The gunner girls' chorus line went down a treat as did the Arthur Askey comedy tribute and the mime artist. The ventriloquist raised a laugh, but more at the terrible act rather than the dialogue between the man and the puppet. He shrugged and waved when it ended. Soon, Kathy and Violet's turn came. With a thudding heart, she put on a smile and took her place on the stage. The familiar Scottish country songs began to play on the piano and her feet found the steps. Then it was only a matter of keeping in time with Violet as they leapt lightly from foot to foot, arms held high, and then spun round in pirouettes, their kilts spinning too and showing their legs to whistles from the soldiers in the audience.

A great round of applause sounded in her ears as they dashed off the stage afterwards. Kathy laughed, grabbing Violet and pulling her along back to the canteen. What fun it was.

'Who's next?' she panted.

Violet's chest was heaving from the exercise. 'Judith.'

Kathy called her name. Judith appeared from the throng and Kathy did a double take. She hadn't seen the other girl that evening in among all the chaos. Judith wore a borrowed dress, a velvet gown with a low neck in a midnight blue shade. It suited her heavy bosom and wide hips. Someone had loaned her a string of paste pearls and these graced her neck. She looked quite different, especially with her face made up and scarlet lipstick making her mouth bow-shaped.

'Gosh, she's scrubbed up rather well,' Violet whispered in Kathy's ear. 'Good for Judith.'

Kathy watched Judith stalk outside and up onto the stage, holding her gown up to avoid tripping on the rough, nailed planks that formed the steps at the side. She found herself hoping that Judith's act went well. Although she looked calm, there was something vulnerable about the nape of Judith's neck, bare where her hair was scraped up into a knot of curls held with pins.

There were appreciative whistles before someone shushed the audience. Then a silence. For one horrible moment, Kathy thought Judith wasn't going to sing. She stood there, her face blank. But then the pianist pressed the first keys and the tune of 'I'll Never Smile Again' rang out. Judith's shoulders sank and she sang the first line. It was croaky. She turned to the soldier at the piano and he nodded and started the song once more. This time, Judith's voice picked up volume and pace and confidence. The lyrics rang out across the yard. Soon, the audience were tapping feet and clapping hands in rhythm and joining in at the chorus.

She sang three numbers and then a fourth as an 'encore' due to popular demand. Back in the canteen, Gladys and the other girls crowded round her to say congratulations. Judith looked stunned. Kathy wanted to say well done too but was distracted by one of the last acts, the disaster-prone scene from Ancient Rome, who had all lost their sandals. By the time she had found the offending articles, shoved under someone's overcoat, it was too late to seek out Judith. She had to wrap up the show and thank everyone for taking part and coming to see it.

-

'You were good.'

The words came from behind her and Judith turned to see Young Wullie. He was dressed in a clean checkered shirt and dark trousers and was cleanly shaven. She could smell the Brylcreem from his slicked-back hair.

'I just… sang,' Judith said. It was hard to put into words the magic of the evening, the touch of the velvet dress on her skin and the taste of Gladys's lipstick on her tongue as she licked her lips nervously before the song took its shape. It was impossible to describe the feeling that enveloped her as the mood of the audience lifted and swayed to the beat and they urged her on.

'Aye.' Wullie looked at his feet then up at her. 'Do you want a wee walk before it gets dark?'

Judith was wearing Lily's court shoes but she nodded anyway. Sure, the soil was dry from weeks of good weather. The shoes might be dusty but she could clean them off. Beyond Wullie, the audience had dispersed. She saw the backs of Auld Wullie and Bess in their Sunday-go-to-meeting clothes as the couple walked affectionately, hand in hand back in the direction of the Muirhead Farm-house.

She glanced around to see if anyone might notice her gone. Cook was nowhere to be seen. At the front of the stage she saw Kathy picking up props and calling instructions. She hadn't even come to say thanks to Judith for her performance. When all the others had crowded round, Kathy had deliberately hung back. She had no liking for Judith. That was just fine. It was mutual. Judith turned her back on the stage and Kathy Dougal, and smiled at Young Wullie.

'I'd like a walk. Where will we go?'

They went round the side of the hill, under the looming presence of the guns, and towards the woods, Wullie leading the way. At some point, he took Judith's hand without speaking. She felt his large grasp, the roughened skin and the strength of him, and liked it. She knew she was no slim wisp of a girl but being with Wullie she felt light and feminine. He could lift entire logs single-handedly and she'd watched him lift boulders off the fields, his shoulder muscles bulging.

Although it was late evening, because of double summer time the sun was still warm and cast a yellow glow over the pine trees which dappled down onto the bluebells and wood anemones under their feet. There was a sweet scent of sap and the chirp of birds on their nests high up in the canopy.

Wullie stopped and put his hands on Judith's waist. He leaned in and kissed her. Judith opened her mouth under the pressure of his lips and responded. It was unlike Frankie's wet kisses or the kisses she'd taken from some of the soldiers. It was tender and passionate, as if Wullie was holding back a force that might be unstoppable. She took his hands from her waist and placed them on her breasts. She knew what to do. Her nipples rose from the contact and she moaned. She reached under her skirt and pulled her knickers down. She expected Wullie to make the next move but as she wriggled to set her hips snugly to his, he froze.

Gently, Wullie set her away, holding her at arms' length and gazing into her face before letting his arms drop. Judith's jaw dropped. She felt foolish standing there, her knickers round her ankles while Wullie's expression was unreadable.

'Slow down, lass. I didn't ask you to walk out for this. I want to do things properly,' Wullie said, and she had never heard him speak so kindly.

She scrabbled for her knickers and turned away to pull them up. Her eyes were burning and before she could stop them, tears welled up and poured down her face. She was bawling like a wean without any control over them.

Wullie sighed and took her in his arms. He hugged her close and kissed her hair as Judith sobbed.

Chapter Seventeen

There had been no more enemy aeroplanes spotted and it was reckoned that Hitler had other things on his mind now that the invasion of Western Europe by the Allies had begun. In any event, the girls were able to get twenty-four-hour passes once every seven or eight days. Those that came from the Midlands or further south spent them happily enough in Glasgow or having walks in the beautiful countryside around Muirhead Farm, and the bluebell woods were a favourite for rambling and courting. Kathy felt lucky that she lived so close to home and could visit her family in Kiltie Street.

She and Violet set off early to walk to the train station to catch a train into the city centre. They could then catch a bus or tram headed out to Maryhill. Some of the other gunner girls were heading into town that day too. Kathy noticed Judith among them. Although the others included her now in their chatter, Judith still kept herself slightly apart, not talking much but nodding and smiling when it was needed. She certainly didn't attempt to come near Kathy, ignoring her entirely. Kathy wasn't sure how Judith felt about her now. The bullying had stopped, but there was the matter of Kathy's secret between them and she got a sense that it still rankled with the other girl.

'Are you sure I'm not going to be in the way?' Violet asked as they stepped onto the carriage amid a blast of white steam.

'Of course not. Mammy loves when you visit. Besides, you want to see Evie, don't you?' Kathy coughed and wafted the smoky steam away.

'I certainly do, so I can report back to Felicity.' Violet took a window seat and sat with a contented sigh. 'Oh, it's good to take the weight off. All those parades take their toll.'

'How is your sister?' Kathy asked, sitting beside her on the upholstered seat.

'Joe says she's doing well. He took me for another visit when I had my last pass.' Violet blushed.

'You've got it badly.' Kathy nudged her wickedly.

She had met Joe when he came to pick Violet up from the camp and thought he was just right for her friend. Even if he was a bit older. Somehow she couldn't imagine Violet with a boyfriend the same age.

'Oh dear, is it that obvious?' Violet said, putting her hands to her hot cheeks. 'Goodness, I must learn to hide it.'

'Why? Just enjoy it. Who knows how long it will last?' Kathy replied. 'Sorry, I don't mean to be gloomy on such a glorious sunny day. I was thinking about Don. Life's for living, Violet, so make the most of it.'

She was thinking about Alisdair Meikle too. Where was he now? And did he ever think of her? She knew she ought to forget him, she had told herself to enough times, but somehow she couldn't. She had been asked out by some of the soldiers but she always declined. Firstly, there was Don and that lingering guilt over their short-lived love affair. Secondly, there was the memory of Alisdair.

245

She hadn't felt that strong pull of attraction for any other man before or since.

The door to number four Kiltie Street was opened by a beaming Mary who pulled them both into a warm embrace. At knee height, they were grabbed on one side by Evie and on the other by Dennis with shrieks of glee. Kathy and Violet, buffeted by warm bodies, returned the hugs with fervour.

'Like wee twins, those two,' Mary laughed. 'Inseparable, so they are, and full of mischief with it. Keeps me young. Come away in the now and get a cuppa.'

'Mammy, how come you're so happy?' Kathy said. 'Last year, you were that tired, you said you couldn't cope.'

Mary smiled as she set the kettle onto the black range. 'It's the weans. They keep me and Harry lively. When we sit down together of an evening, we've all these wee tales to discuss, funny stories of what they've been up to during the day. You'll get to meet Flora in a moment, Jeannie's feeding her in the back bedroom.'

'What a lovely name for the baby,' Violet said.

'Aye, she's named for her other grandmother. Bill's mother over in Canada.'

'Jeannie had better name her second wean after you or Dad or there'll be hell to pay,' Kathy teased. The tea and some home-made biscuits were taken through to the parlour where Dennis and Evie had settled with jigsaws on the floor. Jeannie came in with her baby cradled in her arms. Kathy jumped up to see her.

'She's a bonny wee thing. I can't believe I'm an auntie. What does Bill say?'

'He hasn't seen her yet but he's delighted.' Jeannie smiled tenderly and stroked her baby's soft face. 'I wish he was here and not somewhere in France, fighting.'

'He'll come home safely,' Kathy said. 'You mustn't worry.'

A shriek interrupted what Jeannie was going to say next. Dennis grabbed a piece of jigsaw and hugged it to his chest.

'Mine!' he screamed.

'I need that for *my* picture,' Evie yelled.

'Give it back, Den Den,' Kathy said, trying to take it from her son's fierce grip.

He screamed again and rolled onto the floor, kicking his legs.

'I'll take Evie out for a bit of fresh air,' Violet suggested quickly, taking her niece's hand and edging towards the hallway.

Kathy picked Dennis up and waited until he calmed down. Mary went to see Violet and Evie to the door and Jeannie walked Flora up and down, gently rocking her as the baby cried with all the din going on. Finally both children were quiet. Flora had fallen asleep and Dennis sat on the floor with his jigsaw as if nothing had happened.

'You're a natural with him,' Jeannie remarked. 'I thought you'd pass him quick enough to Mammy to sort out.'

'Aye, it crossed my mind, but Mammy's got enough to be getting on with, hasn't she.' Kathy touched Dennis's red hair. She loved him so much, even when he had tantrums.

'The army suits you,' Jeannie said, watching her approvingly. 'Do you like it then?'

'I love it. I've made so many friends, and the work is hard but fair. I've learned a lot of skills. In a way, I'll miss the war when it ends. Ordinary life will be far too dull for me.'

'Och, that's a terrible thing to say. The war must end soon now that we've entered France. I want my Bill home to see his wee daughter.'

'I know… I just mean… what will I do wi' myself?'

'You'll find something. It was awful that Don died. If he hadn't, you'd be a married woman and you'd keep house for him and have more weans. Did you ever hear from the other lad you liked?'

'Alisdair? That was never going to work out.'

Kathy remembered back to her conversation with Jeannie, oh so long ago, when she had just met Alisdair and fallen in love. She thought of Maggie's Café. Perhaps she might take a wee trip into the city centre and pass by it. Violet's birthday was coming up and she wanted to get a gift for her.

–

Judith was bored. There was nothing to buy in the shops and she didn't have much cash to spend anyway. She should've spent her free day with Wullie. Only Wullie was busy on the farm. Bess was always glad to see her but Judith knew there were other girls visiting the farm that day. She didn't want to share Bess and be one of a crowd. A wee wander round Glasgow had appealed. Except now she'd had enough. She idly glanced in the shop windows. The glass was taped for bomb blast and there were sand-bags against the walls. The barrage balloons, next to the People's Palace at Glasgow Green, glinted silver in the sunlight.

She went past a café. It looked shabby, like most other shops and cafés after almost five years of war, but the waitress looked cheerful. Suddenly, Judith remembered her. That day last year when she'd followed Kathy from the butcher's shop, intending to rough her up, she'd watched her collide with a man in RAF uniform. She'd watched them talk and seen the way the man smiled at Kathy, clearly finding her attractive. It had angered Judith so. No man ever looked at her like that. She'd followed him and seen where he lived. And she'd followed him here to this café where he met Kathy. Afterwards, she'd threatened Kathy that she would tell him about her baby.

Judith peered in and her eyes widened in surprise. As if she'd conjured him up, there he was. The man with dark coppery hair and the smart blue uniform. She was certain it was him. He wasn't alone. A young woman sat opposite him. She had a red cloche hat and a matching red jacket over a brown skirt. Her hair was blonde and curly and she was smiling shyly at him. He'd got over Kathy Dougal then. Judith's mouth twisted.

When she turned back to the street, she couldn't believe her luck. Coming towards her was Kathy. Her gaze was focussed somewhere beyond Judith and she jumped a little when Judith stepped right in front of her.

'You gave me a right start. What are you up to?' Kathy said.

'I'm not "up to" anything. Having a nice day out, are we?' Judith sneered.

Kathy frowned. 'Aye, nice enough. Yourself?'

'Never mind me. You ought to have a peek in yon window there at Maggie's Café. I think you'll find it very interesting.'

'What are you on about?' Kathy sounded impatient.

'Yer man's in there. The RAF chappie that you fell for. Looks like he's forgotten you. He's with his girlfriend. A right looker she is too. What a shame for you.'

Kathy's mouth opened and shut and she went so white that Judith was worried. She brushed past, trying to squash down the sour feeling of guilt. Why should she feel guilty? She hated Kathy. Of course she did. So why did she wish she hadn't said those horrible things? Judith thought of Wullie. He'd be disappointed in her for what she had just done. She knew he would. He only knew the new Judith. The Judith who tried hard to be good and do right. Bess and Auld Wullie and Young Wullie made it easy for her to do so. With them, on the farm at Muirhead, she was… *happy*. But as Judith hurried on, away from Maggie's Café, she had a horrible sense that she had destroyed Kathy's happiness. She ought to be enjoying her victory, but all of a sudden it felt hollow.

–

Kathy walked swiftly towards Maggie's Café. Was Judith telling the truth? Was Alisdair really there? She desperately wanted to see him again. Even though they had parted so badly at the Borders railway station. Even though he despised her. Her steps slowed. His opinion of her was unlikely to have changed. She should walk away and forget about him. But she couldn't. She had to see him once more. To show him what she'd made of herself. Aye, show his girlfriend too. Kathy decided she would be dignified and cool but polite. She nodded. She could do this.

Pushing open the door to Maggie's Café, she was almost overwhelmed by the aromas of ersatz coffee, strongly brewed tea and baking. Oh, how familiar it was. It brought back so many lovely memories of days spent shopping in the city centre and a wee treat of a cuppa and a biscuit before catching the tram back to Maryhill. She had often sat dreamily, chin in cupped hands, watching the rain trickle down the window and the people scurrying past outside.

She glanced around. There was Maggie herself, pencil tucked in her thick brown hair, balancing plates and laughing with the customers as she wove between the tables. A thin girl behind the counter counted out change from the till for an elderly man. Kathy's heart squeezed as she saw the couple in the far corner. Alisdair looked as handsome as ever in his RAF blue uniform and with his slicked back Brylcreemed dark hair. Opposite him sat a slim girl with blonde curls. She was talking earnestly. A sour jab of jealousy hit Kathy's midriff. Alisdair was staring at the girl with his green eyes as if no one else existed.

She couldn't bear it. Seeing him, she knew that she was in love with him. Nothing could change that. Not even Alisdair's opinion of her, nor the fact he was stepping out with another girl. She turned on her heel. There was no way she could sit and swallow anything. It would stick in her craw. Her hand was on the door handle when she heard Alisdair call her name.

'Is it really you?' he said incredulously, reaching her before Kathy could get the door open.

'Aye, it's me. How do you do?' Kathy said stiffly.

'I'm well, but I can't believe I found you…'

'Don't let me keep you from your girlfriend. She's looking over here, puzzled like.'

'Girlfriend?' Alisdair frowned. He looked over his shoulder at the corner table. 'Ah, that's Miss Alison Renfrew. She's…'

Kathy didn't let him finish. She stormed out of the café, not wanting to hear him say it. That Alison Renfrew was his girlfriend, or fiancée. Or maybe they were already married. She took in a deep breath to calm herself. She'd find the tram and go home. What had she been thinking? Judith had warned her and yet she'd gone right in there. And for what?

'At least give me your address,' Alisdair said, appearing beside her. 'Look, I'm busy right now, but I'll call on you this evening if that's all right?'

'Won't Alison mind?' Kathy said acidly.

'Why should she?'

Kathy wrote her address on a scrap of paper. She gave it to him and walked away before he could say goodbye.

—

Alisdair watched her go. Her lustrous red hair shone under her cap and she held herself tall and straight. His gut instinct was to go after her right then in case she slipped away and he never found her again. Which was daft, as he had her address firmly in his hand. He tucked it into his pocket and patted it. Elated, he returned to Alison.

'Is there a problem, Mr Meikle?' Alison asked nervously.

'Not at all, Miss Renfrew. Quite the opposite, in fact,' Alisdair replied cheerfully. 'Now, where was I?'

'You were explaining about your grandmother,' Alison prompted. 'I was telling you about my experience as a companion. I lived in with my previous lady for two years until she sadly passed away last month. I'm used to dealing with forgetfulness and frailty.'

Alisdair had been granted a week's compassionate leave. Beatrice had fallen. She was unharmed except for bruising down one arm but her confidence had gone. His parents apparently were unable to visit her. Alisdair had found his grandmother determined to keep her independence. She was adamant she was not going to live with her daughter and son-in-law. He had thought hard on the problem and all he could come up with was a companion. One advertisement later in the *Daily Record* and here he was, interviewing Miss Renfrew.

'When can you move in? I only have six days before I have to go back to base.'

He had already decided Alison Renfew was perfect. He was sure Beatrice would like her. While they talked through the details, his mind was on Kathy. No wonder she was frosty with him. She had never got his letters. Maggie had given them back to him when he arrived in the café. He couldn't believe it. They had sat here all these months. It was nearly a year since he had met Kathy and left that first hurried note when he was suddenly recalled to duty. What must she think of him? Thank God he would see her that evening and have a chance to explain.

-

'Your young man can come in and meet Harry and myself then the two of youse can go for a wee walk together. It's a madhouse in the parlour.'

Kathy and Mary were in the back bedroom where Mary and Harry slept. It was a small neat room with a dark wood bed covered in blankets and a coverlet that Mary had crocheted in pale pink and rose wool, a walnut sideboard and thick blackout curtains draped at the window. In the parlour, Harry was crawling on the floor with Dennis and Evie riding on his back like a pony. He and Violet had hit it off since they met and Kathy could hear Violet's laughter. Jeannie and Flora were in the middle of it all too. Flora was getting used to the noise and was beginning to be able to sleep anywhere. She was not a fussy baby.

No chance to be in this household, Kathy thought. What would Alisdair make of it all? She tossed her head. Served him right for inviting himself over. She didn't feel that though, not really. Nervous excitement made her skin tingle. Why was he coming? Didn't his girlfriend mind?

'It's only proper that we meet him,' Mary was saying.

'He's not my young man, Mammy,' Kathy protested.

Mammy looked at her shrewdly. 'If a young man comes visiting a beautiful young woman, I cannae think of many other reasons.'

'He's a… friend. I met him before I knew Don. A lot has happened since I first met Alisdair.'

'And you be careful now. You know what I'm saying.' Mary squeezed Kathy's hand.

'Och, Mammy, I'm no that naïve wee girl any more. I can take care of myself.'

'I believe you can. You look that smart in your uniform and you've learned a lot over the last year, what with all the training and that. But if it wasn't for this terrible war, you'd have been living at home until you got married.'

'If it wasn't for the war, I'd never have met Don or Alisdair,' Kathy said. 'And I've learned such a lot by being on the anti-aircraft battery. When the war is done, I'm going to go out and work. I don't know yet what I'll do but I'm no gonnae sit home and knit.'

Mary smiled. 'Aye, things are changing for women, that's for sure. There'll be more opportunities than my generation ever had for you and Jeannie and Isa.'

The doorbell rang and Kathy jumped up. Mary stood up more slowly, rubbing her hip.

'Don't be too eager. Let him do the running,' she advised, kissing Kathy's cheek lovingly before they went out into the hall.

Kathy didn't smile as she opened the door. Alisdair stood there, as gorgeous as ever, with a bottle of camp coffee. He gave it to her with a grin that made her blood pulse.

'This is for your mother. Not quite the same as a bunch of flowers or a box of chocolates but all I could get, I'm afraid, at short notice.'

'Mammy will like it better than flowers,' Kathy said politely. 'More practical. Won't you come in?'

Hark, she sounded like the lady of the manor when what she really wanted to do was to ask him about his girlfriend and why he was here. She turned on her heel and led the way inside, not waiting for him. Luckily, Mary arrived and made a fuss of both Alisdair and the camp coffee and Kathy was able to take a silent breath in and prepare herself for whatever he had to say.

Kathy had to hand it to Alisdair. He managed to remain calm and outwardly confident despite the barrage of questions from all corners and the questing sticky fingers as Dennis and Evie touched his uniform. Harry was asking him about the RAF and the role of the fighter pilots in the D-Day Landings and the ongoing push into mainland Europe. Mary was asking him whether he took a wee drop of milk in his tea. Jeannie wanted to know if there were many Canadians on his airbase. Violet was on her hands and knees gathering up pieces of jigsaw. Kathy waited impatiently. She looked composed as she perched on the sofa but she was desperate to know why Alisdair was back in Glasgow and what his relationship was to the blonde girl in the café.

She caught his amused glance occasionally. The flash in his sea green eyes sent a thrill through her. He looked so smart in his air force blues. He held his cap in strong, capable hands. She saw the attractive creases in his cheeks as he laughed with Dennis and let him try the cap on. He was making it hard for her to stay icy with him. Eventually, tea had been drunk and Mary's pound cake sampled and pronounced delicious.

'Son, it's been a pleasure to meet you,' Harry said, putting out his hand to shake with Alisdair's. 'Look after my step-daughter and you're always welcome here.'

'I will look after her, sir,' Alisdair said, looking directly at Kathy.

'Don't stay out long,' Mary said.

'Mammy!' Kathy cried.

How embarrassing. She didn't want to be treated like a child. Sometimes, family was the worst. She caught Violet's gaze and they exchanged a smile. Violet understood. Her family was worse.

'Shall we?' Alisdair said.

Kathy nodded and led the way out of the Dougals' flat and down the stone steps onto Kiltie Street.

'Where do you want to go?' she asked, her heart pounding at his nearness.

'I don't care as long as we can talk,' he said.

'Without all the shouting and wailing, you mean?' Kathy grinned. 'I apologise for my family.'

'They are all perfectly charming. But I did want to get you to myself,' Alisdair laughed.

'You did? Why's that then?'

Kathy tucked a stray curl behind her ear as they walked together along the street. It was a warm evening and blessedly dry. If it was raining, they'd have been stuck in the flat, no doubt with no privacy. She felt his gaze follow the movement.

'Your beautiful hair,' Alisdair murmured. 'I thought I saw you once at a dance some months ago. I had a glimpse of red hair the very shade of yours.'

'Maybe I saw you too,' Kathy said. 'I wanted to. I thought I'd imagined it.'

Alisdair turned and took her hands. They were right at the end of the street now, where there was a wooden bench overlooking a dusty square of grass. They sat down.

'There's something I need to show you,' Alisdair said.

He reached into his jacket pocket and pulled out a small stack of envelopes. Wordlessly, he handed them to her. Kathy stared at them. Slowly, she opened the top one, took out the letter inside and read it carefully. Tears filled her eyes as she opened each one in turn.

How wrong she had been about him. Oh, if only she'd known... it might all have been so different!

'You never got my letters. I wrote to tell you I had to leave rather suddenly the day we had planned to meet, but I didn't know where you lived so I went to Maggie's Café and asked her to give it to you.'

'She never did... Oh, I didn't give her a chance to. You didn't turn up and I thought you'd stood me up so I left before she could.'

'I wrote a few letters but you never answered and so I stopped. I thought you didn't return my feelings,' Alisdair said, his fingers still wrapped around hers.

The touch of his hands was distracting. She felt their warmth and savoured his touch. Little sparks of desire flickered across her skin.

'Your feelings?' she murmured.

'You must know how I felt... feel... about you,' Alisdair said.

'Hang on a moment.' Kathy wrenched her hands out of his. 'What about that Alison you were with in the café? Does she know you're here with me?'

'Alison isn't my... I was interviewing her in the café. My nana requires a live-in companion and Alison has agreed to take on the role.'

'So she's not your wife or your fiancée or your girl-friend?' Kathy said quickly.

Alisdair shook his head with a cheeky grin that Kathy wasn't certain if she'd like to wipe off his face with a slap or a kiss. The man had put her through purgatory before he'd made all that clear.

He leaned in towards her. 'Now that we've got that sorted, may I kiss you?'

'I don't...' Her words were lost under the gentle pressure of his lips on hers.

The kiss was tender but promised more. There was more than a hint of passion kept in check. When it seemed he might move away, with a groan she pulled him back and deepened their kiss. Now the sparks lit into a fire within her. A cheeky yell from a neighbourhood child made her stop and sit beside him, her mind whirring. Alisdair had kissed her. He... *liked* her. Oh, and she very much *liked* him. She picked up a pebble off the dusty ground and threw it at the urchin making faces. The boy squealed and ran off.

'May I see you again?' Alisdair asked.

'Yes please. But I'm back to camp tomorrow. I've only got a twenty-four-hour pass.'

'And I've got a week to sort Nana out and make sure she's safe and comfortable. After that I'm back to Ayrshire. It may be a while before we can see each other again. But I'd like to. Very much.'

Kathy wanted the moment to stay as perfect as it was, but she had to ask.

'That day I met you at the railway station in the Borders. Were you ashamed of me? When your dad came out to get you. You went in without another word to me. As if you didn't want him to know that we knew each other.'

'I wasn't ashamed of you. I was ashamed of him,' Alisdair said. 'My parents have a difficult relationship, and they had been arguing in the station tea shop. It wasn't the right time to introduce you. I suppose I had imagined how it would be when I took the girl of my dreams home to meet my parents. It was nothing like that day, when my mother was sobbing and my father was being dictatorial. I couldn't do it. We went back inside but I realised I'd made a mistake letting you go. At the very least I needed to know how I could contact you again. But by the time I raced out to the platform you had gone.'

'I have to tell you something,' Kathy said. 'After that, I didn't think we'd see each other again. A while later, I met a pilot, Don, and we got engaged but he died.'

'I'm so sorry to hear that.'

Alisdair's voice was gentle and compassionate. There was no accusing or jealous tone. His gorgeous eyes flickered over her face as if to reassure himself that she was all right.

'The thing is… Don was a good man, and when he died… I went to pieces for a while. But… he was never *my* man, not really. You see, I couldn't love him, not properly the way he wanted me to because you were never far from my thoughts. I tried to move on from you when I thought you didn't return my feelings and, that's why I got engaged, but I knew it wasn't right even while I said

259

yes. Poor Don. He didn't deserve to die that way. He had his whole life ahead of him. He'd have found someone else to fall in love with and spend his life with. But he never got that chance.'

'This bloody war. It changes all of us,' he said quietly.

'It does that. Let's walk a wee bit more before Mammy comes on the rampage to get us.'

Kathy boldly took his hand and they walked on out of Kiltie Street, round the curve in the road and up towards the canal. There was light enough yet and she knew Alisdair would be as good as his word and walk her back home before too long.

Chapter Eighteen

Violet and Joe got married quietly on a Friday morning in late August by the church minister who had visited the camp every Sunday since it was established. The service was held in nearby Bearsden but Bess had insisted that the wedding reception must be held at Muirhead Farm and wouldn't hear otherwise.

'Not that I was going to refuse such a kind offer,' Violet told Kathy, a few days before the wedding. 'It will be super to celebrate in Auld Wullie and Bess's welcoming farmhouse and very kind of them to offer. Otherwise, it was going to be at home in Helensburgh although not a word from Mummy on the subject so perhaps that might have been a difficult one.'

'Are you certain about marrying Joe?' Kathy asked. 'I mean, he's very nice and all, but do you know him well enough? It's awful quick.'

Violet laughed. 'I'm head over heels in love with him. Yes, I'm certain. Besides, with the war on, we don't want to wait. We want to be together, and who knows how many days we'll have as man and wife. Joe might be sent abroad or I might at any time. I want to have a taste of married life before that happens.'

Violet had also been to get Felicity's blessing. She and Joe had again taken the journey across the city and out into the countryside east to Robroyston Hospital. Joe kept taking his hand off the steering wheel to hold her hand until she laughingly told him to stop.

'You'll make us crash,' Violet protested, pushing his hand back towards the wheel, but secretly she liked it. 'And please don't glance over at me like that either. You know very well what I look like.'

'I can't get enough of you,' Joe smiled, but he kept his hands on the steering wheel and his gaze forward on the tarmacked road.

'And I can't get enough of you too,' Violet smiled back. 'But I'd quite like to be alive to enjoy our wedding day.'

'You don't mind this hurried affair, do you darling?' Joe frowned. 'Only, if you do, we can delay it and do it all properly after the war. White wedding gown, proper cake and food and all the right guests.'

'I'd marry you tomorrow if I had the chance,' Violet said firmly. 'I don't care about a fancy dress, and I can assure you if Bess is catering, the food won't be any worse than after the war is over. As for the right guests, most of our friends will be able to make it.'

There was to be no honeymoon as Joe couldn't get the extra time off from the hospital, but they planned to take a weekend in September if they could. They weren't the only couple making do, Violet thought. After all there was a war on. They couldn't expect all the traditions that pre-war had been considered essential.

Joe's brother had promised to be his best man if he could get leave from his post in Whitehall. Joe's parents were dead and he had no other family but he had two good friends, both doctors, who hoped to come to at least the ceremony if their work schedules allowed. As for Violet, it looked as if Evie was going to be the only member of her family able to attend. Felicity was stuck in the sanitorium and Camilla was yet to respond to her invitation. She had invited the Dougals, who had been so kind and taken Evie in as one of their own. She had also invited the girls in her unit.

Felicity had taken a turn for the worse, the matron told Violet when they arrived at the ward.

'She's very tired. You can have five minutes with her but no longer.' Matron turned to Joe. 'Could I have a word with you please, Doctor Gillingham?'

Violet gave Joe a worried glance. He shook his head slightly to signal that he didn't know either what the matron wanted to speak about.

'You go ahead, dear, and speak to your sister. I'll see you when you return.' Joe then bent his head to hear the matron's murmured conversation.

Wondering what the woman was asking, and fretting about Felicity, Violet walked out onto the balcony where the tuberculosis patients were, as usual, taking the air. At least it was now high summer and the air was warm and balmy and full of the scents of the flowers and grass from the ground below. Violet thought she could also smell a hint of rhubarb blowing in from the vast Pinkerton fields beyond.

Felicity was asleep in the end bed. Violet sat on a chair conveniently left beside the bed and waited. She had only been given five minutes. She knew the matron well enough by now to know that she would be marched out of the ward when the clock had ticked the minutes by.

'Do wake up, darling girl,' she whispered, stroking the damp hair off Felicity's brow.

Felicity mumbled in her sleep. There was high colour in her cheeks and her skin felt hot. Violet wondered if she had a fever. Apart from the red flush to her cheekbones, her skin was pale and clammy. At Violet's touch, her eyes opened and she stared up at the balcony cover in an unfocussed way.

'Felicity? It's Violet. Can you hear me? You're scaring me, darling. Do say something.'

Felicity struggled to sit up and Violet helped her. She seemed to weigh nothing as Violet pulled her up to sit against the pillows behind her. Felicity's coughing fit sent shudders through her thin frame.

'I'll fetch the nurse,' Violet said in alarm, jumping up.

'No, no. Do sit down,' Felicity coughed but thumped the side of the bed to tell Violet to stay. 'I'm quite all right.'

'Do you feel awful? Can I get you anything?'

'I'm perfectly fine, thank you. Gosh, back so soon? You must love this place as much as I hate it. How's Evie?'

'Evie is very well and happy and she sends you her love. You must get well, Felicity, you simply must. Evie needs you dreadfully.'

Violet tried and failed to keep the panic from her voice. Felicity looked worse than usual. She had been making such good progress up until now.

'I miss her too, and I'm doing my best to get out of this blasted place. Trust me. Now, enough of my woes. What news of the outside world? The nurses won't tell us about the war in case we curl our toes up immediately with despair.'

Violet couldn't help but smile. Even ill, Felicity had the power to amuse.

'It's all going rather well apparently. We've got Hitler and his army on the run in France. Not just the British Army of course, the Americans and the French too. I read in the papers today that the German troops were waving white flags of surrender at our air force.'

'Oh, never mind the bloody war. You've got something else on your mind. I can read you too well, Violet. Come along, spit it out, as our old nurse used to say.'

'It's Joe. He asked me to marry him and I said yes.'

'That's wonderful, dearest. I thoroughly approve. When are you tying the knot?'

'Oh, Felicity. That's the very thing… we don't want to wait but…'

'I do hope you aren't thinking of waiting for me to help you celebrate. Because we both know that's going to be rather a while yet,' Felicity said, her head sinking back, exhaustedly, onto the pillow. 'I insist that you go ahead. Only promise me that you'll have another party later. One that I can attend.'

'Are you sure?' Violet cried. 'I feel terrible. I want to marry Joe, but I want you there desperately.'

'Violet Stewart, where's your stiff upper lip? Mummy would be appalled at you. Promise me you'll marry your Joe as soon as possible. Promise?'

Felicity's eyelids flickered and before Violet could answer, she had drifted into a slumber. The click clack of heels as a nurse bore down on her made Violet stand up from the chair. Her five minutes were most certainly up. She followed the nurse back into the ward to find Joe waiting.

They didn't speak until they were back in the car.

'Well?' Violet said fearfully. 'What did the matron say? Is Felicity going to be all right?'

'You must brace yourself, darling. It's not terribly good news. Felicity's had a setback. They're not quite sure why. She was getting better but…' Joe's mouth was set in a grim line.

Violet let out a sob. She couldn't help it. It was all very well for Felicity to say she had to be brave and have a 'stiff upper lip', but she couldn't.

'Is she…' She swallowed.

Joe shook his head. 'She's in the best place for treatment. We'll have to wait now and see if she picks up.'

They were silent on the journey back, Violet lost in gloomy thoughts while Joe had to concentrate on driving through the rain showers that poured from the summer sky. Joe parked the car on the lane outside the camp. He came round and opened the passenger door to let Violet out.

'If you want to postpone the wedding, let's do that,' he said.

'Oh, Joe. I don't know…' Violet bit her lip. 'Felicity was adamant we should go ahead. Only… do you want to delay or cancel it?'

She was afraid that he was using Felicity's illness as an excuse. Maybe he had taken cold feet. Maybe he wasn't in love with her after all? Her doubts vanished when Joe kissed her hard on the mouth. He put his hands either side of her face and gazed into her eyes intently before kissing her again more gently.

'I want to marry you and make you mine as soon as is decently possible. I want to tell the world that you're Mrs Violet Gillingham, my wife. But… I do understand that Felicity's condition changes things. It's your decision, my darling.'

'Let's go ahead. Let's get married next week just as we planned,' Violet said. 'I promised her a party later when she's better. We can renew our vows, have a party when the war is over. What do you say?'

'I say the sooner the better.'

Joe kissed her thoroughly, until Violet became aware of the nearness of the camp and the great visibility through the wire fencing for all the soldiers inside.

'I've got to go,' she murmured. 'Until next week.'

She watched his lithe body as he went round and got back into the car and felt pride in her husband-to-be. He looked youthful and strong and athletic, but those qualities weren't as important as his caring nature and their love for one another. In that moment, she knew she was making the right decision and she felt as if Felicity was smiling at her, agreeing and egging her on.

–

After an unseasonable week of damp drizzle and rain showers, the sunshine reappeared on the morning of the wedding, causing much relief to the bride and her friends as they looked out from the barracks. Not all the girls had been given leave to attend the ceremony but Kathy, Gladys, Lily and a few others had been lucky and received permission from their commander. Joe's friends had organised a car to get Joe and Violet to the church and back to the farmhouse. There was a minor panic when word came that Joe's brother wouldn't make it due to an emergency meeting in Whitehall. One of Joe's doctor friends stepped in as best man at the last minute to allow the vows to go ahead.

Violet arrived back at Muirhead Farm as a married woman, glancing at her new husband and at the shining new gold wedding ring gracing the fourth finger on her left hand. Auld Wullie's horse and cart, spruced up for the day, was bringing him, Bess, Mavis Lafferty and Mary and Harry back. Jeannie had declined the invitation, volunteering to stay home to look after Flora and Dennis. Kathy and the other gunner girls were returning by bus.

Violet's only sadness on this happy day was that Felicity and her mother weren't there. Camilla had sent a short letter stating that she was unwell and couldn't attend. She hadn't wished the couple well but warned Violet of the pitfalls of marrying a man she had met so recently.

'You must forgive your mother,' Mavis Lafferty said, patting Violet's hand as they all went in to the farmhouse. 'She wanted to see you wed but she was suffering from her joints and her stomach problems. She does love you, Violet. In her own way.'

'She has a jolly funny way of showing it,' Violet remarked. 'I'm glad you're here though. It wouldn't have been the same without you.'

Because, really, when she thought about it, the woman standing there in front of her with such a look of loving concern on her lined face was the nearest she had to a proper mother. Mrs Lafferty had been there throughout her childhood and the Stewarts' kitchen had been the warm, safe place that Violet and Felicity had always gone to tell the housekeeper about their day and their problems and worries and the nice things too. Mrs Lafferty had been the provider of birthday cakes, biscuits and hugs and kisses.

'I was so very glad to hear about William,' Violet said, kissing Mrs Lafferty on her soft, powdered cheek.

William, lost at sea, had been picked up by the German navy and was now a prisoner of war in Germany.

'I had a letter from him,' Mavis beamed. 'And I've sent a couple of parcels through the Red Cross. His war is over but it's wonderful. When he comes home, he has a place with my brother and me in Lochgilphead. It's so beautiful there, he will be able to recuperate and build up his health.'

Bess was at the range, heating up a rabbit stew and a large ham to feed the wedding guests. A black kettle was whistling, ready to make pots of tea. Auld Wullie and Bess didn't drink but the minister had brought two bottles of elderflower wine. Violet watched as Mavis went to help Bess. She had insisted she wanted to be useful. Soon, the two women were organising the feast onto the long, sturdy wooden table which was draped with Bess's best white linen tablecloths.

Joe was chatting to Harry and Mary. The land girls brought in more chairs and Joe's friends helped. Perhaps there was a little flirting going on too. From outside, there came the sound of laughter and Violet knew that her gunner girls had arrived. Evie had insisted on travelling on the bus with them. She had made a lovely flower girl and taken her role very seriously. Violet smoothed down her pale blue dress, ready for her guests and looking forward to a happy afternoon with them all.

'Look who we found at the bus stop.' Kathy burst in, her grey eyes sparkling.

Behind her, Jennifer and Bridie waved and grinned. Evie pushed between them and ran to cuddle Violet.

'How wonderful to see you both,' Violet exclaimed. 'We didn't know if you'd make it.'

'Sorry, I did write but it was all so rushed,' Jennifer said. 'We're awfully busy up in Aberdeenshire and they didn't tell me I could go until the last minute.'

'I can't believe you're both real,' Kathy said. 'It's all very well getting letters, but it's not the same as being together.'

Bess called everyone to the table at that moment. Violet and Joe sat together as befitted the newly married couple. Auld Wullie sat at the head of his own table with Bess at the other end, ready to ladle out food and pass dishes with a keen eye for when someone wasn't eating and needed a second helping.

Kathy was happy to sit between Jennifer and Bridie. Jennifer's familiar hooting laugh soon rang out among the loud chatter of the wedding party as she described life on the ack-ack station on the rural Aberdeenshire coast.

'How is Howard?' Kathy asked, after they had heard a few hilarious tales about being chased by cows and mistaking a scarecrow for a German soldier one night.

'I haven't seen him in months. He's in Europe fighting but his letters can't say much, what with the censor and all.' Jennifer shrugged. 'I think he must be in France or Italy. Anyway, as long as I hear from him, I know he's alive.'

Kathy admired her attitude. It couldn't be at all easy to get married, have one day's honeymoon and then be apart from your new husband while he was in danger every day.

'How are you?' she asked Bridie.

Her friend looked much better than when they had parted last Christmas. Then, Bridie had been ill and mourning. Eight months on, her black hair was shiny and she looked stronger with a healthy colour to her face.

'I'll always mourn my baby but I'm learning to live with it,' Bridie said, keeping her voice low so that only Kathy could hear. 'In fact, I've applied for nursing with a view to becoming a midwife. I want to help other women going through what I experienced.'

'That's wonderful. You'll make a brilliant nurse. I'm so glad.'

A clink of cutlery tapping on glass made them look up. Joe coughed and set his wine glass back down on the table.

'Ladies and gentlemen, can I have your attention please for the wedding speeches.'

Kathy enjoyed Joe's speech and that of his stand-in best man very much; they were light-hearted with gentle teasing and the audience laughed along with the newly married couple. There was a tender moment when Joe asked the assembled company to raise a toast to absent friends. She saw Violet's eyes glisten and knew her friend was thinking about Felicity. Kathy raised her glass towards Violet and saw her grateful smile.

Bess and Mavis cleared the table and one of the land girls began to play the piano in the parlour. They all went through to listen and join in the songs. Kathy sang along for the first number before heading outside for a breath of air. She didn't realise Violet had followed her until she felt the bump of her friend's arm as she leaned on the farmhouse wall.

'Are you missing Alisdair?' Violet asked.

'Aye, I thought he'd be here by now. I wrote a couple of weeks ago and he hoped to make it.'

'I daresay he's terribly busy. The RAF have a huge role to play in Europe.'

'I haven't seen him since I met him in Glasgow nearly six weeks ago. I knew we might not meet again for ages but I hoped he'd make it today. Anyway, why are you out here? You're just married, you should be in there with Joe, singing your hearts out,' Kathy said.

'I will in a minute. But I saw my best friend looking a little bit sad so I followed her outside,' Violet replied.

'Och, you don't need to worry about me,' Kathy said, feeling glad that Violet cared about her.

'There is something else, though.'

Violet turned to her and her expression was serious. Kathy leaned on one shoulder so she could see Violet's face better. What was this 'something else'?

'It's about Alisdair...' Violet paused awkwardly.

'What about him?' Kathy felt a prickle of unease.

'If it's serious between you, don't you think you should tell him your secret?'

Kathy bit her lip. She didn't answer Violet immediately. Sure, hadn't she asked herself the same question when she woke in the night, as she had done quite a few times recently? She had wrestled with it since she knew how deeply in love with Alisdair she was.

'I remember talking to Jeannie about it a long while ago before I joined the ATS,' Kathy said slowly. 'She told me there should be no secrets between a couple, especially if they were married. But I disagreed. There are some secrets that could destroy a couple's happiness. Could destroy a marriage before it had even really begun.'

'And now? After all you've experienced in the last year. Do you still feel the same way?'

'Yes, I do. I've made my mind up. Alisdair can never know...'

'Know about what?' A deep voice made them both startle.

Kathy spun round to see Alisdair grinning at her. He had come round the side of the farmhouse as they had been deep in conversation. His green eyes looked puzzled. Kathy shrieked and threw herself into his arms. Violet discreetly vanished back in to the house. Kathy gave herself up to Alisdair's kisses until he gently put her from him with a slight frown as if he didn't quite know who she was.

'You're late,' Kathy said quickly. 'I thought you weren't going to come at all.'

'Transport difficulties.' He dismissed it with a shake of his head. 'You're changing the subject. What is it that Alisdair can never know?'

'How much I love you,' Kathy said, reaching for him.

But Alisdair stepped back from her touch. 'There has to be total honesty between us, Kathy. I assumed we both believed in that. You're the girl I want to marry. I haven't asked you yet because life is hectic and uncertain, but we love each other and I want to spend the rest of my life with you and I very much hope you feel the same way.'

'Of course I do. Is that a proposal?' Kathy teased weakly.

She didn't like the stern look he was giving her.

'What you have to understand is that I grew up with lies and secrets,' Alisdair said evenly. 'My parents' relationship was built on them. When I'm with them, they often speak to each other through me. They hate each other, but will never divorce or separate as for them that is socially unacceptable. Whatever the discussion, my father will tell one story and my mother another, usually blaming the other. What is true and what is false, I can never tell.

'The day I met you at the station they were at each other's throats because my father was selling one of their shops. Mother claimed she hadn't known about the decision to sell. I found out later from their solicitor that it was my mother who had made the first enquiry about selling. It's confusing and infuriating and I've lived with it since I was a little boy. So you can see why I refuse to live with it in my own life and with whoever becomes my wife.'

Kathy was torn between compassion for the boyhood that Alisdair had experienced and a sudden terror because he'd said 'whoever becomes my wife' instead of 'when you become my wife'. He was distancing himself from her. But it could only be worse if he knew the truth about Dennis. She couldn't bear it if he turned away from her in disgust. He'd never want to marry a girl who was already a mother but not a widow. She drew on all her resolve and her inner strength. It was for the best. One wee white lie now and the rest of their lives together would run smoothly. She'd see to it. She'd make it all right.

'I don't know what you're talking about,' she said. 'There's no secret for me to share. You misheard me and Violet havin' a blether, that's all.'

His mouth twisted and she saw the sudden anger on his face. Without another word, he turned on his heel and walked smartly away. Kathy wanted to run after him but she was frozen to the spot. Then she stumbled away from the shadow of the farmhouse wall and ran after him.

'Alisdair! Come back. You only just got here. Talk to me.'

He stopped as she reached him. 'There is nothing more to be said, is there? You're keeping something from me. I've had a sense of it since I met you but you confirmed it yourself today. Unless you want to tell me right now, then there is no future for us.'

There was a heart-stopping silence as they stared at each other. Kathy was the first to look away. When she looked up again, he was out of view behind the hawthorn trees that fringed the path. She hardly saw the hedge through her tears. Wiping them away with the back of her hand she ran into the woods and sat on a tree stump. With no one except the birds to hear her, she gave herself up to hot tears of pain and loss.

Chapter Nineteen

'I'm no great catch, lass, but I'll inherit the farm one day. I can't offer you a life of luxury, mind. A farmer's wife is always busy. Meals to be made, house to be kept clean. Responsibilities for the chickens and milking the coos. And helping during the lambing season.'

Judith was only paying half a heed to Wullie as they walked in the woods in a rare hour of free time. She knew Violet's wedding party had been held at the farmhouse the day before. She had been invited but Cook had said she was needed at the canteen so she hadn't been allowed to go. Not that she cared much about the actual wedding. Violet was marrying an older man and she couldn't see the attraction of that. But she regretted missing out on Bess's company and the food. She was always hungry. Wullie hadn't been at the event either. He'd told her he had gone to fix the drystane dykes that formed the boundaries of the fields.

'What do you say?'

She turned to see Wullie wringing his cap in his big, working hands. She'd never seen him nervous before. It did something funny to her heart. She felt a tenderness that mixed in with the love and attraction she had towards him, like stirring a pudding mix until it was all the same perfect consistency.

The meaning of his words sank in as she caught their echo. She hadn't been paying attention but now she did.

'Are you... Are you asking me to marry you?' Her throat was tight, as if a lump was stuck in it.

'Aye, lass. That I am.' Wullie's voice was patient but his hands were still clamped on his cloth cap. 'But I'm a believer in a long engagement. Let us get to know each other better.'

'Yes, I will,' Judith said simply.

She took his cap and smoothed the wrinkles out of it before placing it on his head. Wullie grinned sheepishly. Judith smiled back. She was doing more of that these days. Ever since she'd sung at the show. And now she was going to be Wullie's wife. She'd be Mrs Campbell. Just like Bess.

'Do Bess and Mr Campbell know that you're asking me?' Judith asked. 'Will they... will it make them happy?'

'Aye, they're pleased as punch.'

Young Wullie, being a man of few words, didn't say more, but Judith didn't need him to. That was all she had to know. Bess and Auld Wullie were pleased she'd be part of their family. And she'd get to live at Muirhead Farm, enjoying the fresh air and hard, honest work of the farm. Best of all, Wullie loved her.

She walked Wullie back to the farm, where Bess beamed at her and took her into a bear hug. Wullie had to go back to work. Judith had a cup of tea with Bess and reluctantly walked back to camp where she knew that Cook had a mountain of carrots to be scrubbed and pies to be filled with oatmeal and mince.

On the way back round the side of the gun site hill she met Kathy.

'Skiving off?' Judith said as they passed.

'Och, give it a rest with your big mouth, will you,' Kathy snapped back.

Judith saw the dark circles under the other girl's eyes.

'What's the matter with you? You've been like a cat wi' a sore paw since yesterday,' she said.

'What's it to you? You hate me, so why do you care if I'm unhappy?'

She was right, but with surprise Judith found she did care. Maybe because she was so happy herself right now. She was engaged to Young Wullie and she was going to be Bess's daughter-in-law. She saw a rosy future ahead.

'Can we come to a truce? We might never be friends, but can we agree not to be enemies?' Judith said.

'So you don't hate me then?' Kathy's fists were on her hips, challenging her.

'I did hate you. You got me into trouble with my aunt and she battered me for it. I hated you for a long while. But I hated you most because you had what I wanted.'

'What did I have?' Kathy's arms dropped to her sides.

'A close family in Kiltie Street. A ma who cares about you. And friends. I huvnae had any of that.'

'Well, you've not exactly helped yourself there.'

'Aye, I realise that now. I was so unhappy I was lashing out at everyone. It's different now. I've discovered how much I like the countryside and I'm going to be part of a family that I'm that fond of, I couldn't tell ye how much.'

'A family?' Kathy sounded curious.

Judith blushed. 'Young Wullie and me, we're engaged.'

'Congratulations. I'm not sure you deserve him, but I hope you'll both be very happy.'

'I'm not going to let your snippy tone drag me down,' Judith said. 'Besides, you owe me one. You let the rest of them think I was a liar.'

'You were mean enough to tell them about my wee boy.'

'It was true what I said. You did have a wean and weren't married. And they turned on me instead of you.'

Kathy's sigh was loud enough to drown out the birdsong for a second. She shook her head.

'You're right. I shouldn't have lied about it. I've discovered that keeping a secret can destroy relationships. I thought I was doing the right thing, keeping it from everyone so they couldn't judge me, but I'll put it right. Tonight, in the barracks. I'm sorry.'

Judith was taken aback by Kathy's apology. It was raw, as if something else was eating her up.

'I'm... I'm sorry too,' she offered. 'For tripping you up and being horrible, but you weren't so nice yourself. When I sang at the show, all the girls came to congratulate me but not you.'

'I was going to, but I was that busy organising stuff. When I'd sorted it, you'd gone away with Wullie. I loved your singing. You've got a real talent.'

So she'd got it wrong. Kathy hadn't ignored her maliciously. Anyway, what did it all matter now? She felt light as a feather. She stuck her hand out to the other girl.

'Mebbe not friends exactly, but a truce?'

Kathy grinned and shook Judith's hand. 'Aye, we Kiltie Street girls have to look out for each other, don't we. We should've done this before. Life at camp will be a lot more pleasant now.'

In the barrack room that evening, Kathy was as good as her word. She waited until the room was peaceful. Gladys was sewing, the other girls were writing letters and Violet was reading a book that Joe had lent her. Judith wasn't writing or reading. She lay on her bunk, looking up at the ceiling and dreaming about Wullie and being a farmer's wife. She sat up when Kathy clapped her hands and called them all to attention.

Gladys put down her latest work, a set of embroidered napkins she was making as a belated wedding present for Violet. There was a rustling of paper as letters were set down on the beds.

'I've got something to say to youse all,' Kathy announced. 'I want to apologise to Judith and I want youse to know that I'm… well, I'm a liar. I lied to youse.'

There was a murmur of protest and Judith felt their glances. She looked away, waiting for Kathy to make it right.

'You'll remember that Judith told you that I had a wean… a baby… And it's true. I made a mistake when I was younger with a man I thought was going to marry me. I've got a wee boy called Dennis.' Kathy paused and took in a deep breath in the quiet room before continuing. 'I'm not ashamed of him. I was ashamed of myself and I didn't want youse all thinking the worst of me so I denied him. I wish I hadn't because I love him very much and I'm his mammy. So there.'

Kathy's chin was held high but her face was white. There was a terrible silence in the barrack. When Judith dared to look, she saw shocked faces. All except Violet, who was smiling encouragingly at both Kathy and Judith. Of course, Violet had known all along. Judith waited to see how she felt about that but the expected pain and anger didn't materialise. Instead, she realised how lucky Kathy was to have such a friend as Violet who knew her secrets and loved her anyway.

Slowly, Judith got up from her bunk and went over to where Kathy stood, trembling slightly. She took Kathy's hand in hers and faced the others.

'I want to say sorry too,' Judith said. 'I was angry at everyone and I wanted to hurt Kathy. She's no the first to be an unmarried mother and she'll no be the last.'

They stood together, but they weren't alone. The others surrounded them with hugs and no one, it seemed, was judging them. Instead, there was sympathy and friendship.

'That was difficult for you to tell us and we don't think any less of you,' Lily told Kathy, and the other girls all nodded.

'Sorry we said you were a liar,' Gladys said to Judith. 'We misjudged you and that was wrong. We were wrong.'

Judith flushed, but smiled as the others apologised too and Lily squeezed her arm gently in sympathy.

'Are you going to tell them?' Kathy said to Judith.

'Tell us what?' Gladys asked and the others crowded in.

'I'm engaged to Wullie.'

Now there were cries of delight and warm congratulations and Judith basked in their attention. It was good to feel part of the group. Why had she disliked them all so much when she first arrived? Her anger had faded along with her memories of life with her Aunt Irene.

'That wasnae so bad,' she remarked to Kathy when all the women had returned to their activities. There was a happy atmosphere in the barrack room.

'There's someone else I have to tell,' Kathy said. 'I don't know how to do it.'

'The way you did just now. It cannae be that bad, can it?'

Whatever Kathy was about to say was lost, because there was a loud knock on the door. Violet got up to answer it. Joe stood there and his face was sombre. Kathy ran and caught Violet as her friend crumpled to the floor.

–

'How will I tell Evie?' Violet asked, late that evening.

Her face was swollen and sticky from the many tears she had shed into Joe's shoulder. Felicity was gone. She couldn't believe it. How could someone as vibrant and devil-may-care as her sister have succumbed to that dreadful disease?

'We'll tell her together,' Joe said gently.

They were standing outside the Robroyston Hospital in the darkness. Violet was glad that Joe had dealt with all the paperwork and whatever else the hospital demanded when a patient died.

'There's the funeral to arrange and the wake. Oh, and Mummy… I'll have to tell her. Goodness only knows how she will react. She loved Felicity, even if they did argue incessantly. Mavis will…'

'Violet, you'll make yourself ill if you concentrate on all that has to be done. One step at a time, my darling. You're not alone. I'm here.'

She loved him so much. His strength and calm nature made her feel better. She wasn't alone, but there was a Felicity-shaped hole in her soul that would never be filled. No one now to share and remember all their childhood memories. No one to tease her wickedly like Felicity did, nor to bring that biting sarcasm to bear, always, but always, laced with love. And Evie. What about Evie? Losing a mother at such an early age was beyond imagining.

'We'll adopt Evie, won't we, Joe? I can't let anyone else bring her up. It's what Felicity would want, I know it.'

'Of course we will. I've always wanted children. Perhaps we might produce a little brother or sister for Evie too.'

'I love you, Joe. I can't tell you how much I love you, there aren't enough words.' Violet smiled through her tears.

Driving back to camp gave her time to think. She must visit Kiltie Street as soon as possible to see Evie. There was also the question of where Evie would go. Violet didn't want to give up the Royal Artillery and her gunner girls but she couldn't see an alternative if they were to give Evie a proper home. She had been staying with the Dougals only until Felicity got better. What now?

–

'You're like a bear with a sore head, Alisdair. Do sit down and have a slice of this Dundee cake,' Beatrice said.

Alisdair ceased his pacing at the window with a sigh and sat at the small table with his nana. His knee jigged up and down in frustration. Damn it! He had been all set to propose to Kathy at Violet's wedding and instead he'd made a cock-up of the whole damn thing. She was hiding something. He found he didn't care what it was. What hurt was that she didn't trust him enough to tell him.

'It's delicious cake. That girl made it. Fiona is it? I can't recall her name or why she's here. Alisdair?'

'Sorry, Nana. I was miles away. It's Alison who made the cake. She lives with you now for companionship and to make sure you don't fall again.'

'It was a tiny wee slip, that was all. I don't need Alison living in my house. It must be terribly boring for her living with an old lady.'

'Alison's very happy living here. You mustn't worry about that.'

The 'tiny wee slip' had been a full length fall onto the floor and a suspected fractured hip which thankfully had not been broken, just badly bruised. Beatrice's memory was also slipping.

'It's wonderful to see you. Will you stay for long?' Beatrice asked.

'I have to report back to base this afternoon but I'll be back to see you next week if I can.'

He had managed to wangle some extra time so that he could check on his grandmother.

'Are you going to tell me what's bothering you?' Beatrice finished her slice of cake and set her napkin down on her knee.

'It's nothing, honestly.'

What an understatement. His whole life was in turmoil. He had lost the woman he loved. His carefully thought-out plan was in ruin. He had thought they would get engaged and then married once the war was over. He would return to his career as a mathematics teacher and they'd set up home and have a family. He wanted children. He wanted to give them what he had never had, a stable home where they knew they were loved and wanted. And it was all gone. Over a stupid argument.

'Is it your highland lassie?' Beatrice asked. 'Have you had a lover's tiff?'

'Something of the sort,' he admitted, running his hands through his hair distractedly. 'It's over, Nana. I have to accept that.'

'Nonsense, Alisdair. Where's your fighting spirit? As a wee boy I worried that you were too serious and prone to shying away from conflict. You've made me proud as an adult, flying for your country. If you can face Hitler, then you can make it up with your red-haired girl. Whatever the argument, make it up. Life's far too short, I can tell you that.'

Alisdair stared at his frail grandmother. Beatrice might be failing physically and mentally but she still had her strong days. When he was a small boy she had fought his corner with his parents and he had loved staying here with her. She had a joy in life that had enthused him then and, it seemed, could enthuse him still.

'Nana, would you mind awfully if I didn't see you next week when I'm in Glasgow?'

'Alisdair, I would mind awfully if you did,' Beatrice replied drily.

Chapter Twenty

It was noisy at number four Kiltie Street. Flora was teething and letting everyone in the family know about it. She had been passed from Jeannie, who had had no sleep the night before, to Harry, who had finally escaped to his beloved allotment, and then to Mary. The thin wailing grated on the nerves.

'Poor wee thing. She's got a hot red cheek,' Mary crooned to her grand-daughter and rocked her as she walked up and down the short stretch of carpet in the parlour.

'Dinner, Mammy,' Dennis yelled, tugging at Mary's skirt, clearly unhappy that his Mammy's attention was being taken up by the new baby.

'Heavens, he's right. I need to get the tatties on if we're to eat a midday meal.'

'Give her to me,' Kathy said, reaching out for the hot, wriggly bundle that was her niece. 'I'm sure I can settle her and that lets you get the dinner on.'

Mary handed Flora over gratefully.

'Mind you get that cloth tucked under her wee chin. She's dribbling enough to fill the Forth and Clyde Canal.'

'Och, don't you worry about me. I know what I'm about,' Kathy said confidently. 'If I can shoot planes out of the sky, I can handle a wee baby.'

'Do they let you shoot the planes down?' Mary paused on her way.

Kathy shook her head with a laugh. 'Not exactly. We gunner girls aren't allowed to load the shells or pull the trigger. But let's face it. Without our calculations, the men wouldn't be able to target the enemy planes, would they now.'

'You're doing a very valuable job. Harry and I are so proud of you.'

'Thanks, Mammy. That means a lot to me.' Kathy managed to kiss Mary's cheek without squashing Flora in between them. 'Is Evie coming home for lunch? I forgot to say that Violet is coming to see you.'

Evie had been enrolled at the local St Mildred's primary school and was enjoying her lessons and making new friends.

'Poor Violet. She must miss her sister very much. Such losses these days. The O'Learys' nephew was killed last week, he was in the army. And I heard that Mr Heaney, the butcher, his son is gone too in a navy vessel that sank after being bombed.'

'It's good that Violet has Joe. He's helping her through it all. They want to adopt Evie but Violet doesn't want her to live with Camilla. I don't blame her, it's a rattling empty sort of place for a wee girl and now the housekeeper's gone, I think Evie would be very lonely. But it means Violet leaving the army.'

'Why should she do that?' Mary sounded surprised.

'Well, she can hardly bring Evie up while she's in the Royal Artillery.' Kathy rocked Flora and was pleased to see the baby's eyelids flutter down into sleep.

'Evie's settled into school here. It would be a shame to move her. Do you think Violet would let us keep her until the war is done?'

'Let you? I'd say she'll jump at the chance. Oh, Mammy, I love you so,' Kathy grinned.

'What have I done the now?' Mary smiled back.

'Only been the most generous and kind woman in Scotland. You've solved all Violet's problems, so you have. I wish…' Kathy sighed. 'I wish you could solve mine.'

'Harry and I didn't want to say anything in case you snapped our heads off, but we can see something's eating at you, love.'

Mary sat on the nearest armchair, the midday meal momentarily forgotten. Dennis had wandered off to find Jeannie in the back bedroom.

'Och, it's nothing you can fix.' Kathy stroked the soft lock of hair from Flora's brow. 'Me and Alisdair had a falling-out and it can't be sorted.'

'If you love each other, it can,' Mary said. 'You don't want to lose the man you love over an argument.'

'He was going to ask me to marry him. But I made a mistake and I can't make it right.' Kathy bit her lip.

'We all make mistakes. If he truly loves you, he'll forgive you. What mistake did you make?' Mary leaned forward to touch Kathy's hand.

'I didn't tell him about Dennis.'

Mary glanced at the door. Beyond, in the back bedroom, they heard Jeannie's voice telling Dennis a story and him occasionally interrupting with a question. He loved stories.

'Dennis is your brother. That's all anyone ever has to know.'

'I sense a "but",' Kathy said. She looked at Mary. In her arms, Flora slept peacefully, unaware of all the troubles that make up an adult life and that she had yet to experience.

'Perhaps there's an exception to be made for the man you'll share your life with. But it's your choice to make. No one else's. Make it wisely, love, because you'll live with it for a very long time.'

'Won't you tell me what the right thing to do is?' Kathy cried.

Mary shook her head. She took the sleeping Flora and put her down on a blanket on the sofa where she'd be safe until Jeannie had had her rest and came to claim her.

'I must away. Those tatties will have sprouted by now and Dennis's tummy won't wait for his dinner.'

Dennis. Her dearest wee man! Kathy's own tummy lurched. What was she to do? What was the right choice, as Mammy put it? And had she lost her chance with Alisdair? He'd been so angry with her. He hadn't waited to patch things up. He hadn't written either in the last week to apologise. But then, neither had she. It was all so confusing. At least she'd made things right with Judith. But that was easier than doing the same with Alisdair and possibly losing him forever.

Hadn't she lost him already though?

'Kaa,' Dennis yelled, staggering through to the parlour.

He laid his head on her knees where she sat on the sofa beside Flora. She kissed him tenderly. The doorbell rang.

'That'll be Violet,' she called through to Mary. 'I'll get it. Come on, Dennis. You can help me open the door. You like Violet, don't you?'

Dennis ran gleefully to the door. Mary didn't usually let him open it in case he ran out and fell down the steps or wandered off. Kathy was looking forward to telling Violet that Evie was going to be well looked after here in Kiltie Street. She opened the door and gasped. It wasn't Violet standing there. It was Alisdair.

'Hello, Kathy. Can we talk?'

'Let's take a walk,' Kathy said warily. 'I'll get my cardigan.'

She took Dennis's hand and pulled him back inside. 'Go and see Mammy. You'll get your dinner soon.'

'He's a bright little lad.' Alisdair smiled.

She glanced at him but couldn't detect a deeper meaning beneath his words. He hadn't figured it out. He was simply being nice. She shrugged on her green cardigan over her thin summer dress. She should be wearing her uniform, but who was to know. She led the way down the stone steps and along Kiltie Street.

'Where to?' Alisdair asked, his hands casually in his trouser pockets, as if they had never argued, flung accusations at each other and stormed apart only a week before.

'Harry's allotment,' Kathy decided. 'It's near the river and it's nice down there.'

They walked beside each other. Kathy was only too aware of him. At last she couldn't stand it any longer. She halted and Alisdair had to stop too.

'Why have you come? Don't you hate me?' she cried.

'I came because I'm in love with you, and I don't care if you are keeping something from me. I trust it must be important to you and when you're ready to share, I'll listen.'

'You might not want to be with me if I tell you. But I'm ready to share now,' Kathy said. 'I've been ready for the last week, but I don't know how to.'

'It can't be that bad.' Alisdair took her hand.

His touch was both comforting and exciting.

'My nana reminded me today that life is short,' Alisdair said earnestly. 'Too short to let arguments get in the way when we love each other. I want to marry you, Kathy Dougal, and have a life with you. I've never felt this way about any other woman. I want the home, the children, the whole caboodle.'

'The children...' Kathy said, staring first at her shoes and then forcing herself to look Alisdair straight in the eyes. 'I already have a child.'

He dropped her hand and staggered back in shock. 'You're married?'

Kathy gave a bitter laugh. 'No, I'm not married.'

Relief swept across his features. 'Thank God.'

'Did you hear me? I've got a wean. Dennis is mine.'

'Ah, that explains his hair. It's the exact same shade as yours.'

'Aren't you shocked? Do you still want to know me?' Kathy said.

'It doesn't change the fact that I love you. Do you want to tell me about it?'

Kathy walked on, unsure how to start, and Alisdair came with her. The sounds of the river wafted towards them. Gurgles from the sluggish water, the quacks of the ducks and the shouts of small boys bunking off school to catch minnows with twine tied to twigs. Further along, on a large area of what had been mown grass, allotments had sprung up for the 'Dig for Victory' campaign. Kathy could make out Harry's large figure bent over a spade near to his hand-built shed.

'I thought I was engaged to this soldier.'

She began to tell the sorry tale. Alisdair didn't interrupt her. When she finished, he pulled her close into his arms and held her.

'That bastard took advantage of you. If I ever meet him, he'll get what he deserves.'

His voice was so fierce, Kathy hardly recognised it. There was a savage, protective edge to it that made her thrill and want to cry all at once. He kissed her upturned face and then her lips.

'Harry and Mammy are bringing Dennis up,' Kathy explained, as they drew slightly apart, both breathing fast.

'When we're married, I'd like very much to adopt Dennis and be his father,' Alisdair said.

Kathy knew in that instant that she wanted it too. She wanted to be Dennis's mammy, not his older sister. She was ready. She knew that Mary and Harry would understand. And that if they were prepared to look after Evie until the war was won, then they'd keep Dennis safe too so that Kathy could play her part as a gunner girl and bring that victory closer more quickly for them all.

'I'd like that too,' she said simply.

Alisdair slung his arm around her shoulders gently.

'Is that Harry I see digging?' he asked, squinting into the sun.

'Aye, it is. Shall we go and say hello?'

'I'll do more than say hello. I want to ask him for your hand in marriage,' Alisdair said.

'It's not Harry who makes that decision, it's me!' Kathy cried in indignation. 'I'm a modern woman. I'm a gunner girl. I don't need anyone's permission to marry who I like.'

Alisdair gave a roar of laughter. In the distance, Harry heard it and raised his head from where he was digging up his crop of lettuces. He smiled at the couple and waved.

'You're my fiery red-haired highland lassie,' Alisdair teased, picking her up and spinning her round until she squealed with laughter. 'Poor Harry doesn't stand a chance. Will you give the man his due respect as your step-father and let him have the honour of giving me his permission to marry you, please?'

'Oh, very well.' Kathy pretended to grumble but couldn't stop her mouth curling up in pure pleasure as they walked swiftly, hand in hand towards the lush green of the allotment and their happy, loving future.

A letter from Carol

Dear Reader

I hope you are well. Thank you for choosing *Kathy's Courage*, which is the third in the Kiltie Street Girls series. If you haven't discovered them yet, you might enjoy reading the first and second books – *Jeannie's War* and *Elsie's Wartime Wish*.

The inspiration for Kathy's story came from an article I read in the *Glasgow Times* called 'When the Army Took Over a Drumchapel Farm' about ATS women stationed at an anti-aircraft mixed battery on what is now Jedworth Avenue. In those days the area was farmland outside the city. Now it's part of a housing estate and the city has spread around it. I walked up the streets to the top of the hill and tried to imagine the gun emplacements and the army barracks and the potato fields, and I knew then that I had an exciting, authentic setting for Kathy's story.

I have taken a few liberties to allow for fictional characterisation and plot twists. The real farm was called Garscadden Mains. I've called mine Muirhead Farm. Kathy and her friends have to defend the area from German aeroplanes in April and May 1944. In reality, the last raid on Glasgow, according to *Luftwaffe over Scotland* by Les Taylor was on 25th March 1943.

As usual I referred to a huge stack of non-fiction books for research. Of these the following were particularly useful: *Girls in Khaki* by Barbara Green, *Sergeant* by Elsie M. Crossley and *Glasgow, A City at War* by Brian D. Osborne and Ronald Armstrong.

If you enjoyed *Kathy's Courage* please do leave a review – I try to read them all! Reader reviews are very much appreciated and make the book more 'visible' for other readers too.

Thank you for your support and I hope you will enjoy the next in the series which will be about Jeannie's best friend, Eileen, and will be out in spring 2025.

You can get in touch with me on my social media pages on Twitter and Facebook.

Best wishes and happy reading,

Carol x

Website link www.carolmacleanauthor.com
Facebook link www.facebook.com/carolcmaclean
Twitter link www.twitter.com/carolcmaclean

Acknowledgements

Thank you to Keshini, Dan, Miranda and the rest of the Hera team for all their hard work – the suggestions, corrections and sharp-eyed editing – all of which have made for a stronger story. Many thanks to Ann Fotheringham, journalist at the *Glasgow Evening Times*, for her article on the gunner girls which inspired my story, for answering my emails and not only putting me in touch with local historian, Eric Flack, but also interviewing me about the Kiltie Street Girls series. Special thanks to Eric Flack for sharing his knowledge of Drumchapel history and particularly of the anti-aircraft battery and the people who lived and worked there during the second world war. Finally, thanks, as always, to my family for understanding my need to write and for giving me the space to do it.